Blue at the Mizzen

Blue at the Mizzen

Patrick O'Brian

Thorndike Press • Chivers Press
Thorndike, Maine USA   Bath, England

This Large Print edition is published by Thorndike Press, USA and by Chivers Press, England.

Published in 2000 in the U.S. by arrangement with W. W. Norton & Company, Inc.

Published in 2000 in the U.K. by arrangement with HarperCollins Publishers Ltd.

U.S. Hardcover 0-7862-2046-5 (Basic Series Edition)
U.S. Softcover 0-7862-2047-3
U.K. Hardcover 0-7540-1388-X (Windsor Large Print)
U.K. Softcover 0-7540-2292-7 (Paragon Large Print)

The text of this Large Print edition is unabridged.
Other aspects of the book may vary from the original edition.

Set in 16 pt. Plantin.

Printed in the United States on permanent paper.

British Library Cataloguing in Publication Data available

Library of Congress Cataloging-in-Publication Data

O'Brian, Patrick, 1914–
 Blue at the mizzen / Patrick O'Brian.
  p. cm.
 ISBN 0-7862-2046-5 (lg. print : hc : alk. paper)
 ISBN 0-7862-2047-3 (lg. print : sc : alk. paper)
 1. Chile — History — War of Independence, 1810–1824 — Fiction. 2. Great Britain — History, Naval — 19th century — Fiction. 3. Large type books. I. Title.
PR6029.B55 B57 1999b
 823'.914—dc21   99-048283

I dedicate this book, *donum indignum*, to the Provost and to all those many people who were so kind to me while I was writing it in Trinity College, Dublin

The sails of a square-rigged ship, hung out to dry in a calm.

1 Flying jib
2 Jib
3 Fore topmast staysail
4 Fore staysail
5 Foresail, or course
6 Fore topsail
7 Fore topgallant
8 Mainstaysail
9 Main topmast staysail
10 Middle staysail
11 Main topgallant staysail

12 Mainsail, or course
13 Maintopsail
14 Main topgallant
15 Mizzen staysail
16 Mizzen topmast staysail
17 Mizzen topgallant staysail
18 Mizzen sail
19 Spanker
20 Mizzen topsail
21 Mizzen topgallant

Illustration source: Serres, Liber Nauticus.
Courtesy of The Science and Technology Research Center,
The New York Public Library, Astor, Lenox, and Tilden Foundation

Chapter One

The *Surprise*, lying well out in the channel with Gibraltar half a mile away on her starboard quarter, lying at a single anchor with her head to the freshening north-west breeze, piped all hands at four bells in the afternoon watch; and at the cheerful sound her tender *Ringle*, detached once more on a private errand by Lord Keith, cheered with the utmost good will, while the Surprises turned out with a wonderful readiness, laughing, beaming and thumping one another on the back in spite of a strong promise of rain and a heavy sea running already. Many had put on their best clothes — embroidered waistcoats, and silk Barcelona handkerchiefs around their necks — for the Surprises and their captain, Jack Aubrey, had taken a very elegant prize indeed, a Moorish galley laden with gold, no less — a galley that had fired on *Surprise* first, thus qualifying herself as a pirate, so that the prize-court, sitting at the pressing request of Captain Aubrey's friend Admiral Lord Keith, had condemned her out of hand: a perfectly lawful prize, to be shared according to the usage of the sea, or more exactly according to the Prize Law of 1808.

And now they were all on deck, radiating joy and facing aft on the larboard side of the quarterdeck in the usual disorderly naval heap, gazing at their captain, his officers, the purser and the clerk, ranged athwartships and facing forward on either side of some charming barrels. These had been brought aboard by a guard of Marines, heavily sealed: but now their heads had been taken off (though carefully numbered and preserved by the cooper) and it was apparent that their bodies were filled with coin. The gold was somewhat unorthodox, it having been captured in small uneven ingots which the Gibraltar goldsmiths had cast into smooth shining disks each marked 130g Troy: one hundred and thirty grains Troy weight: but the silver and copper were in their usual homely forms.

The echo of the fourth bell and the cheering died: the clerk, catching his captain's nod, called 'John Anderson'. Since no one else aboard *Surprise* in this commission had ever come earlier in the alphabet it was no surprise to John Anderson or his shipmates; and although

8

he was ordinarily shy and awkward he now stepped aft quite happily to the capstan-head: taking off his hat, he touched his forelock and cried, 'John Anderson, sir, if you please: ordinary, larboard watch, afterguard.' The clerk followed this conscientiously in the book though he knew it all by heart; said, 'Very well: one hundred and fifty-seventh part of a half-share: hold out your hat.' And plunging his right hand into the barrel of gold he drew out first one handful of disks and counted them into the hat, 'One, two . . . ten.' Plunged again, counted out seven more, said 'Wait a minute' to Anderson and to his little dark shrewish assistant at the other two barrels, 'Seventeen and fourpence.' Then to Anderson again, 'That makes seventeen pound, seventeen shillings and fourpence: and here is your witnessed paper asking for three hundred and sixty-five pound to be remitted to Mrs Anderson. Are you content?'

'Oh dearie me, yes,' said Anderson, laughing. 'Oh yes, sir, quite content.'

'Then sign here,' said the clerk: but seeing Anderson's uneasy look, he murmured, 'Well, just make your mark in the bottom corner.'

And so it went, right through the list:

there were a few men with no dependants of any kind, and they walked off with the entire hundred and fifty-seventh part of half the splendid prize; but most over thirty had yielded to the representations of their captain and divisional officers to send at least some money home; and all eagerly agreed with the clerk's reckoning. At one time Stephen Maturin, the frigate's surgeon, had been calculating the degree of literacy aboard; but melancholy, no doubt helped by the increasing wind and the spindrift, had welled up and he lost count among the names beginning with N. 'How I do wish,' he murmured to Jack in a moment's pause, 'that William and his Ringles might have been here.'

'So do I indeed: but, you know, as a privately-owned tender to what is in fact a hydrographical vessel I do not think they would stand in line for more than fourpence. In any case I could not refuse Lord Keith — he had no other suitable craft at hand — he asked it as a personal favour. And I owe him a great deal: I owe both of them a great deal.'

'Of course, of course: it was only that I should have liked some of the younger ones to accept a gold piece, by way of memento,' said Stephen. 'How the waves increase! The darkness thickens.'

'They will rejoin at Madeira,' said Jack. 'And then you can give them their gold pieces.' They talked on quietly until Jack realized that Willis and Younghusband had been dealt with, and that once Moses Zachary, one of *Surprise*'s very old Sethian hands, had stopped chuckling over the coins that he obscurely insisted upon stuffing or trying to stuff into a variety of little inadequate triangular pockets it would be time for him as captain to wind up proceedings.

But the proceedings would not be wound up: in spite of the gathering darkness and the now quite vicious driving rain some hand, probably Giles, captain of the foretop, called out 'It's all along of the unicorn's horn — it's all along of the glorious hand. Huzzay, three times huzzay for the Doctor.'

Lord, how they cheered their surgeon! It was he who had brought the narwhal's tusk aboard: and the severed hand, the Hand of Glory, was his property: both symbolized (and practically guaranteed) immense good fortune, *virility*, safety from poison or any disease you chose to name: and both had proved their worth.

Jack Aubrey was a taut captain: he had

been brought up by commanders who looked upon exact discipline and exact gunfire as of equal importance in a man-of-war, but on this occasion he knew that he had nothing whatsoever to say; and speaking privately to his first lieutenant he observed, 'Mr. Harding, when things are a little calmer, let us weigh and proceed south-west by west with all the sail she can bear. If any King's ship hails or signals you will reply *carrying dispatches* and pursue your course, touching neither sheet nor brace.'

'South-west by west it is, sir: and *carrying dispatches*,' said Harding, and Jack, steadying Stephen by the elbow — the frigate was pitching quite violently by now — guided him to the great cabin, where they sat at their ease on the cushioned stern-lockers that ran across the ship under the elegant, remarkably elegant sash-lights that gave on to the sea.

'I am afraid it is going to turn out a truly dirty night,' said Jack. He stood up and in his sure-footed seaman's way walked over to his barometer. 'Yes,' he said. 'Dirtier than I had thought.' He came back and gazed out at the darkness, full of rain and flying water from the ship's bow-wave, more and more as she increased her way.

'But, however,' he went on, 'I am most heartily glad to be at sea. At one time I thought it could never be done . . . indeed, without Queenie and Lord Keith it never would have been done.' The stern-lanterns were now lighting up the frigate's wake — exceptionally broad, white and agitated for a ship with such fine lines — but in spite of the brilliance just aft he could still clearly make out the distant red glow above Gibraltar, where they were still keeping it up in spite of the wind and the rain.

For his own part he had had quite enough of the junketing, especially that part of it which consisted of patriotic songs, self-praise and mocking the French, who had after all gone down fighting, outnumbered, with the utmost gallantry — gibes that very often came from those who had had nothing whatsoever to do with the war. Even Maturin, though he loathed the whole Napoleonic system root and branch, could not bear the obscene, gloating caricatures of Bonaparte that were everywhere to be seen, a penny plain and up to as much as fourpence coloured.

'Do you remember Malta, when there was a payment of six dollars a head for one-share men?' asked Jack. 'No, of course you do not: you were at the hospital, looking after poor Hopkins's leg. Well, I thought it would answer, with a settled, steady crew of seamen: and they certainly expected it, the bag of silver having been hauled out of the trabacolo's cabin and spilt on deck. But I was wrong: once ashore they kicked up Bob's a-dying to a most shocking extent and then set about the soldiery.'

'Indeed I remember it. My colleagues and I had to treat many of them: contusions, mostly, and some quite important fractures.'

'So you did . . .' said Jack, shaking his head: then he stopped, listened intently, and ran on deck. Coming back, he wiped the foam and rain from his face with an habitual gesture and said, 'Fore topmast staysail carried away — a damned awkward veering wind and as black as the Devil's arse. But young Wilcox was up there before I reached the fo'c'sle and they were tallying the new sheet aft as though it were broad daylight and the sea as smooth as a pond. But there you are: that is your seaman. He can put up with uncommon dirty weather, endure great hardship and very short commons — a good, steady, courageous, uncomplaining creature under officers he can respect. He will bear all that, and sometimes harsh punishment, shipwreck and scurvy. What he cannot bear is sudden wealth. It goes straight to their heads, and if there is the least possibility they get drunk and disorderly, and desert in droves. In Malta it was not so bad. With the help of the whores their six dollars were soon spent; and on an island there was no chance of deserting. But now the case is altered, and each damn-fool hand with fifty guineas in his pocket would have been blind drunk, poxed and stripped before Sunday, had we not got away: besides — what is it, Killick?'

'Which we shall have to ship washboards athwart the coach door: green seas is coming aft as far as the capstan, and getting worse every minute. I doubt we'll ever get your toasted cheese up dry, without I bring up the spirit-stove and do it here.'

'Who has the deck at the moment?'

'Why, the Master, sir, in course: and he's just sent Mr. Daniel and a couple of strong hands aloft with a spare lantern. Which the top-light came adrift again. And sir —' addressing Stephen — 'your mate — I beg his pardon: Dr. Jacob as I ought to say — has had a nasty tumble. Blood all over the gunroom.'

Stephen tried to leap to his feet, but the

roll of the ship pressed him back: and when he made a second attempt on the larboard heave it flung him forward with shocking force. Both the captain and the captain's steward had the same notion of Stephen's seamanship, however: between them they held him steady, and Jack, grasping his windward elbow, guided him through the coach — the anteroom, as it were, to the great cabin — and so out on to the deck, where the blast, the utter darkness, thick with racing spindrift, rain, and even solid bodies of sea-water, took his breath away, used though he was to the extremities of weather.

'Mr. Woodbine,' called Jack.

'Sir,' replied the Master, just beside the wheel, where the faint glow of the binnacle could be made out by eyes growing accustomed to the darkness.

'How is the top-light coming along?'

'I am afraid we shall have to rouse out the armourer, sir: I doubt Mr. Daniel can fix the bracket without heavy tools.' Then raising his voice he called to the quartermaster stationed to windward, watching the weather-leeches. 'Higgs, hail the top and ask if Mr. Daniel would like the armourer.'

Higgs had an enormous voice and very

keen ears: through all the shrieking of the wind in the rigging and its roaring changes he conveyed and received the message. By this time Stephen could make out the small hand-lantern high among the pattern of sails, all as close-hauled as ever they could be, with the frigate plunging westward through the tumultuous seas. He could also see the faint light reflected from the companion-ladder; and towards this he crept, holding on to everything that offered, bowed against the wind and the blinding rain. But with each tentative step he took down, the frantic uneven roll grew less — a question, as Jack had often told him, of the centre of gravity. Yet a most discreditable scene it was when he opened the larboard door of the bright-lit gun-room. Here were men, accustomed to bloodshed from their childhood, now running about like a parcel of hens, mopping Jacob's arm with their napkins, giving advice, proffering glasses of water, wine, brandy, loosening his neckcloth, undoing his breeches at the waist and the knee. The purser was literally wringing his hands.

'Pass the word for Poll Skeeping,' cried Stephen in a harsh peremptory tone. He thrust them aside irrespective of rank, whipped out a lancet (always in a side-pocket), slit Jacob's sleeve up to the shoulder, cut the shirt away, uncovered the spurting brachial artery and two other ample sources of blood on the same limb. In turning a complete somersault over both his chair and a small stool with a glass in his hand, at the moment of a double rise on the part of the frigate followed by a sickening plunge, Jacob had contrived not only to stun himself but also to shatter the glass, whose broad, sharp-edged sides had severed the artery and many other smaller but still considerable vessels.

Poll came at a run, carrying bandages, gut-threaded needles, pledgets and splints. Stephen, who had his thumb on the most important pressure-point, desired the members of the gunroom to stand back, right back; and Poll instantly set about swabbing, dressing and even tidying the patient before he was carried off to a sick-berth cot.

All this had called for a good deal of explanation and comment: and when Jack came below, telling Mr. Harding that they were making truly remarkable way, barely six points off the wind, the whole tedious thing seemed to be happening again, with people showing just what had happened and how it had happened, when a truly enormous, an utterly shocking crash checked the frigate's way entirely, thrusting her off her course and swinging the lanterns so violently against the deck overhead that two went out — a crash that drove all discussion of Jacob's injuries far, far from the collective mind. Jack shot up on deck, followed by the whole gunroom.

He could at first see nothing in the roaring darkness: but Whewell, the officer of the watch, told him that the forward starboard lookout had hailed 'Light on the starboard bow' seconds before the enormous impact; that he himself had seen a huge, dark, and otherwise lightless craft coming right before the wind at ten knots or more, strike the frigate's bows, cross her shattered stem and run down her larboard side, her yards sweeping *Surprise*'s shrouds but always breaking free. A very heavy Scandinavian timber-carrier, he thought: ship-rigged. Could see no name, no port, no flag. No hail came across. He had roused out the bosun and the carpenter — they would report in a moment — the ship was steering still, though she sagged to leeward.

Jack ran forward to meet them. 'Bowsprit and most of the head carried away, sir,' said the carpenter.

19

'Nor I shouldn't answer for the foremast,' said the bosun.

A carpenter's mate addressed his chief: 'We'm making water: five ton a minute,' in a tone of penetrating anxiety that affected all who heard him.

Harding had already called all hands, and as they came tumbling up Jack put the ship before the wind, furling everything but the main and fore courses and manning the pumps. She answered her helm slowly, and she sailed slowly; but once Jack had her with the very strong wind and the short pounding sea on her uninjured larboard quarter she no longer gave him that desperate sense of being about to founder any minute; and he and the carpenter and Harding, each with a lantern, made their tour of inspection: what they found was very, very bad — bowsprit, head and all the gear swept clean away — headsails gone, of course; and there were certainly some sprung butts lower down. But by the end of the middle watch, with the carpenter and his mates working as men will work with water pouring into their ship, the pumps were holding their own, or even very slightly gaining on the influx. 'Oh, it's only makeshift stuff, you know, sir,' said the carpenter. 'And if ever you can bring her inside the mole and so into the yard, I shall forswear evil living and give half my prize-money to the poor: for it is only the yard that can make her anything like seaworthy. God send we may creep inside that lovely old mole again.'

They did creep inside that lovely old mole again, and there they spent the remaining hours of the night in relative peace, the wind howling overhead but sending no more than wafts of foam and sometimes even webs of seaweed into their part of the harbour.

Early in the calm of the morning they made their way down the New Mole and the Naval Yard, doing what little they could to make the ship more nearly presentable (though for all their labour she still looked like a handsome woman who has been very severely beaten and had her nose cut off short), and Jack having sent to ask after Jacob — 'Tolerable for the moment, but it is still too soon to speak, and Dr. Maturin begs to be excused from breakfast' — sat down to his steak; and as he ate it so he made notes on the folded piece of paper by his side. Then he ate all the toast in his own rack and trespassed on Stephen's, drinking large quantities of coffee: more nearly human now, after a

21

night almost as rough as any he had known (though mercifully short) he passed the word for his clerk. 'Mr. Adams,' he said, 'should you like a cup of coffee before we begin Lord Barmouth's letter and the report?'

'Oh yes, sir, if you please. The berth drinks tea, which is no sort of a compensation for such a night.'

The letter was simplicity itself: Captain Aubrey presented his compliments and begged to enclose his report of the previous night's events and the damages caused thereby; and it ended with a request that Captain Aubrey might have the honour of waiting on his Lordship as soon as might be convenient. 'And please have that taken up directly by our most respectable-looking midshipman.'

Adams pondered, shook his head, and then observed, 'Well, I have heard Mr. Wells described as a pretty boy.'

'Poor little chap. Well, when you have written the report fair, let Mr. Harding know, with my compliments, that I should like Mr. Wells to be washed twice: he is to put on his number one uniform, a round hat and dirk. And perhaps Mr. Harding would send . . . would send some reliable man to see him there and back.' Bonden's name had been in his throat and the checking of it caused an oddly searing pain: so many shipmates gone, but never a one to touch him for true worth.

Harding's choice, a grave quartermaster, brought Mr. Wells back, and Mr. Wells brought Captain Aubrey word that the Commander-in-Chief would receive him at half-past five o'clock.

Jack was there with naval punctuality, and with naval punctuality Lord Barmouth turned his secretary out of the room: yet no sooner had Jack walked in than one of 'the two doors behind the Admiral's desk opened and his wife appeared. 'Why, Cousin Jack, my dear,' she cried, 'how delightful to see you again so soon! Though I fear you had a very horrid time of it, with that blackguardly great merchantman — Barmouth,' she said in an aside, laying her hand on her husband's arm, 'the Keiths will be charmed, and Queenie asks may she bring Mr. Wright? Cousin Jack, you will come, will you not? I know how sailors detest a late dinner, but I promise you shall be fed at a reasonably Christian hour. And you must tell us every last detail — Queenie was terribly concerned to hear how poor *Surprise* had suffered.' Isobel Barmouth was and always had been a spirited creature, not to be put down easily nor yet made to leave the room. But she was by no means a fool and it was clear to her that obstinacy at this point might do Jack more harm than anything Barmouth could inflict on her. The Admiral was a brave and capable sailor; he had had a remarkable career; and as her guardians had pointed out he was an excellent match. But for all his courage and his admitted virtues, she knew that he was capable of a shabby thing.

When the door had closed behind her, Barmouth sat down to Jack's report: he said, 'I have given orders to all the few cruisers I have at sea to watch out very carefully for any vessel remotely resembling the ship that crossed your bows: judging by the shocking amount of damage you received' — tapping the long, detailed list in Jack's report — 'she should be pretty recognizable. Even a liner must have suffered terribly from such an impact, and from what I gather she was not much more than a fair-sized Baltic merchantman. However, that is another matter: what I am really concerned about is the present condition of *Surprise*: I wonder you can keep her afloat.'

'We are very fast to the mole, my Lord;

and we keep the pumps going watch and watch.'

'Yes, yes: I dare say: but what worries me is this. Having fulfilled — and very handsomely fulfilled — Lord Keith's orders, you now revert to your former status: a hydrographical vessel — I think a *hired* hydrographical vessel intended by the appropriate department for the survey of Magellan's Strait and the southern coasts of Chile. You are completely detached from my command in the Mediterranean; and although I should like to — what shall I say? — to virtually rebuild your ship, if only in recognition of your most spirited capture of that damned galley, I cannot wrong my men-of-war who are waiting for urgent repairs, by giving a hydrographer precedence. A man-of-war must come first.'

'Very well, my Lord,' said Jack. 'But may I at least beg for a somewhat less exposed berth?'

'It may be possible,' said the Admiral. 'I shall have a word with Hancock about it. But now,' he went on, rising, 'I must say good-bye until dinner-time.'

Jack arrived, neat and trim: in good time, of course, but time not quite so good as the Keiths. He was very kindly greeted by Queenie and Isobel Barmouth, yet with the brutality of childhood acquaintance he broke away from them and strode over to Lord Keith, whom he thanked very heartily indeed for his intervention with the prize-court functionaries. 'Nay, nay, never speak of it, my dear Aubrey: no, no — these gentlemen are very well known to me — I am acquaint with their little ways — and they are aware that they must not practise upon me or my friends. But Aubrey, I must beg your pardon for keeping *Ringle* away from you: she would have been wonderfully useful in pursuing that vile great Hamburger or whatever she was that so cruelly stove in your beak and bows. I was looking at *Surprise* this morning, and I wondered that you ever managed to bring her in.'

'We were blessed with a following wind and sea, my Lord; and with a mere handkerchief spread on the fore topsail yard we just had steerage-way: but it was nip and tuck.'

'I am sure it was,' said Keith, shaking his head. 'I am sure it was.' He considered for a while, sipping his glass of Plymouth gin, and then said, 'But I must tell you what an excellent young man you have in William

Reade. He handled his schooner admirably, and he did everything I asked. But I am afraid you must have missed him sadly when you had to make the mole, and when you hoped to identify the villain.'

'We did, sir: but what really grieves me is that I find that as the commander of a privately-owned tender, *and* being absent, he scarcely shares in the prize at all; and with the Navy being laid up again now that Boney is taken, or put into ordinary or just left to rot, he is very unlikely to get another ship in the near future, if indeed at all, and an ordinary lieutenant's share would have been uncommon useful. Peace is no doubt a very good thing, but . . .'

At this point Lady Barmouth greeted two late arrivals, Colonel and Mrs. Roche; and introductions were barely over before she was told that dinner was served.

This was not a formal party, arranged some time earlier, and there were not enough women to go round. Jack found himself sitting on Isobel's left, opposite Lord Keith, while his other neighbour was Colonel Roche, obviously a newcomer. 'I believe, sir,' said Jack to him, after a few inconsequential exchanges, 'that you were at Waterloo?'

'I was indeed, sir,' replied the soldier,

'and a very moving experience I found it.'

'Was you able to see much? In the few fleet actions I have known, apart from the Nile, I could make out precious little, because of the smoke; and afterwards most people gave quite different accounts.'

'I had the honour of being one of the Duke's aides-de-camp, and he nearly always took up a position from which he — and of course we underlings — could see a great stretch of country. As you know, I am sure, the whole engagement took several days, which I think is not usual with fights at sea, but the one I remember best was the eighteenth — the eighteenth of June, the culmination.'

'I should take it very kindly if you would give me a blow-by-blow account.'

Roche looked at him attentively, saw that he was in earnest, very much in earnest, and went on, 'Well, during the night there had been very, very heavy rain — communications had always been extremely difficult on both sides, with messengers being shot or captured or merely losing their way — but we did know that the Prussians had been very severely handled at Ligny, losing about twelve thousand men and most of their guns, that Blücher himself had had his horse shot under him and had been ridden over in the cavalry-charge. Many of us thought that the Prussians could not soon recover from such a blow; and that even if they did, Gneisenau, who would replace the injured Blücher and who was no friend of ours, could not be expected to bring them to battle. During the night a message came saying that Blücher was coming with two or possibly four corps: it pleased some people, but most of us did not believe it. I think the Duke did: anyhow, he decided to accept battle, occupying Mont Saint-Jean, Hougoumont and La Haye Sainte with about sixty-eight thousand men and a hundred and fifty-six guns as against Napoleon's seventy-four thousand and two hundred and forty-six guns. The French cavalry regiments were much hampered by the rain-soaked ground, the artillery even more so, and it was not until after eleven in the morning that the enemy, drawn up in three lines on the opposite slope, about three-quarters of a mile away, sent a division to attack Hougoumont. They were beaten back: but now the real battle began, with eighty French guns drawing up to batter La Haye Sainte, the centre, to weaken the forces stationed there before the more serious attack, and . . .'

'Should you like some more soup, sir?' asked the servant.

'Oh go away, Wallop,' cried Lord Barmouth: the whole table had in fact been listening closely to Roche's account, by far the most informed and authoritative they had yet heard. 'Sir,' went on Lord Barmouth, as Wallop vanished, 'may I beg you to place a bottle or two, or some pieces of bread, in the vital places, so that we mere sailors can follow the manoeuvres?'

'Of course,' said Roche, seizing a basket of rolls. 'This is just a rough approximation, but it gives the general sense — Hougoumont, La Haye Sainte, the emperor's centre right over on that side of the table, the Paris wood and some other woods beyond it at Lord Barmouth's end. Now this piece of bread is Hougoumont, and upon the rise stood the base of a ruined mill: I was on top of it, gazing at the general array, sweeping the countryside with my glass, and I saw a curious movement at the edge of the woods by Chapelle Saint-Lambert: a dark mass, a dark blueish mass — a *Prussian* blue. I counted the formations as soberly as I could and then leapt down. I said, "By your leave, sir: at least one Prussian corps is advancing from Saint-Lambert, some five miles away." This was at about half-past four. The Duke nodded, took my glass and directed it at the emperor: within a few minutes French staff-officers were galloping in various directions. Cavalry squadrons and some infantry left their positions, moving in the direction of the Prussians; while within a very short time Marshal Ney attacked the Allied centre. But his men failed to storm La Haye Sainte and two of Lord Uxbridge's cavalry brigades rode right over them, capturing two eagles, but paying heavily when fresh enemy squadrons took them in the flank.'

'Pray, sir,' asked Mr. Wright, a scientific gentleman, 'what are eagles, in this sense?'

'Why, sir, they are much the same as colours with us — a disgrace to lose, a triumph to win.'

'Thank you, sir, thank you. I do hope I have not checked your flow — that would be a catastrophe.'

Roche bowed, and went on, 'Then Ney was required to attack La Haye Sainte again: after a most shocking cannonade the Allies withdrew for better cover. The French mistook this for a genuine retreat and launched forty-three squadrons of cavalry. But on this uphill, yielding ground the horses could do no more than trot, and their riders found the Allied infantry formed in impenetrable squares: they were swept by gunfire and the Allied cavalry drove them down the slope. But now the French cuirassiers and the Imperial Guard cavalry were sent forward, their retreating friends falling in behind them — eighty squadrons in all. Eighty squadrons, sir! It was the most furious attack imaginable: such fighting I have never seen. But they could not break the Allied squares: and at last they too were driven down the hill. And now Bülow engaged the forces Napoleon had sent against him — this was about a quarter to five — at first with some success, taking Placenoit: just by the centrepiece, ma'am. However, reinforcements drove him out, and Napoleon ordered Ney to take La Haye Sainte: this he accomplished, the troops holding it having used up all their ammunition. But the Duke, undisturbed by the loss of his key-position, sent all he could to strengthen the centre; and by this time two other Prussian corps had joined the battle. I will not go into details — I have talked myself hoarse and you almost to death from starvation — yet I will just say that with Zeiten's Prussian corps coming up, the Duke could move two fresh cavalry brigades from his right wing to strengthen the centre: a point of the very first importance. But now Napoleon attacked with his utmost strength all along the line, sending in the Imperial Guard. They fought with very great courage, but they no longer had enough men. As the Guard fell back, Zeiten's Prussians drove through part of the French front, right through: and that was the end. Some battalions of the Guard held firm, but then they too had to join the total rout. I do beg your pardon, ma'am,' he said to Isobel Barmouth.

'Not at all, Colonel, not at all. I thought it perfectly fascinating, all the more so that I could make out the various directions. Thank you very much indeed.' She gave the attentive Wallop a secret nod, and dinner resumed its stately pace.

When it was over and the men were sitting over their port, the two admirals and Mr. Wright at the top of the table talking eagerly about the problems of scour as it related to the problem of the new mole, Jack said to Roche, 'I have never had the honour of meeting the Duke of Wellington: surely he must be a very great man?'

'Yes, he is: and he can say some very fine things, just straight off, like that — not studied.'

'Could you tell me one or two?'

'Alas, I have a wretched memory, above all for quotations. In the middle of the night they may come back to me, but not at command. Still, I do remember that as we rode about the field afterwards, and when we had seen the wreck of the Inniskillings' square and its shocking number of dead, he said to me, "Next to a battle lost, the greatest misery is a battle gained". And then again, much later, when we were moving down into France, "It has been a damned serious business — Blücher and I have lost thirty thousand men. It has been a damned nice thing — the nicest-run thing you ever saw in your life . . . By God! I don't think it would have done if I had not been there." '

There was a longish pause, in which the sailors and the expert talked passionately about the various currents between the European and the African shores and Jack and Roche walked up and down the terrace outside, smoking cheroots. After half a dozen turns Roche said, 'Once he also said that his men *Were the scum of the earth,* or perhaps *Mere scum of the earth.* That was well before Waterloo: he said it quite often, I believe, and I first had it at second hand. I rather resented the words, forming my judgement from the men I had served with; but I do assure you they came back to my mind, carrying full conviction, on the march back to Paris, escorting the sick and wounded there was no room for in Brussels: the drunkenness, riot, insubordination, theft, looting and open rape — and we in a nominally friendly country — were utterly sickening. The provost-marshal's men were very active and they set up the triangles every morning — we use them for flogging, you know — but it did no good, and I was heartily glad to have them all clapped up in the Coligny barracks and to be rid of the whole shooting-match. In the end I came to the conclusion that men subjected to very strong discipline may behave like devils the moment they are released from it. Anyhow, that matches my experience.'

Jack nodded, saying, 'Yes, yes, I am sure.' But his tone implied that although the words were quite true of the army, sailors were, upon the whole, of a different nature.

'Come in, dear Coz,' called Isobel at the open door, 'or your coffee will be no more than just tepid.'

On his way up from the dockyard to Lord Barmouth's house, Jack Aubrey had been aware of a dark, sullen, dogged, ominous cloud at the back of his mind: but in spite of its almost tangible presence he had enjoyed his evening. He was very fond of Queenie and (though in another way) of Isobel. He had thoroughly relished Roche's account; and even his last microscopic cause for discontent — the lukewarm coffee — had been dispelled by the appearance of a fine strong pot, almost too hot to drink, and then some capital brandy.

But now that he was going down towards the outer batteries, the dockyard and of course the town, the sullen cloud moved to the forefront of his mind, and his spirits sank with the road. In places it had been blasted out of the rock to allow the passage of heavy guns, and in these hollow stretches he was quite sheltered from the breeze and the diffused murmur of the town, though not from its glow, reflected from the high, even cloud.

He had just settled on a boulder in one of these sheltered corners when he found that he had given Roche the last of his cigars: it was a vexation, but only a moderate one, and it turned his mind back to the soldier's remarks about men being released from strong discipline and their subsequent excess. 'No,' he said. 'The sailor is a different animal.' He stood up, walked on, and turned out of the cutting on to the plain hill-side, and there the breeze brought him the very powerful, perfectly familiar voice of Higgs. 'There ain't no martial law,' cried the sailor, apparently addressing a fair-sized group in the still unfinished eastern end of the Alameda Gardens. 'There ain't no martial law. The war is over. In any case, *Surprise* ain't a man-of-war no longer, but a surveying vessel. They can't do nothing to us. We've got our money and we can do what we damned well please. There ain't no martial law, and we are free.'

'Wilkes and liberty,' cried someone, drunker than most.

'There are merchantmen crying out for hands, weeping for hands. Eight pound a month, all found, free tobacco and prime victuals. I am going home.' A good deal of hallooing followed this, but Higgs' enormous voice drowned it with the cry 'There ain't no martial law. We are not slaves.'

'We are not slaves,' cried the others, stamping the ground with a rhythmic stress.

This falling apart of the frigate's crew, this disintegration of a community, was of

course the darkness that he had kept back
through the dinner and his happy evening
with Isobel and Queenie. It could not but
have been there, Jack being of the sea
briny, deeply aware of its motions and of
the motions of those who sailed upon it.
He had been conscious of the hands' discontent even before it was formulated: naturally, with the war over, they wanted to
go home and have a good time. But he was
not going to lose his ship or his voyage if
he could help it.

They were a motley lot, the present Surprises: the Admiral had had to bring her
up to war-time strength when Jack was
given his squadron, and no captain in his
senses was going to hand over his best
men: some of the unhappy pressed objects
that came across were more fit for a chari-
table foundation than a man-of-war, but
most were of the lower, more stupid, least-
skilled kind of seafaring man, good for
hauling on a rope, but little else: natural
members of the afterguard. Now, however,
full of life, full of gin and admiration for
Higgs, they were forming up behind him,
and within moments they were marching
into the town, all bawling 'There ain't no
martial law.'

'Can it be true, Captain Aubrey?' asked

a voice just behind him. 'Can it be true that there ain't no martial law?'

'Mr. Wright? How very pleasant to see you. As for the state of the law, in this case as in almost all others, I am profoundly ignorant: but if I were at home, as a magistrate I should feel inclined to read the Riot Act.'

They walked along behind the seamen: and when the cry about slavery was suddenly cut short by the sight of an immense fire at the crossroads — two whole carts and countless empty barrels — with people dancing round it anticlockwise — Jack said, 'I know that Maturin would be very sorry not to see you. I cannot invite you to the ship, she having been sadly damaged in a collision. But he and I are to sup together at the Crown, and we should be delighted if you were to join us.'

'The Crown? Very happy indeed. As it happens I am staying at the George, and I shall have to call in there first . . . and if you will forgive me, sir, this lane takes me to the side courtyard, avoiding the crowded square.'

'So it does,' said Jack. 'So it does: then shall we say about ten o'clock? Maturin and I will come and fetch you, the streets being so full of people.'

Jack Aubrey, a tall, solid and even massive figure in his post-captain's uniform — gold epaulettes broaden a man wonderfully, particularly by firelight — made his way easily enough through the revolving throng and pushed on towards the Surveyor's office, where, if he did not find any of the senior officials present, he meant to leave a note: but at the turning into Irish Town his way was blocked by so compact a mass of people and by such an enormous discordant volume of sound that even his sixteen stone could not advance: and very soon he was blocked from behind as well. In the middle there was a furious battle going on, between Canopuses and Maltas as far as he could make out, while on the right hand a determined body of seamen were breaking into a large wine-shop defended by an equally determined body of well-armed guards; while over on the far side it was clear that a brothel — quite a well-known brothel — had been taken by storm, and its naked inhabitants were trying to escape over the roof, pursued by yet more determined sailors.

Standing there, wedged, unable to advance or retreat, coughing with the smoke of various fires, he reflected on his hitherto conviction that soldiers and sailors were, upon the whole, quite different creatures. 'And perhaps they are, too: yet perhaps drink, in very large quantities, may make the difference less evident.'

At this moment a heart-stirring blast of trumpets away on the right cut through the animal bawling and shrieking in the middle and within minutes a large, perfectly disciplined and resolute body of troops with fixed bayonets emerged at the double from three streets, clearing the place with wonderful speed and efficiency: they were followed by mere constables and the like, who seized obvious malefactors and dragged them, bound, to a mule-cart used for night-soil.

Jack walked across the silent square, saluted now and then by soldiers: blessed ordinariness seemed to have descended upon Gibraltar (though there were still distant fires and what was probably far thunder rather than a raging mob) and it became almost perfect when the few porters and junior clerks in the Surveyor's office declared that none of the higher officials had been in the building for the last three hours. A fine ordinariness in the hospital, too, where Jack sat on a bench outside, drinking an iced mixture of wine, orange and lemon juice through a straw and watching Arcturus growing clearer every minute.

'Oh Jack, how I hope you have not been waiting long. The infernal whores never told me you were there, and I have been exchanging the smallest of small talk this age and more. Brother, you are low in your spirits.'

'Yes, I am. I had a delightful dinner — dear old Mr. Wright was there: we are to fetch him at the George this evening to sup with us — and a Colonel Roche, one of Wellington's ADCs, gave me such an account of the battle — how I wish you had heard him. But as I walked back I came close to a bunch of Surprises: and I tell you what it is, Stephen — the Surprises as a ship's company no longer exist: I fear the new drafts and above all this ill-timed and excessive prize-money have destroyed it. How I wish our Marines had not been taken from us.' He fell silent. Then after a while he said, 'I had thought of speaking to the officers and asking each how many in his division he could count on. I had thought of mustering the people and telling those who wished to carry on with me to move over to the starboard rail, the others to larboard. I thought of many

42

things: but the position in naval and civil law as far as *Surprise* is concerned, and my powers aboard her, is deeply obscure and I shall do nothing before I have spoken to Lord Keith tomorrow morning.'

'I am sure that is wise,' said Stephen, seeing that Jack did not intend to go on. 'The law is a terrible thing to be entangled with. I shall rejoice in Mr. Wright's company, however. We fetch him at the George, I believe you said?'

'Yes: and I shall take Killick and Grimble to protect him from the press.'

But at the George the people of the house stood aghast. 'You are a doctor, sir, I believe?' asked Mrs. Webber. Stephen agreed. 'Then please would you step up and see him? The poor old gentleman was knocked down and robbed by three drunken sailors at our very door. Webber took a horse-pistol to one, but it would not fire. Still, our men did bring him in and carry him up. This way, sir, if you would be so kind.'

When Stephen came down again he said, in answer to Jack's enquiring look, 'A few bruises and a grazed elbow, but nothing broken, I am happy to say. But for a very aged man, the emotional, the spiritual disturbance is almost the equivalent of a broken limb for a lively youth. Yes: he is certainly over eighty — he was elected to the Royal before either of us was breeched — and the ancient, when they are not wholly self-absorbed . . .'

Killick stood swaying in the doorway, but seeing that the Doctor was not likely to stop for some time, he burst in with 'Which Mrs. Webber says would the old gentleman like a little thin gruel? A caudle?' His voice was heavy and slurred, but a sense of what was proper in a post-captain's steward kept him more or less upright, and when he had received and understood Stephen's reply, he said, 'Then I shall tell Grimble to cut along to the Crown and call for your supper to be set on table in half an hour: which I must go and fetch your clean nightshirts.'

The Surprises, their ship being barely habitable, were scattered about the town, most of the officers at the Crown, the master's mates and the superior warrant-officers at the Blue Boar, while the greater part of the ship's company were lodged in a disused set of barracks, food and beer being supplied by the dockyard in exchange for stores removed from the frigate — 'Nothing for nothing, and precious little for fourpence' being the invariable doctrine of the Victualling Office — barracks that were guarded with a certain amount of pomp in front, but whose laundry and sculleries opened on to a squalid lane.

The Crown, however, being a civilized place where Jack had often stayed when he was in funds — a place that provided him and Stephen with a handsome parlour and with a bedroom apiece — was not at all unlike a ship, so that it came quite naturally to Captain Aubrey to invite two of his officers to breakfast with him, Harding, the first lieutenant, and Whewell, the third. From about two in the morning the town had been, and still was, almost preternaturally silent: all hands had slept well after an extremely trying day, and now all hands were laying into their breakfast with a splendid zeal.

'May I trouble you again for the sausages, Mr. Whewell?' asked Jack; and, taking the dish, 'Good morning, Mr. Somers. Will you join us?'

'Good morning, sir,' said the distressed young man. 'I am very sorry to trouble you — very sorry to bring such wretched news — but I am afraid most of the hands have deserted.' He had seen all the men except

45

those granted shore-leave into their hammocks at lights out: he had spoken to the responsible bosun's mates and quartermasters, and he had left proper orders with the sergeant commanding the soldiers at the outer gate. There were still a couple of score old Surprises in the barracks: they complained bitterly of the dockyard food, but they knew nothing about their shipmates' disappearance: nothing whatsoever.

'They have probably gone over the Lines into Spain,' said Jack. 'Many of them would venture upon it for a passage home. Sit down, Mr. Somers, and take at least a cup of coffee and a piece of toast. I shall send to the Convent — their people are almost certain to have news of the deserters. And Mr. Harding, please arrange for a muster aboard at noon. Now, if you will forgive me, I must go and pay an early morning call on the Admiral.'

The Admiral in question was not Barmouth, who, though civil, was neither very well inclined nor, in matters of this sort, with their odd, ambiguous responsibilities, a fount of wisdom: not Barmouth, but Lord Keith, Jack's friend from very early days and a man of immense naval and administrative experience.

It was at Keith's door that he knocked,

46

therefore, and the anxious, downcast servant (an old acquaintance) showed him into the breakfast-room, where Queenie was sitting, mechanically dipping into a bowl of porridge. 'Oh Jack,' she cried, 'such wretched news from Tullyallan . . .'

Tullyallan was a very considerable estate in Scotland belonging to the Admiral — an estate he prized extremely — and it appeared that the factor who looked after it, a man with very wide powers and responsibilities, had made the most of them, absconding with a very large sum of money and leaving Tullyallan in debt and heavily encumbered. 'I have never seen Keith so affected,' said Queenie. 'It is as though he had been struck by a disease . . . he sits there writing letters as fast as his pen can fly, and then tearing them up. But I shall tell him you called, dear Jack.'

Returning, hot and tired from his bitterly disappointing walk under a sun blazing from very near the zenith — a broadcloth uniform coat a prison rather than a protection — returning as ignorant of his exact legal status and powers as when he set out — Captain Aubrey found Stephen and Dr. Jacob sitting on the Crown's veranda, smoking a hubble-bubble. Both Stephen and Jack were used to Jacob's sudden appearances and disappearances: Jack put it down to his being a naturalist as well as a medical man — he had once found Jacob gazing with affection at a remarkably fine plant of henbane, whose qualities he explained with much the same vigour and with an approval almost amounting to enthusiasm as Stephen might have used — a naturalist who could come and go as he pleased.

'How happy I am to see you, Dr. Jacob; I trust you are tolerably recovered?'

'Perfectly recovered, I thank you: a mere blood-letting, sir.'

'I am heartily glad of it,' he said, sitting wearily down on the step. 'I dare say Maturin has told you of our misfortune?'

'Yes, sir: and I told him where they had gone.'

'Over the Lines, I suppose?'

'No, sir: they traversed the entire Rock and dropped down to Catalan Bay, where the fishermen packed them all into three boats and took them across to the Spanish shore under San Roque and there landed them. It cost two and a half ounces of silver each.'

'Pray, how did you find out?'

'Why, I asked a fisherman, sir.'

'Sir,' said Harding, 'forgive me for interrupting, but the muster you called for will take place at noon, if that is convenient.'

'Perfectly convenient. Make it so, Mr. Harding: and if you pass by the bar, please ask them to bring a jug of very cold sangria, with at least four glasses.'

The muster was not a very cheerful occasion, to be sure — the inevitable first name to be called was answered by a heavy, embarrassed silence, and a capital R was placed by Anderson's name, R for run, one of the very few deserters Jack had known as a commanding officer — but he had not asked for numbers, and judging by his officers' tone he had expected things to be much worse. Most of the old and valuable Surprises were there: he greeted each by name — 'Well, Joe, and how are you coming along?' 'Davies, I am happy to see you; but you must take that head of yours to the Doctor' — and they answered with such evident and personal good will that it cancelled the absence of many a good seaman, to say nothing of waisters and members of the afterguard.

This oddly heartening muster took place aboard a docked ship, her bows in an impossible position to allow carpenters —

49

hypothetical carpenters — to deal with some of the sprung butts; and it ended with Harding's most agreeable words, 'Sir, Mr. Daniel tells me that *Ringle* has just made her number.'

'I am very glad to hear it,' said Jack. 'Mr. Reade will no doubt have a message for Lord Keith: please leave word that when he has delivered it, I should be happy if he would dine with me. In the meantime, let us look at the wreck of the bows with Chips.'

There they stood, or rather crouched, right forward and what ordinarily would have been far below: by now their eyes were used to the darkness, and by what light the lanterns could be induced to shed they gazed at the breast-hooks — at the horrible gashes round the breast-hooks — and sighed. 'Listen, Chips,' said Jack to the carpenter, 'I think you know perfectly well that the yard is going to do nothing to all this for a long, long time. Have any of your fellow-carpenters on the commercial side both the timber and the skill to allow us to put to sea and creep to Funchal, to da Souza's place?'

'Well, sir,' said the carpenter, 'I do know a little firm of private shipwrights just below Rosia Bay — I sailed as mate with the top man once, and the other day he showed me some lovely wood in his yard. But they are what you might call carriage-trade, and very expensive. And to do anything here, in the royal yard, they would have to come surreptitious, and sweeten many a palm.'

'Can you give me any sort of a figure?'

'It would not be less than ten guineas a day, I am afraid; and the wood on top.'

'Well, Chips, pray lay it on,' said Jack. 'And pray tell your friends that they shall have a handsome present if upon their conscience we can swim before the new moon.'

He and Stephen left the ship and walked along the mole, gazing eastward at the white spread of *Ringle*'s sails as she beat against the wind, making good progress; and in this total privacy Jack said, 'I think I have made up my mind. It is very probable that Chips's friends will patch her up well enough for us to hope to reach Madeira and a pretty good yard, which should see us home.'

'Home, brother?'

'Why, yes: to Seppings' yard in the first place, the best yard in the kingdom, that practically rebuilt her. And in the second place, to gather an adequate crew, a crew of real seamen. Our South American caper absolutely calls for a strong crew, even without paying any attention to our engagements with the Chileans. Surveying, really surveying these coasts — but then you know about the weather and the tides of the Horn — requires truly able seamen aboard the surveyor's ship.'

'It was the world's pity that those wretched fellows ran off.'

'Yes, it was: by the time we had rounded the Horn, the bosun and his mates, to say nothing of the officers' efforts and my own, might have turned the rag-tag and bob-tail half into something like real seamen. I do not really blame them, however. We had nothing much to offer them except for hard work, short commons and hard lying — no possibility of prizes and no home leave. It is true that once even indifferent seafarers are no longer in demand — which will be in a month or two — and once their money is spent, which is likely to be sooner by far, a berth in *Surprise* might be something to be envied. But as far as we are concerned, I am pretty sure of being able to pick up enough truly able-bodied seamen paid off from King's ships with the coming of peace to form a strong crew, capable of fighting the ship.

At present we can handle her with those good souls who have stayed, but we could not fight her. You do not seem quite happy, brother?'

'It is the Chileans who worry me. All this — the present repair, the dillying in Madeira — all this will take a whole almanac of time: and the Chileans are in a high revolutionary fervour, eager for immediate or almost immediate results. Will they wait?'

'They have no choice. It is not every day that Government fits out a man-of-war to chart their waters, and do little acts of kindness on the way.'

'Well, I hope you are right, my dear. But do not forget that they are foreigners.'

'To be sure, that is very much against them, poor souls. Yet from what you have told me, they have been very steadily set upon independence for many years now. Nothing very flighty or enthusiastic in that, I believe? When we are in London, or elsewhere for that matter, should you like me to speak to the heads of the mission and put the case to them in plain seamanlike terms? They could not fail to be convinced.'

Chapter Two

To a casual observer it would have seemed difficult if not impossible to carry on an affair in so small and tight-knit a community as Gibraltar; yet it was done or attempted to be done by those who did not mind mixing levity and love, done on a quite surprising scale; and when Lord Barmouth's current mistress, an exceptionally vicious woman who hated Isobel, told him that she and Jack Aubrey met daily in a hayloft or at the house of a complaisant friend, it did not surprise him very much. He by no means wholly believed it: an affectionate, easy familiarity was not at all surprising in those who had been children together. Yet he did not like having it said — where horns were concerned he far preferred giving to receiving or even appearing to receive — and although no one had ever questioned his courage in battle, domestic war was another matter entirely. Not only was his own conduct exceptionable to a very high degree, but Isobel, if angered, had a flow of language that he quite dreaded: she was an exceptionally courageous woman, and once her temper had risen beyond a certain degree she was as wholly determined and unshakeable as one of those terriers that will let itself be killed before losing hold. He was also, in his way, deeply attached to her, and very willing that she should be in a good humour with him.

He reflected, therefore: and among other things that occurred to him was the fact that Aubrey was one of Keith's rare protégés. Keith, though resting from his labours at the moment, had very great influence and might easily return to high office. Presently, having walked up and down, Barmouth sent two discreet men to the yard. They confirmed his impression that almost all the remaining Surprises were actively engaged with caulking, painting, and rerigging her boats; and that the frigate herself was still in that improbable position, given over to her captain, carpenter, his mates and auxiliaries.

He threw a shabby old cloak over his uniform, and making his way down to the yard, threaded through those vessels last on the list for repairs until he dropped from the mole on the *Surprise*'s deck. A few people stared at him open-mouthed but he moved rapidly forward and below until he reached the dim, crowded forepeak. Above the sound of mallets he called, 'Captain Aubrey, there.' And in the appalled dead silence, 'How are you coming along?'

'Admirably well, sir, I thank you. Some of my carpenter's old shipmates and friends are bearing a hand. And if I may hold this lantern, my Lord, and beg you to look at the lower breast-hooks I think you will agree that they are making a very pretty job of it indeed.'

'Uncommon pretty,' said Barmouth, gazing with narrowed, knowing eyes. 'Uncommon pretty. Let them carry on, while we take a turn upon the mole.'

Upon the mole, the deserted mole, he spoke quite easily: 'I am glad to see you so forward with your repairs, Cousin Jack; for there is a certain amount of uneasiness in Whitehall about your ultimate destination, and I think I must relax the rigour of my order on precedence and get *Surprise* to sea a good deal earlier than I had thought. The moment you think it safe to take her off the slips we will step your foremast anew, rattle down the shrouds and send you on your way with adequate stores, to say nothing of munitions. Powder and shot is by no means in short supply.'

'You are very good, my Lord,' said Jack with lowered eyes, keeping the suspicion out of his tone and expression with tolerable success. 'I shall look forward to it exceedingly.'

'I shall look forward to it exceedingly, I said to him, Stephen: but I do assure you, I found it quite hard to utter the words, being close on dumbfounded, reduced to silence, I was so amazed by this strange sudden turn. Yet in a flash, it occurred to me that this might be your doing, with — what shall I say? — your connexions.'

'Never in life, my dear,' said Stephen, gazing upon him with real affection — and silently, within his own bosom, 'Did it never come into your mind that the freedoms you have taken with the gentleman's wife — these twilight rambles, this sea-bathing under the moon — however innocent, could scarcely pass unnoticed in this idle peacetime population of lechers, and that the glad news would have been conveyed to the ear most intimately concerned?' Aloud he went on, 'Though I must confess that now the peregrines have hatched, I too should be more than happy to be on the wing. Shall we steer directly for Sierra Leone?'

'Oh dear me, no, Stephen. This is no more than a patching to allow us to reach a yard in Madeira, a professional yard that will give its full attention and allow the barky to face the high southern latitudes and their ice — you know all about that, dear Lord alive — how nearly we were crushed south of the Horn and on the Horn itself, quite apart from the wicked American. Madeira for a thorough repair and a full crew. At present we can just about handle the ship: but to fight her, to fight her both sides, and to sail her in the worst parts of the far South Atlantic, we need another forty really able seamen. Ordinarily we should be able to find them without much difficulty in Funchal.'

'Oh,' said Stephen.

'I fear I have disappointed you?'

'To tell the truth, I had hoped that we should *slope away* for the Guinea Coast, for Sierra Leone, as soon as these admittedly dreadful leaks were staunched and the foremast replaced: that we should slope away directly.'

'Dear Stephen, I did tell you about this necessary pause in Madeira before; and many and many a time have I warned you that in the service nothing, nothing whatsoever, takes place directly.' A pause. 'Pray

58

tell me: where did you learn that term *slope away*?'

'Is it not a nautical expression?'

'I am sure it is; but I do not remember to have heard it.'

'I take the words to refer to that slanting progress, with the breeze not from behind, nor even sideways, but from ahead or partially ahead, so that the vessel *slopes* towards its goal. Yet no doubt I mistake: and no doubt I have used the wrong term.'

'No, no: I follow you exactly — a very good expression. Pray do not be so discouraged, Stephen.'

'Never in life, my dear.' But going to his room and his unfinished letter he wrote, 'This is the third time I have added to these many sheets since my earlier letters in which I acknowledged your extreme kindness in sending the dear potto's bones — so beautifully prepared — to me at the Royal Society, and the others in which I applauded your resolution of staying in Sierra Leone until you had come a little nearer to completing your account of the avifauna of Benin or at least that part of it studied by our great predecessor. How I pray that they reach you safely, in the care of the present Governor. But to come at last to this often-delayed message I am most unwillingly obliged to confess that it amounts to but another dismal postponement. Perhaps I had not attended with sufficient care or understanding to Captain Aubrey's remarks — often when he speaks of sea-going matters in the sailor's jargon my mind tends to wander, to miss some vital point — but whereas I had been convinced (or had convinced myself) that on leaving this port we should steer for Freetown, and that presently I should have the happiness of seeing you, of hearing your account of the new-hatched chanting-goshawks, I now find that I was mistaken — it is no such thing. All this more or less covert hammering, disorder, even devastation is a mere preliminary to far worse in Funchal, where Captain Aubrey declares we must certainly go, to be put into truly naval order for the southern hydrographical voyage, and to pick up some score or so of mariners to make the ship more amenable in the austral tempest.

And so, my dear Madam, I cut this thoroughly unsatisfactory message short, in the hope of renewing it with more definite tidings in a week or so: in the mean time I take the liberty of sending you this hermaphroditic crab, whose singularity I am sure your keen eye will appreciate, while in closing I beg you will accept the most respectful greeting of your humble, obedient servant S. Maturin.'

Yet although S. Maturin had a perfectly good sailcloth wrapper at hand (sea-going letters could not be trusted to paper, least of all in the Bight of Benin) he did not fold the many pages directly but read carefully through the whole to check for any expressions of undue familiarity, in spite of the fact that the earlier sheets were second or even third draughts, recopied from corrected pages.

'Come on, sir,' cried Killick. 'Ain't you finished yet? Tom Wilden says the Guineaman, is fiddling about with the hoist of a Blue Peter. She will sail within the hour, and you won't get another this month or six weeks.'

'Oh dear, oh dear,' said Stephen in an undertone, and he read faster and faster. The dread of an impropriety, of an unwarranted evidence of affection — indelicate in the last degree on the part of a man in his condition, fairly haunted him. But rather than lose the letters' carriage he thrust the whole, far too hastily and imperfectly re-read, into the wrapping, sealed and corded it.

Dissimulation was nothing remotely new

to Maturin: to it he owed his continuing existence. Yet this particular *suppressio veri* was by no means his province. Christine Wood had in fact dwelt in his memory, his mind, his recollection since their first meeting in Sierra Leone: not so much her striking good looks — slim, long-legged, almost androgynous — as her modesty, clarity of mind, and quite exceptional breadth of knowledge, covering most of the areas in which he took most delight.

Stephen was of course discreet: but in spite of a discretion carried to something not far from an apparent frigidity, he had strong, even very strong male impulses and a recollection of Christine swimming in stark innocent nakedness across a clear African stream to bring back a wounded ibis — swimming under the eyes of a perfectly indifferent and almost equally naked black servant-girl — had very often inhabited and indeed tormented his mind, preventing incipient sleep. But more than her Greek or African nakedness — bare flesh, after all, being less to an anatomist than to most — was the slight but clearly perceptible pressure of her hand when they last parted years ago that dwelt with him now, abed in the Crown, when he was not rehearsing passages of that interminable letter in which he may have blundered. Just before he went to sleep much the same part of consciousness that presented careful paragraph after careful paragraph called upon him to 'State a quality common to all those women for whom, as an adult, you have felt a strong tenderness'.

'A strong *amorous* tenderness?'

'Of course, you lemon.'

He reflected, and said: 'In all cases they have held themselves well: they have, all, without the least consciousness or affectation, taken quite long strides for a woman, placing each foot directly in the line of its fellow — a wholly natural grace.'

All this had been a weary, anxious task, and the contemplation of his hastily, partially re-read, almost certainly over-voluble and ill-considered series of letters bounding over the ocean wave (for the breeze was favourable) so wrung his weary spirit that for the first time in a great while he turned to his old friend and enemy laudanum, the alcoholic tincture of opium, and plunged into a sleep, guilty for the first few fathoms and then pure balm.

'Oh come on, sir,' called little Wells, his adolescent voice soaring with indignation. 'You'll miss it all, snorting there . . .'

Stephen gazed blinking at the brilliant sun, and the boy urged him to his feet, to the window, the extreme left-hand side of the window which commanded part of the yard. 'There, sir: do you see?'

Yes, indeed he saw: *Surprise* still rocking from her violent run astern, but upright, trimmer every rnoment, but for the ill-looking gap where the sheers had plucked out her foremast. Volubly, with a wealth of detail, Wells recounted the whole event. '. . . and if you lean a little this way, sir, you can just make out the sheer-hulk going crabwise towards her . . . she makes fast . . . hush.'

And from over the still water far below came Harding's powerful voice: 'Silence, there. Silence fore and aft' — an urgent, imperative cry that from long habitude imposed an instant, remarkable calm, through which Jack's hurried step could be heard. 'Just in time,' he exclaimed. 'There, Stephen, do you see? The sheers raise the mast clear — they swing it over — they clap on — they lower away — handsomely, handsomely now — Harding gives the word — she is home!' All the other operations followed their natural course — shrouds, stays, top; and then the topmast itself swayed up.

'There,' said Jack. 'As pretty as could be wished. You would not have liked to miss a moment of that, I am sure.'

'No, indeed,' said Stephen.

'And I am sure Mr. Wells explained what little you had not seen before?'

'With the utmost clarity: I was extremely gratified.'

'Very good, very good, Well, cut along, Mr. Wells, and tell Mr. Harding that the Doctor saw it all, and was extremely gratified. I tell you what it is, Stephen,' he went on as the boy could be heard going down the stairs like a hundred of bricks, 'the Admiral has altered course most surprisingly: 180°, no less, and now he is bundling us off as though we were carrying the plague. They are busy at the ordnance wharf this very minute, and I make no doubt that as soon as the galley fires are dowsed and cold, the powder-hoy will be alongside. He spoke of some uneasiness at home about our delay in reaching Chile.'

'I trust there was no hint of reprobation? After all, it cannot be said that we trifled away our time in thoughtless or even wanton play.'

'No. I think it was just ordinary official impatience. His Majesty's ships are often expected to be in two places at once, whatever the difference of longitude — see, a lighter is putting off with round shot. What joy!'

For much of the rest of the day stores and munitions came aboard, wearing the meagre crew if not to a shadow then at least to total rock-salt soberness; and the existing midshipmen's berth was strengthened by three young gentlemen, Glover, Shepherd and Store, two of them sons of Jack's former shipmates, the third imposed by Lord Barmouth. In spite of their fine new clothes they were instantly required to 'Bear a hand, there, bear a hand: and roundly, do you hear me, now?' by Mr. Harding.

A few minutes later, with the sun almost touching Africa, Jack's barge was lowered down (with a new coxswain, Latham: a capital seaman, but one who could never fill Bonden's place in his own, his captain's or his fellows' affection). 'Although it is untimely, I must pay my respects to Lord Keith,' said Jack in an undertone.

'If I may come with you, I too have a message to leave in the town,' murmured Stephen. The message was a deeply cryptic note for Dr. Jacob, begging him to send any word he had gathered on the presence or absence of Chileans: and if either was of any consequence, to come to Funchal himself.

He left this in the discreet, capacious bosom of the woman of the house, and he was walking back to the waterside when he heard a voice cry 'Dr. Maturin!' and turning he saw Lady Barmouth, accompanied by Mr. Wright and followed by a maid.

After greeting made, Mr. Wright said, 'This falls very well. By your leave, Lady Barmouth, I shall resign you to Dr. Maturin and hurry off to the Surveyor.' With this he did indeed literally hurry away, his handkenchief falling from his pocket.

'Dear me, what an old savage,' said Isobel mildly. 'Pepita!' she cried in Spanish, 'the gentleman has lost his handkerchief — pick it up and catch him, for the love of God. Dear Dr. Maturin, I am so happy to see you: and please may I get you to give me a sorbet at Bomba's just over there? I die of thirst.'

'And I am happy to see you, Lady Barmouth,' said Stephen as he offered his arm, 'yours indeed was the name I was revolving in my mind.'

'How pleasant. In what connection, pray?'

'I was wondering whether the shortness

67

of our acquaintance would bar my calling to take leave: sure, it might be thought presumptuous.'

'It would certainly never be thought presumptuous, my dear Doctor: but why in Heaven's name should you think of taking leave? I had thought we were sure of you for a great while yet.'

'Alas, I understand that we are to sail rather late this evening, if the breeze lies as Captain Aubrey could wish. He is making his farewells to the Keiths at present, and I am sure he will have done all that is proper at headquarters.'

'When I was not at home.' She reflected and said, 'I should be sorry not to say good-bye: Jack Aubrey and I are very old friends. Perhaps I shall meet him as he comes down. Come, Pepita. Dear Dr. Maturin, thank you very much for my delicious sorbet: do not move, I beg.'

He did move, but only to stand as she walked off, followed by her maid — walked off with just that lithe pace he had had in mind.

It was the same, the very same step he recognized that night, when at last the breeze came true and *Surprise*, filling her fore and main topsails, glided along the outside of the mole, her lanterns faintly lighting the veiled figures upon it, one of them discreetly waving — a sight so usual on the quay of partings as to excite no attention among the odd, scattered, immobile fishermen.

For the next few days they had some very sweet sailing on a warm, moderate breeze whose only fault was that it varied from west-north-west to north-north-west, so that at times they were close-hauled and at times they were fetching, but always with a fine array of headsails: very sweet sailing had they not been in a hurry. But the more or less clandestine work on the frigate's bows had not fully restored her windward qualities — quite outstanding until that vile collision — and again and again *Ringle*, who in any case was schooner-rigged, had to ease her sheets or even take in sail not to shoot ahead — discreet manoeuvres, but never unnoticed, never unresented by the Surprises. Yet in spite of these drawbacks and the comparative slowness, upon the whole this was a happy time, a kind of homecoming and the restoration of what even to Maturin seemed the good and natural life, with its immutable regularity (whatever the weather might say), its steady though not very appetizing nourishment, the association with men who, if not brilliant company, were almost all sound, solid, professional seamen and far more agreeable than any mere chance gathering of the same size.

With all its disadvantages of close quarters, lack of privacy, and desperate shortage of post, to say nothing of books, newspapers, magazines, it was indeed a return to order, to that unquestioned order so absent in life, above all urban life ashore. In a very little while they might have been back in a sea-going monastic order — monastic, but for the shocking prevalence of pox in its dismal varieties that kept Stephen, and at a certain remove his loblolly girl, so busy.

How quickly the old train of life, ruled by bells and pipes, the swabbing of decks, by quarters, lights out, the cry of sentinels and all the rest came back — all the rest including an excellent appetite, particularly among the young, who, when invited to the captain's breakfast-table (which often happened if they had had the morning watch) would eat four eggs without a blush and then finish whatever happened to be in the bacon-dish. Good appetites, together with a longing for a change of diet and, among the older seamen, a dread of running out of stores, so that now, when they had scarcely sunk the high land behind Rabat, they cheered the foretopmast look-out when he hailed the quarterdeck with the news of a body of tunny-fishers standing along the Moroccan coast; and when the Captain altered course to meet the boats even the grizzled old fo'c'sle hands capered like lambs on a summer's green.

Here the *Surprise* bought a fine great fish, still quivering, hoisted him aboard, cut him up on the fo'c'sle, carried the massive pieces to the galley in tubs, washed the red blood off the deck, swabbed and flogged it dry, and ate an improbable amount for dinner. A very great deal: yet even so, the wind veering northerly, they were still eating him for supper the next day, officers, men, boys, and the few women they were allowed, such as Poll Skeeping and Maggie Tyler the bosun's wife's sister, eating him steadily with active pleasure and what little Gibraltar beer they still had aboard, when the cry came down from the starving masthead: 'On deck, there, on deck. Land very fine on the starboard bow. Sort of reddish, like,' he added in an undertone.

'I believe that must be our landfall almost to the minute,' said Jack, looking at his watch with great satisfaction.

A brief-lived satisfaction, however, for when they cut their meal short, carrying coffee up on to the quarterdeck, they found the whole gunroom and most of the midshipmen's berth already there. On seeing their Captain, the officers cast a guilty look aft and sidled forward along the starboard gangway. Only Harding, as in duty bound, remained. 'It may not be as bad as it looks, sir,' he said.

It did indeed look bad: very bad. The 'sort of reddish' was now a great crimson blaze all along that part of the town where ships were built, including Coelho's famous yard: a great blaze with huge flames soaring and even cracking off to soar alone.

The ebbing tide and falling wind kept the frigate well off shore until first light, when it was already apparent that the fire was growing sullen. At slack water the breeze revived a little and they stood on, pumps and fire-hoses ready. But it was clear that the townsmen had the upper hand, and there was nothing that strangers could do but keep out of the way until ordinary life resumed; if, indeed, it ever did. There was scarcely a man aboard *Surprise* who had not seen a dockyard, a shipbuilding yard, ablaze, together with all its stores of timber, its rigging-lofts and all the vessels on the stocks: but this outdid anything the Adriatic or the Aegean had had to offer on their last campaign.

After a silent breakfast, with all hands gazing at the blackened ruins and the vessels burnt to the water-line, with smoke still rising over all, they approached the good holding-ground where they usually checked their way with a kedge in order to salute the castle handsomely, broadside on.

The castle already had its colours flying, still, as Jack noticed with the British next to the Portuguese; but the gunners within, presumably exhausted from their night's labours, could not gather their wits to return the civility for close on five minutes; and during this time a small, dirty, unofficial boat put off and pulled for the frigate. A very thin young man, in what could still just be described as naval uniform, came up the side, and taking off his hat to Captain Aubrey, said in a fluting, intensely nervous voice, 'Wantage, sir: come aboard, if you please.'

'Mr. Wantage,' said Jack, looking attentively into his face, in part familiar, yet strangely altered. 'There is an R against your name.' The young man, a master's mate, had not responded to the ship's repeated signals, and she had left Funchal without him. It was known among his shipmates that he was much attached to a shepherdess in the hills, and his absence was attributed to this liaison.

'Yes, sir. But it was not my fault. A gang of men took me far into the mountains and kept me shut up. They beat me every Sunday, taking turns, until a monk said it was hardly right. And they were very cruel to me, sir: they cut me.'

Certainly he was very much reduced: and very deeply embarrassed. Most of those aboard had some knowledge of the countryside, some acquaintance with the practices of shepherds; and they were aware of his, present condition.

'Pass the word for Mr. Daniel,' said Jack: and two moments later, 'Mr. Daniel, here is a colleague for you, Algernon Wantage, master's mate, who was detained in the mountains when the ship was called to Gibraltar, but who has now rejoined. Take him below, show him the new members of the berth, remind them of his seniority, and make him as comfortable as our limited space allows.'

'Yes, sir,' said the one, and 'Thank you, sir,' said the other.

'And now I come to think of it, Mr. Wantage,' he called after them, 'I believe we carried off your sea-chest and other belongings. Jason, tell one of the holders to rouse them out. Mr. Harding, as soon as I have paid my duty-call on His Excellency, I believe we must talk to the port-captain. Doctor, you will be so very kind as to interpret for us, as you did before?'

Stephen bowed: but when they had put on formal clothes he said, 'Interpret, is it? As I told you before I do not speak — not as who should say *speak* — Portuguese. Still less do I understand the language when it *is* spoke. No man born of woman has ever understood spoken Portuguese, without he is a native or brought up to comprehend that strange blurred muffled indistinct utterance from a very early, almost toothless, age. Anyone with a handful of Latin — even Spanish or Catalan — can read it without much difficulty but to comprehend even the drift of the colloquial, the rapidly muttered version . . .'

The captain of the port, however, was a master of the lingua franca spoken over most of the Mediterranean and even beyond, as well as the archaic Catalan still current in his mother's part of Sardinia, and it took him very little time indeed to destroy Jack Aubrey's hopes entirely, speaking with the utmost loquacity, sometimes in one language, sometimes in the other — the different versions each shedding a dismal light on the other. He addressed himself entirely to Stephen, but at the same time he gazed upon Jack with unfeigned astonishment and concern. 'Had not the gentleman seen with his own eyes that Coelho's yard, the glory of Funchal, of Madeira, of the western world, was utterly destroyed? That there was not another in the whole island to be mentioned in the same breath? And that even Carteiro's could not possibly accommodate anything above a hundred and twenty tons?' The captain of the port shook his saddened head. He called for madeira of the famous year 1775, and when they had drunk a couple of glasses each, he observed in a gentle side-voice directed at Dr. Maturin, though his eyes still dwelt upon Jack, that 'he wondered where the gentleman had been in his youth, and during all the years since then, not to know that at this time of the year there was not a seaman in Madeira, with two hands and both legs, to be had. The fleets bound for both the Indies, East and West, had sailed a little early, because of Nostradamus; and all who did not go with them were on the Banks for cod or in the tunny-boats along the African shore. And even the few odd remaining cripples could not possibly be tempted by a hydrographical voyage to survey the Horn and its terrible passages, with no possibility of taking a prize.'

Here Stephen did his discreet best to convey the notion that, in certain circumstances, prizes might not be altogether out of the question. 'After all, there were always, or at least very often, pirates — legitimate quarry — beyond the Straits of Magellan.'

'Oh, certainly,' replied the port captain. 'Prizes on the far side of the world. Beyond the Straits of Magellan: but, my dear sir,' he added with civil triumph, 'you will remember what happened to Magellan himself.'

'Indeed,' said Stephen, 'and how I regret that great man's untimely death. But I clearly see that I shall have to disillusion my superior officer: allow me to thank you however for your luminous, wholly convincing statement of the position, and to beg your acceptance of these few pairs of English worsted stockings.'

'Well,' said Jack, as they walked through the unburnt part of the town — some streets slightly charred on the left-hand side, but no outright ruin — 'I suppose there is no help for it: but it was a damned unlucky stroke, the Indies fleets going off like that. Who is this Nostradarnus?'

'Oh, a sort of prophet, like our Old Moore; but not quite so wise. May I ask whether you have made up your mind what to do?'

'Oh yes: I have no doubt of it. I should have liked some new breast-hooks here, in Coelho's yard, and some more diagonal bracing; but I am reasonably sure that *Surprise* will carry us back to Seppings' yard for an overhaul that will allow us to face the Horn without terror: at least without absolutely paralysing terror. And that, after all, is what I had wanted from the start.'

After a while, Stephen, speaking hesitantly, said, 'My dear, have you reflected upon mainland Portugal and Atlantic Spain, with their famous ports, and shipwrights who turned out such beautiful vessels as the *Santa Ana*, which Nelson himself so much admired?'

'Yes,' said Jack. 'Harding and I turned the matter over before ever we shaped our course for Funchal: at the time the wind would have served for either, whereas now it is awkwardly east for the main. Yet I am sure our choice of Funchal would have been perfect, but for that infernal blaze. Certainly the Spaniards can build a noble first-rate, noble ships of the line; but they are not so happy with frigates, and in any event I do not think that a small English hydrographical vessel would be really welcome in a Spanish yard, nor very briskly attended to. And as for crew, I should not care for so large a proportion of Spaniards: there has been too much ill-feeling for too long. Whereas the Portuguese, in my experience, are just as good seamen, and kinder, less likely to fly into a passion. More easy-going, if you understand me. And then again, Funchal was accustomed to moderate-sized ocean-going yachts, vessels quite like the *Surprise*: which is not the case in Vigo, nor at the Groyne. No. What I think is the clever thing for us to do is to lie here for a few days while Chips, who knows the town well, will see if he can find some prime timber in the outlying stores, and if he can, to bring some master-shipwrights — there will be many, many

out of employ at the present, poor souls —
and set them to work on our bows. Then
hey for Seppings' yard, a thorough
overhaul, and a full crew of right
West-country seamen . . .' He would have
added 'and England, home and beauty, of
course,' but for the fear that the mention
of the first two might bring the third into
Stephen's mind aind wound him cruelly:
his expression was already far from cheerful.

In fact the sombre look was caused by
his knowledge of the extreme impatience
of any revolutionary force and by his per-
suasion that if they did not come to a solid
agreement with the Chileans they knew,
having met them by appointment in this
very town, an agreement with set dates,
undertakings and statement of forces in
being and above all if they did not make an
appearance in their well-armed
hydrographical ship — these first Chileans
might lose faith, might let their impatience
overcome them, or — another strong probability — might be superseded by some
new, even more enthusiastic and impatient
body, with even less knowledge of the
facts. All this amounted to little more than
a presentiment: a somewhat more informed presentiment than most, but cer-

tainly nothing to be set against the considered opinion of two experienced sea-officers.

They walked along, each deep in his own thoughts, passing through the sad, dirty, worn-out people on either side, many of whom had obviously toiled all night: no gaiety whatsoever, so that the hoots of silly laughter at the far end of the street seemed more than usually offensive. Hoots of laughter, then another imitation of a man's falsetto, and hoots again. The crowd cleared somewhat and Jack saw that the imitator was the heaviest, hairiest, most pimpled of his new midshipmen, Store, accompanied by the admiring smallest, a first-voyager called Shepherd. For the sake of his father, a former shipmate, Jack had invited Store to dinner and had been surprised by his uncouth, silent barbarity, until he remembered that Admiral Store — Rear-Admiral Sir Harry Store, to be exact — had spent almost the whole of the war on the Indian and South African stations. At present it was obvious that the reefers were following Wantage and a carpenter's mate, some fifty yards ahead, and openly mocking them. He called out in his strong, sea-going voice. The tall youth turned, looking guilty, ashamed, defiant: he made his unsteady way back accompanied by the little one, but at least he had wit enough to stand up straight and pull off his hat. 'Who gave you leave to come ashore?' asked Jack.

'Mr. Harding, sir,' they said in unison,

'Go back to him at the double and tell him that on my orders you are to go to the foremast head and Mr. Shepherd to the mizzen, there to stay until I return.'

Wantage had stopped short on hearing Captain Aubrey's hail, and now that the midshipmen were running off he came up. 'What is your errand, Mr. Wantage?' asked Jack.

'Sir, the carpenter asked me to go along with his mate' — the mate touched his forehead with a knuckle — 'and cheapen some pieces of dragon-wood for him.'

'You speak the Portuguese, I collect?'

'Yes, sir: my father was a wine-merchant here in Funchal, and I used to come and stay with my grandmother.'

'That is a capital accomplishment, to be sure. I shall call upon you, if I may, when the ship needs an interpreter. I hope you are successful in your bargaining: but do not stick for a dollar or two — the ship comes first. Good day to you.'

He returned their salute, and after a

pause he went on to Stephen, 'There is your point to the very life. Wantage may not be a Newton or a Halley or a Cook — how I honour that man! — but he did have a Portuguese grandmother, when he was a little fellow, and now he has the Portuguese, ha, ha, ha! And to think I never knew it.'

'Perhaps you never asked,' said Stephen, somewhat put out.

'On the other hand, that might have been his loss too. Without the Portuguese he could never have cuckolded the shepherd. But I must not speak lightly of serious things . . . I shall have a word with Harding.'

Back to the ship — the ceremony of boarding her — to the great cabin, and the word passing for the first lieutenant.

'Mr. Harding, pray take a seat. May I offer you a glass of Madeira?'

Harding bowed his agreement, and having drunk a sip, he said, 'Capital Madeira, sir, capital.'

'It is pretty good, is it not, though I say it myself: but where can you get capital Madeira if not in Funchal itself?' They drank in a grave, considering way, and refilling their glasses Jack went on, 'But I tell you this, Mr. Harding, our midshipmen's berth is not what it should be.'

'No, sir: it is not.'

'I watched them on the way from Gibraltar. The newcomers have no idea of their duty and except for the little fellow, the first-voyager, no wish to learn it. But what really angered me extremely was Store's conduct ashore. He followed that poor unfortunate Wantage, crowing like a cock in an affected eunuch's voice. For God's sake, a gentleman's son behaving so in public! I have told him very clearly that if he ever ventures upon such a caper again I shall first have him made fast to a gun and beat him very hard indeed and then put him ashore at the nearest port, in whatever country it may be. I think that has calmed him for the moment: but he is a thoroughly undesirable influence on the mere boys, and since we cannot inflict him on the gunner, I believe we must return to the old way of asking him to look after youngsters, which will leave Daniel, Salmon, Adams — who must be thirty-odd — and Soames to keep Store in order: to say nothing of poor Wantage, who must make the wretched fellow anxious.'

'I quite agree, sir. You would not consider putting him ashore here?'

'No. I did think of it; but his father and I

84

were shipmates. Yet at the very first hint of a repetition, out he goes. You and the bosun and the bosun's mates must keep him very busy — he cannot even manage a clove-hitch. And whenever he presumes to start a seaman with fist, foot or rope-end let him go straight to the masthead. In any case, if we recommission in England after the repair, I very much doubt that I shall invite him to come with us.'

'Stephen,' he said much later, when they had finished their rather dull game of piquet — not a really interesting hand since the very first deal, and only fourpence won or lost — and they were sitting at their ease, drinking Madeira, 'I rarely, or *tolerably* rarely, bore you with the miseries of command: a good ship, a happy ship — and the two are much the same — pretty well runs herself, once all the people are settled down, above all if they are mostly old man-of-war's men.'

'Certainly. One can see that particular ethos come into being: and what has struck me quite forcibly is that it differs from ship to ship.'

'Ethos is not a Christian word, brother.'

'I beg pardon: I should have said something like *tribal sense of right conduct* but for the fact that sea-officers usually employ *tribal* to signify a group of black or red men created only for the comic or picturesque effect — I mean, leaving slavery aside. However, since nothing else occurs to my wine-fuddled mind, let us go on with *tribal,* using tribal in the noble sense of Boadicea's Iceni.'

'I have no objection whatsoever.'

Stephen bowed and went on. 'This tribal nature, which is of course most obvious towards the end of a long commission, may be likened to that which one senses in London clubs. No one could mistake an habitual member of Boodle's for an habitual member of Black's. It is not necessarily a question of better or worse. The Bactrian camel with two bunches is a valuable creature: the Arabian with but one is also a valuable creature.'

'I should not deny it for a moment — though I could wish that Black's did not have what some people might call an almost Whiggish complexion — but my real point is that in peace-time everything becomes much more difficult. You cannot distinguish yourself; and although as a captain it is your obvious duty to do your best for the people under your command, how can it be done? Getting a ship at all, when so many are being paid-off, is a near impossibility, like. . . .' He searched for the word.

'Making a mountain out of a molehill?'

'Even worse, Stephen, even worse. These three young fellows who came aboard were able to do so only because they have very highly influential fathers; two of whom were my old shipmates anyhow. And boys, youths, with very highly influential fathers have to be handled with tongs: above all in peace-time . . . No, I don't mean for myself, Stephen — I shall tell you about that on Sunday — but if any of the lieutenants or the master or any of the warrant-officers comes down on them heavy, it might cost him very dear. I have known it: some miserable little scrub writes to his mother, "Mr. Blank boxed my ears so cruelly in the middle watch that I can hardly see out of my right eye at all." And if Father Scrub votes for the ministry and knows someone in Whitehall, in peace-time Mr. Blank may whistle for a ship until Kingdom Come.'

Jack Aubrey could never have been described as enthusiastically evangelical, but he did possess a sort of disseminated piety, sometimes expressing itself in mere superstition, sometimes in a very powerful singing of his favourite psalms, and sometimes in little private rites, such as keeping presents or good news for Sundays.

Sunday, and a very welcome pause from the hellish beating of mauls and square-headed mallets in the forepeak. Wantage, who knew Funchal through and through and who was recovering some of his self-possession with the familiar life of the Royal Navy going on all around him, had told Harding of the best eating-house in the town, and there the first lieutenant was entertaining Reade of the *Ringle*, Whewell, Candish and Woodbine of the gunroom, and the two master's mates, Daniel and Wantage. He had hoped to invite Jack and Stephen too, but his servant, sounding Killick first, had learnt that the Captain and the Doctor were engaged to eat a young wild boar, roasted according to the Madeiran fashion, in the hills.

'Please tell the Senhor that I have never eaten better porco in my life,' said Jack, holding up a bare white bone. Jack had a variety of little imbecilities, but none irritated Stephen more than his way of tossing in the odd word or two of a foreign language.

'Oh mind your breeches, sir,' cried

Killick, interposing a napkin, a napkin too late. 'There: now you've gone and done it.'

'Never mind,' said Jack, and he tossed the bone into the glowing embers. 'What now?' he called, addressing a nervous horse-borne midshipman on the edge of the picnic dell.

'If you please, sir, Mr. Somers thought you might like to know that a packet is come in from Gibraltar.'

'Thank you, Mr. Wells. Ride back and tell him that we are just about to take our leave.'

A packet it was, and a fine fat one too, with English letters of various degrees of antiquity, a great parcel of dockets for Mr. Candish the purser, post for the cabin, gunroom and midshipmen's berth, and two waxed sailcloth rolls for Dr. Maturin.

'Forgive me,' said Stephen, and as he went he heard orders given for the general distribution. It was long before he came back: his first roll had contained some curious feathers of an unidentified nocturnal bird, probably cousin to the red-necked nightjar, and a particularly agreeable note from Sierra Leone, written before Christine Wood had received his letter; and the second was a coded message from Jacob, written according to a system they rarely used — a system in which Jacob had clearly lost his way, for although the first section spoke of certain Chileans and their arrangements (apparently with some anxiety), the second, third and fourth could not be induced to yield any meaning at all, whatever combinations were applied to them.

The attempt at decoding took much time and spirit, and well before he abandoned all hope the ship was alive with steps and voices once more, sounds that died as the letters were read; yet when he walked into the cabin he found Jack still smiling over his post. 'There you are, Stephen,' he cried. 'I do hope your letters were as pleasant as mine? I had a very agreeable foretaste on Friday, and I meant to keep it for today: but here is a confirmation,' holding up a sheet — 'so I shall contain no longer. You remember that dear man Lawrence?'

'Faith, I shall not soon forget him. He did his profession infinite credit.' Mr. Lawrence was the barrister who had done his utmost to defend Jack Aubrey when he was charged with rigging the Stock Exchange — a completely false charge brought by those who profited by the fraud and a trial conducted on political motives by one of the most prejudiced and unscrupulous judges to have sat on the English bench. Lawrence had worked extremely hard to save his innocent client, and his failure to do so had marked him deeply.

'He did indeed. We often dine together when I am in town; and long ago, oh very long ago, before ever we went to Java and New South Wales, he happened to say that a nephew of his who had worked for years with Arthur Young had set up as an agricultural consultant and agent, but found it difficult to get a start. "I am the man for him," I said, and I told him about the little estate my cousin left me.'

'The place with a glorious spread of fritillaries in the water-meadows and the borough you represent in Parliament?'

'Just so. I have nothing against fritillaries: but I do assure you, Stephen, that with their sodden fields, the few farms and small-holdings produce nothing whatsoever except the ten or eleven electors and their families and just enough for them to eat. Every Lammas they send me a petition begging to be forgiven their rent *this* year, and please may they have twelve loads of stone for Old Hog Lane? It is an estate that costs me half a guinea for every snipe I have shot there: not that I have ever gone down much — it is far away, over vile roads, and there is no pleasure in looking at those barren fields and those coarse rank pastures. My cousin only bought the place because of the parliamentary seat. Indeed, the borough may be rotten, but the land is very much worse. Killick,' he called, barely raising his voice at all.

'Sir?' replied Killick, almost immediately.

'Light along a pot of coffee, will you?'

After a pause, Jack went on, 'One really should keep a log-book, you know; a diary: after some years it is difficult to put your ideas in order. At least, that is what I find. Well, the nephew — his name is Leicester, by the way: John Leicester — went down and reported that things were bad, very bad, but not incurable, and given the lie of the land, draining would answer very well. It would take time, it would take years; but most of the tenants would give their labour according to a scheme he had devised which would allow them time for their farming, and there would be no great outlay of money. So since at that time there had been some elegant prizes I told him to carry on: but there were to be no evictions, no distraints . . .'

'Pot of coffee, sir,' said Killick.

'Where was I? Told him to carry on, which he did; and we sailed away. I almost entirely forgot it . . . to be sure, Leicester, who was acting as agent as well, did send annual reports, but with so many things happening I am afraid I neglected them until last year, when he paid in rents of I think nearly forty pounds; and this year he spoke of the likelihood of a really abundant wheat harvest, ha, ha! However, I did not mention it, for fear of ill-luck: but today I have the truly welcome news that he has given the tenants a Lammas dinner of roast beef and plum pudding, at which they drank my health, and that he had placed £450 to my credit at the bank. £450, Stephen! More than my pay as a post-captain. There: that was my good news.'

'And very good, very welcome news it is, my dear. I give you joy with all my heart. There you are . . . I am very glad of it.'

So he was; but Jack, though not preternaturally sharp, detected the uneasiness, not so much in Stephen's expression as in a kind of particular tension in his attitude, and he said, 'Forgive me, Stephen, for boring you with all this personal and rather commonplace talk about money — you are uneasy.'

'No. You mistake: I was not in the least degree bored, weary, inattentive. And if I am at all uneasy, it is from another cause. Jack, tell me how long will these repairs take before you can sail?'

'With two saint's days coming and the vast amount of work to be done in so many of the shipwrights' own houses, eight or nine days.'

'Then I must beg for *Ringle* to carry me to England. And if she could sail tonight how happy I should be.'

It was at once clear to Jack that the request and the Gibraltar packet were connected: he asked no questions but passed the word for Mr. Reade, and when he came, said, 'William, how soon can you be under way?'

'In twenty minutes, sir, if I may sail without my carpenter.'

'You have his mate aboard?'

'No. He is aboard you, sir.'

'Then I shall send him over directly. Good-bye to you, William: you have the breeze as fair as ever you could wish.'

Almost all voyages, from that of Noah's Ark to the sending of the ships to Troy, have been marked by interminable delays, with false starts and turning wind and tide; perhaps the schooner *Ringle* was too slim and slight to count as a worthy adversary, because she gently sailed her anchor out of the ground and then bore away a little east of north with a wind that allowed her to spread every sail she possessed, other than those reserved for foul or very foul weather.

It was indeed almost perfect sailing, the captain rarely leaving the deck, and all hands (a select body by now) perfectly ready to clap on to any rope or line that showed the least inclination to heave slack and recall it to the most rigid sense of its duty — anything for an extra eighth part of a knot.

Most of this time Stephen spent in his low triangular berth, vainly applying various formulae to Jacob's meaningless groups of seven: he did however share his meal with William Reade, who reminded him of a wonderful run they had made racing up the Channel and reaching the Nore just in time for the first stirring of the flood tide that swept them up to the Pool in some period of time so wonderfully short that Reade had had the record signed and witnessed by several eminent hands.

'How I hope we may do the same this time, sir,' he said.

'I hope so, indeed,' said Stephen.

But alas for their hopes: the Channel, awkward as ever, had had enough of south-west breezes in all their variety, and now indulged itself in strong rain from the north and north-east, combined with adverse tides that ran with great force long after their legal time. It was a worn ship's company that set Dr. Maturin ashore in the Pool of London, comforted only by the thought that they should now lie snug at harbour-watch, with sailors' pleasures a short biscuit-toss away — would lie snug until orders came down from Whitehall.

Whitehall, and the noble screen before the Admiralty, with appropriate mythological figures adorning its higher part, and an undeniably shabby Pool of London cab drawn up outside, with an equally shabby figure standing by it, slowly sorting English from Irish, Spanish and Moorish coins to pay the deeply suspicious driver, who had got down from his seat with the reins over one arm to make sure that his rum cove of a fare did not scarper.

Stephen's extraordinarily rapid departure had caught Killick at a disadvantage: with Grimble, his mate, he was entertaining two ladies of Funchal to a light collation, and the Doctor went over the side into *Ringle's* boat confident (as far as he

96

thought of it at all) that his sea-chest was in its usual perfect order. During the voyage from Madeira Stephen had not seen fit to dive into the chest lower than the till which held a primitive sponge, a case of razors, brush and comb, and an increasingly dubious towel. The rest of the time he spent wrestling with his code or urging the vessel up-Channel with all the moral force at his disposition.

But when *Ringle* was alongside at the Pool and a ship's boy had brought the cab, the best he could find, Stephen thought it time to put on fine clothes for his official call. There were no fine clothes: no clean shirts, even; no neck-clothes, drawers, silk (or cotton) stockings: no silver-buckled shoes. Everything, *everything*, had been taken away for a thorough overhaul. And the Admiralty's under-porter, peering through his hatch, said, 'There's a rum cove a-paying off a nasty Tower Hamlets cab, Mr. Simpson. Shall I tell him to go round to the tradesmen's entrance?'

Simpson peered over his shoulder for a while, watching with narrowed eyes, while the last groats were counted out: he elbowed his assistant aside, and when the rum cove came to the hatch, greeted him with a civil 'Good afternoon, sir.'

To this Stephen replied, 'And a good afternoon to you, to be sure. I do not appear to have a visiting-card about me, but if Sir Joseph is in the way, please be so good as to let him know that Dr. Maturin would be glad of a word at his earliest convenience.'

'Certainly, sir: I am not quite sure, of course, but I believe he is in. Should you care to wait, sir? Harler, show the gentleman into the *inner* waiting-room, and carry his chest.'

Chapter Three

'My dear Stephen, how happy I am to see you,' cried Sir Joseph, clasping his hand most affectionately. 'Tell me, have you eaten yet? Shall we hurry over to the club and call for broiled chops? But no . . .' he said, on consideration. 'No. I have a little room here, and you may wish to speak without informing all the nation?'

'A little small private room would suit admirably. But please, dear Joseph, may a messenger be sent round to the Grapes, in the Liberties of the Savoy, to tell them of my presence here? Not only shall I stay there, which Mrs. Broad and the little girls do not yet know, for I am come straight from the Pool, but there at least I have some respectable clothes — I keep a room there permanently, you know. I am not what would ordinarily be called a dressy man, as you are aware; but I should not have presented myself here in the utmost degree of squalor . . .'

'No, no . . .'

'. . . had it not been a matter of some

urgency. Though,' he murmured, looking at his cuff, 'this was quite a good shirt, some years ago. Of some urgency,' he resumed, and plucking the undeciphered message from his pocket he laid it on the desk, smoothing the paper flat.

'I cannot make it out offhand,' said Sir Joseph. 'What were you using?'

'Ajax with one shift,' said Stephen. 'It worked perfectly for the first page.'

'I cannot make it out at all, though I know Ajax with a shift quite well.' Blaine rang a bell and said, 'Ask Mr. Hepworth to step this way.'

Mr. Hepworth glanced at Stephen with discreet curiosity and quickly looked down. Sir Joseph said to him, 'Mr. Hepworth, be so good as to take this away and determine the system upon which it was based. Will it take you more than half an hour?'

'I hope not, Sir Joseph; I think I see some familiar combinations.'

'Then please to send the title and a transcript to my little room.'

The tension was too great for either of them to eat chops with any real appetite, and they abandoned their meal entirely when Mr. Hepworth came back, looking grave and carrying his transcript. 'The gentleman who encoded this, sir,' he said, 'was using the new book: and both book and code being unfamiliar he turned over a whole gathering, taking it for the direct continuation of Ajax three. It looks very like: I have known this happen before, when the encoder was hurried, or uneasy in his mind.'

'Thank you, Mr. Hepworth,' said Blaine, and when the door had closed he went on, 'shall we read together? I am afraid our forecast was all too accurate.'

They thrust their chops away — already congealed — and Blaine pulled his chair round to sit next to Stephen. They read intently, and from these short, nervous passages they learnt that an important and reasonably well-supplied body of Chileans had entered into contact with Sir David Lindsay, formerly of the Royal Navy, a most enterprising officer, who had undertaken to come out and command their naval forces. The informant gave particulars of his sources, and although Blaine murmured a few names aloud — known allies or conceivably agents — he was perfectly mute about Bernardo O'Higgins and José San Martín, with whom Stephen had been so intimately well acquainted during his attempt, his very nearly successful attempt, to induce the Peruvians to declare themselves independent of Spain. Some of the names Stephen saw with pleasure — the names of the sources rather than those of the committee — the latter with distaste, anger, and sometimes distrust and once again, once again he realised the fragility of these movements for liberation — so many who wished to be leaders, so few to follow.

When they had finished, Blaine said, 'No wonder Dr. Jacob strayed into the wrong code. We had indeed some remote notion of this possibility, but none whatsoever of its imminence . . . come in.'

'I beg pardon, Sir Joseph,' said Hepworth. 'I just thought you would like to know that the same signal is coming through by semaphore.'

'Thank you, Mr. Hepworth. What is its source?'

'*Hebe*, sir; in Plymouth.'

There was a silence, and then Stephen said, 'The name of Sir David Lindsay has a familiar ring, a naval ring, but I cannot connect it with any particular event.'

'He is certainly a very able sailor, and he gained his reputation on some fine single-ship actions: but constitutionally he was perhaps more willing to give orders than to

102

receive them, and he did less well on reaching post-rank and being obliged to submit to the discipline of fleet manoeuvres. There was some story of an improper challenge in India, I believe — possibly even of assault — the charge being withdrawn on an undertaking to leave the service. But I make no assertions. I only know that he has not served in a King's ship since, and that some people are a little shy of him.'

'I think I remember now,' said Stephen, perfectly aware that though his friend had told the truth, it was by no means the whole truth.

'Returning to Dr. Jacob's lapse — dear me, I wonder it does not happen more often — I believe I am right in saying that none of the names of *his* Chilean committee are those of the gentlemen who first approached us?'

'That is so: and although I know too little of the country to assert it, there may well be a difference, as between north and south.'

'Very true.' Sir Joseph considered the proposition for some time; and then, having gazed at the long, thin extent of Chile on a revolving globe, he went on in quite a different voice. 'Of course, I shall have to submit whatever I have to say to my superiors, but I think the general feeling will be that Captain Aubrey should carry on with the original plan, in spite of the unfortunately necessary delay in Seppings' yard, making the best of his way to Valparaiso, where you will feel the ground — assess the possibilities — and proceed accordingly. In spite of everything we have a representative in Buenos Aires who is very well with the authorities, and who can ensure reasonably brisk communication — brisker, at all events, than messages that have to come back round the Horn. It is extremely unlikely that Sir David will already be there: but whether or no, some degree of cooperation would seem the wisest course; though he must be given no official countenance. He is unlikely to have any vessel equal to *Surprise*; but I must admit that until we have the naval attaché's report from Madrid we remain ignorant of the present Chilean government's strength and of the number of armed merchantmen at their disposal. The attitude of the Peruvian viceroy is naturally of the first importance, but that you know as well as I, indeed probably far better. However, let me consult those who must be consulted and deliver the sum of our collective wisdom tomorrow. Will you drink tea with me in Shepherd's Market — I have one or two trifles to show you — and then perhaps we could sup at Black's?'

'I should be very happy. Joseph, would you have the goodness to lend me half a crown?'

Stephen was greeted with the utmost kindness at the Grapes. His little black god-daughters, Sarah and Emily, had so shot up, had grown so leggy, that he did not have to bend to kiss them, and both were in fine spirits, since they had spent the last half hour in the company of William Reade, Stephen's supper guest, who had shown them the Royal Navy's version of Puss in the Corner, a more complex and subtle game than was usual in the Liberties.

But Mrs. Broad, though as welcoming as could be, was very much shocked by Stephen's appearance, which indeed would have done no credit to a hedge-creeper. 'Well, as for that Killick and his capers,' she said when all was explained, 'don't he wish he may have anything at all to eat or drink in this house, to serve the Doctor so. And I shall tell him, ho, ho, don't you fear — I shall let him know.'

Her natural good humour returned, nevertheless, as she laid out his fine London clothes — black, elegant severity and gleaming Hessian boots — and it was in this splendour that he sat in the parlour while the little girls nervously showed him their copy-books, their sums, and their geographical exercises, with maps. In faltering voices, prompting one another, they recited mediocre verse in English and French, and with more confidence, showed their knitting, sewing and samplerwork. They were not very clever girls, but they were wonderfully neat — their copybooks would have pleased a fastidious engraver — and they were most affectionate to one another, to Mrs. Broad and to Stephen. There was one thing that did puzzle him, however: they were still capable of speaking both lower-deck English (now somewhat tinged with Billingsgate, where they did much of the Grape's shopping) and the quarterdeck variety, slipping effortlessly from one to the other; yet neither could manage even tolerable French.

But it was at supper-time that they showed their real, and very considerable talent. Mrs. Broad was away with her cook, cook-maids, tapsters and waiters looking after the ordinary occupations of a fairly busy inn, and Stephen and Reade played backgammon, drinking brown sherry and discussing the pitiful state of their fellow-sailors in a dissolving Navy, when Sarah and Emily came in, wearing long aprons, and laid the table.

A pause. 'Now, gentlemen, if you please,' they cried, placing chairs. Stephen was draped in a remarkably broad napkin: Reade was allowed to look after himself.

The first dish was simply fresh, perfectly fresh green peas, to be eaten with a spoon: then, borne in with some anxiety, a great oval plate sizzling at the edges and containing filleted soles, lobster claws and tails, with here and there a great fat mussel, the whole bathing deep in cream.

Sarah filled the plates; Emily poured the wine, a pale golden hock.

'Oh my dears,' cried Stephen, having gazed, smelt and tasted, 'what a sinful delight! What a glorious dish! My dears, how I do congratulate you both!'

'I ask no better in all my days,' said William Reade. 'No, not even if I hoist the union at the main.'

'I hope you had a hand in it?' asked Stephen.

'Sir,' said Ernily, 'Sarah and I did every last thing, except that Henry in the snug broke the claws with the side of his cleaver.'

'Well, I am heartily glad of it. You are dear good girls, and uncommon talented. Bless you both.'

Drinking tea with Sir Joseph in his very comfortable house in Shepherd's Market could not conceivably be compared to supping at the Grapes: but there was a pleasure, though of a wholly different kind. Blaine, passing by Somerset House, had looked in to see the conscientious man who received and looked after specimens sent to the Royal Society to be kept for members — both Blaine and Stephen were Fellows — and he had brought Christine Wood's parcel, addressed to Dr. Maturin, back with him. It was the skeleton, very delicately dissected and reassembled, of his potto, a rare and curious little West African creature, nominally one of the primates, though quiet, slow, harmless, and remarkably affectionate. Stephen had been much attached to his potto, and now he opened the case, gazing upon the anatomy with a mixture of friendship and scientific interest — the very singular formation of the index-finger and of the lower thorax were strangely moving all over again, but even more so the strong link of affection.

'I believe you do not take sugar?' asked Sir Joseph.

'No sugar at all, I thank you,' replied Stephen, closing the box and bracing himself for immediate close attention, persuaded by Blaine's expression and attitude that he was coming to the important matter. Yet to his surprise Sir Joseph went on in a falsely casual tone, 'I gather you are well acquainted with the Duke of Clarence, with Prince William?' Stephen bowed: he had treated Prince William several times, but he was not a physician who discussed his patients. Somewhat embarrassed Blaine went on, 'I happened to run into him at the Admiralty this morning. Some extraordinarily indiscreet person had told him that the hydrographical voyage was to go ahead, with Captain Aubrey in command — just that: no mention of anything remotely political. The Prince, as I dare say you know, has an almost reverential awe of Captain Aubrey — too great a respect to present himself unasked, though ordinarily he is not at all shy, not at all backward in such matters.'

'A bounding, confident, foul-mouthed scrub,' said Maturin: but very low.

'. . . and he was intimate with Nelson,

who liked him well. However, the point is this: he has a son.'

'I have seen the little FitzClarences, and an ill-bred set of swabs they are: which is odd, when you consider what a dear, cheerful — and indeed beautiful — woman their mother is.'

'You know Mrs Jordan?'

'Moderately well: and I have often seen her on the stage.'

'But it is not one of those that I have in mind. It is a boy by another woman, a child he does not openly acknowledge, perhaps from fear of angering Mrs. Jordan, a son he calls Horatio Fitzroy Hanson. He is about fourteen or fifteen: he has decent manners, a tolerable education, and I think he is the only one of his children that Prince William really likes. Horatio, I ought to say, has no idea of this relationship: the acquaintance, or more than acquaintance, with Clarence — Uncle William — is perfectly acknowledged, but solely on the basis of his being a former shipmate of the boy's putative father. The mother, I am sorry to say, was rather unstable, and she went off to Canada when Horatio was two or three: his grandfather, a severe rural dean, brought him up. Clarence is all you say and I am aware that neither you nor Captain Aubrey could esteem him: but he does nevertheless have some respectable qualities: he is affectionate, fairly generous, and good to former shipmates. Furthermore, he fairly worships the service; and he has the greatest respect for Captain Aubrey. In short he desires me to ask you to use your influence with Aubrey to have the boy admitted to his midshipmen's berth for this coming voyage.'

'Are you prepared to tell me any more about Horatio's parentage?'

'Mr. Hanson, his nominal father, was a sea-officer: he and Prince William served together in the West Indies. Horatio's mother was staying in Kingston with relatives. She and Mr. Hanson became engaged: they nevertheless quarrelled furiously. But there is said to have been a more or less irregular marriage. In any case Hanson was lost in the *Serapis* and his wife went home, pregnant. I have this from three sources, none of them capable of providing a consistent or even a coherent account. The only thing I know is that Clarence provided consolation and that he is persuaded the child is his.'

'I am sure Jack will at least look at the boy, if only for his Christian name. I shall speak of him when I write to tell about the voyage: perhaps it would be better not to mention the alleged connexion. But tell me, did the extraordinarily indiscreet person who told the duke that the hydrographical voyage was to go ahead have any grounds for his assertion?'

'Oh, certainly . . . I am so sorry. I should have told you that at the very beginning: after all, it concerns you more than anyone else. I grow sadly muddled these days — as though you must know it by intuition — and then I will admit that the endless uninformed arguments for and against the project, topped by Clarence's indecently prolonged and public harangue about this boy, quite upset me. Yes, yes: you shall go: but I must warn you, Stephen, that now the war is over, rigid economy is the order of the day, and you will not be furnished with anything like the means you carried to Peru.'

Stephen nodded and said, 'Since we are to go, I think I must write to Captain Aubrey at once. His tender, *Ringle*, is an extraordinarily swift-sailing vessel, and will certainly outstrip any packet. I shall send her off tonight, with the falling tide, and desire Jack to put into Seppings' yard for the repairs that are still needed without the loss of a minute. If you could induce your colleagues to cast these words into the form of an order properly signed and sealed, I might enclose it in my letter.'

'Shall you not go yourself?'

'I shall not: I am going down into the country to see my daughter Brigid, Sophie Aubrey and her children.'

'Please give them all my love: but before going you will accompany me to the Foreign Office and Treasury for technical details?'

'Certainly. And Mrs. Oakes will almost certainly be there: you remember her, I am sure?'

'Indeed I do, and with much gratitude — the clearest, most valuable information imaginable; and an unusually handsome woman too, unusually handsome. So are some of my latest acquisitions, sent by an intelligent ship's surgeon from the Seychelles.'

Some of the beetles were indeed truly remarkable; but for beauty it seemed to Maturin that his daughter, Sophie, and even her children surpassed them in everything but colour. His unpredictably time-eating interview with people in and about Whitehall had made it impossible for him to give notice of his arrival, and he found them wholly unprepared, playing cricket of a sort in a new-mown paddock by the house.

Brigid, who was at the wicket, being bowled to by George, was the best-placed to see the chaise stop in the lane and a figure step out. 'It's my Papa,' she cried, flung down her bat and ran like a hare across the grass, leaping up to catch him round the neck — no shyness, no hesitation — it fairly touched his heart. 'My dear, you have grown almost pretty,' he said tenderly, putting her down to greet the others. 'Dearest Stephen,' said Sophie, 'I do hope you will put up with an egg — there is almost nothing else in the larder: but tomorrow . . . Do you see Clarissa coming up with a gentleman? He is her husband, the rector of Wytherton, a great scholar. They were married from here last month. Clarissa, you remember Dr. Maturin, I am very sure?'

'I give you all the joy in the world, my dear,' said Stephen, kissing her. 'Your servant, sir: and my very best congratulations,' shaking the parson's hand. 'My dears,' he went on, 'it is delightful to see you sporting in the sun, and on so pure a green. Forgive me for a few moments while I fetch what few trappings may have survived the voyage.'

'I will carry your bag, sir, if I may,' said George, on leave from *Lion*, 74, commanded by Jack's old friend Heneage Dundas.

What pleasant days they were — an English summer at its best, and English countryside at its best, enough night-rain in the hills to keep the trout-streams fine and brisk, and there were reports of a hoopoe seen three times at Chiddingfold parsonage. This year was happy in unusual numbers of birds (nesting-time had been particularly favourable) and Stephen and Brigid wandered about the smooth hay-meadows, by the standing corn, and along the banks, he telling her the names of countless insects, many, many birds — kingfishers, dippers, dabchicks, and the occasional teal: coots and moorhens, of course — as well as his particular favourites, henharrier, sparrowhawk and kestrel and once a single splendid peregrine, a falcon clipping her way not much above headheight with effortless speed. A hare in her form: two dormice: an infant weasel, unalarmed: and such quantities of butterflies. He found with lively pleasure that she was much more receptive now: but she was a very tender creature, and he was not at all sure how she would like his hunting, shooting and fishing. But that would not be for a great while yet: and there was the force of example — all the people she loved and respected were more or less passionately concerned with these pursuits.

Then again there was the mild, agreeable social life. Old friends to dinner once or twice; a few morning calls; and Mr. and Mrs. Andrews came over in their gig to spend a few hours in the library, a noble collection built up by some generations of Aubreys with good black ink in their veins.

Yet there was a certain sadness too: the end of the war had meant that almost all the soldiers and sailors and those multitudes who had kept them in activity were now obliged to find civilian work, and obviously wages dropped, when there were any wages to be had at all. And now with the cry of 'Economy, economy!' taxes soared to extraordinary heights — Jack's agent on the Milport estate wrote in anguish that the one fair-sized farm — three hundred acres — which was just coming into good heart after all the draining, was required to pay £383 11s 4d in rates and taxes. Fortunately neither Cousin Edward's nor the Aubrey land had ever been enclosed, so the villagers and outlying cottagers, together with their returning sons and younger brothers, got along moderately well in the traditional way: it is true that Jack's game dwindled strangely; but on a nearby estate, which had been subjected to rigorous enclosure — no common land with rights of grazing, cutting fern, taking turf — there was not so much as a single rabbit to be seen. Then again, although the Corn Laws endeavoured to keep the price of wheat at £4, taxing imports accordingly, a great deal of American and Continental food now came in, legally or illegally, and farming was no longer a very profitable business. The landowners suffered, of course; and most of the farmers suffered even more; but the people who were really ground right down into misery were the men, women and children who worked the land — those who had not so much as a decent garden left after enclosure.

Clearly this was not the case immediately around Woolcombe, but it was most emphatically the case quite near; and it diminished the joy of living there.

Then again, like most naval wives, Sophie had looked forward with the keenest delight to an almost indefinite time of perfect peace in her husband's company, and she heard of this hydrographical voyage, this *certain* hydrographical voyage to the uttermost point of the inhabited globe, with the most intense disapproval and vexation of spirit. Stephen timidly put forward the proposition that it would greatly enhance Jack's likelihood of a flag: but even repeated it seemed to have little good effect.

'I think,' he said, after one of these useless and indeed rather irritating attempts at consolation — consolation, after all, does imply a superiority of experience or just plain intellect on the part of the consoler: a superiority which an intensely discontented mind is unlikely to accept — 'I think I shall ride over to Shelmerston this afternoon.'

'Do not forget that the Andrews are coming to spend the evening with us.'

'Who are the Andrews?'

'Clarissa and her husband.'

'Dearest Papa,' cried Brigid in her fearless way, but speaking English, Irish not being allowed in the house any more than Maltese aboard a man-of-war. 'Dearest Papa, was you to take the dog-cart, we could both go.'

'Four of us could go,' said George — 'The back dog-boards take up.'

'Five,' cried his twin sisters. 'We are very thin, and will squeeze close.'

'But what about Padeen?' asked Sophie, who had almost never been in the fast, rakish, high-wheeled dog-cart.

'Oh,' they replied, but quite kindly — no scorn for her ignorance. 'He runs by the dog-cart, you know.'

'He always gets up behind the coach,' said Fanny, 'but he runs by the *dog-cart*.'

'Is he not the finest runner in all Connaught?' asked Brigid.

Stephen had long been on good terms with the slim, leggy, yellow gelding: a gelding not to be disturbed by mares or fillies, obviously, but not by voluble children either, and they bowled pleasantly down to the coast, then turned left-handed along the sandy roads to Saint Peter's Pond, where men were already working on the canals that would drain it, but where at the far distant upper end innocent water-fowl swam, waded and dived. 'There,' said Stephen, clapping his glass to with infinite satisfaction, 'the purple herons have brought off their brood again: the only pair in the three kingdoms.'

The gelding and the children, trained to motionless silence during these usually brief sessions, expanded, breathed again

119

and laughed aloud at the lively expectation of tea at Shelmerston, now almost at hand.

A few gentle miles more and the gelding lifted his head to the wind, to the homely scent in the wind, and mended his pace: the sandy roads were left behind, the narrow way (taken cautiously, with Padeen at the horse's head) led winding down to the awkward, rock-strewn bay on whose shore stood Shelmerston, an indifferent port inhabited by fishermen, deep-sea sailors and other seamen, any one of whom would turn smuggler, highly-skilled and enterprising smuggler, at the drop of a hat or a private signal from a French chasse-marée in the offing (flags by day, lanterns by night) — a port with tricks of the tide peculiar to itself, a damned awkward bar, and yet surprisingly well-liked by those who lived there. It was at Shelmerston that Jack Aubrey had fitted out and manned *Surprise* as a privateer during his naval eclipse before reinstatement, filling her not only with man-of-war's men who had followed him in his heavy misfortune but also with Shelmerstonians, rare seamen and perfect for a private ship of war. He and Stephen knew the place and its people well — the ladies of the town had been particularly kind to the children, much smaller then, and apt to do themselves harm — and a journey there, even a stay of a week or so, was considered a finer treat than Bath or Lyme.

The memorious gelding paced into the stable, and while Padeen tried to extricate the rear-children from the dog-boxes, where in their squabbling they had contrived to entangle themselves in a half-bale of close-meshed netting, Stephen walked into the William's Head. 'Mrs. Hake,' he said, 'good day to you, ma'am. How do you do?'

'Why, it is the Doctor!' cried she. 'Very well, sir, I thank you: and I trust you are the same?'

'Tolerably so, ma'am: and I should be even more so if you would feed the children. They have been quarrelling and whining this last half hour, but tea and those round things with cream will mend their temper — they are not fundamentally vicious. I have just run down to see whether you have any news of *Surprise* and Captain Aubrey.'

'Captain Aubrey, sir?' she replied with a look if not of actual horror then of the very deepest pale stupidity mixed with alarm and as it were distress. '*Surprise* and Captain Aubrey?' She sat down heavily, still gazing at him. 'But they was here this

121

morning — snapped up a score of old shipmates, oh ha, ha, ha! They was right happy
to go, too, ha, ha, ha! And rode pretty over
the bar at three-quarter ebb with the
breeze as fair for Seppings' yard as ever
you could wish. And you never knew. Oh,
ha, ha, ha ha!' She beat her knees and
laughed and laughed. 'God bless you, sir,
and please forgive me. I'll feed those
vermin childer right away. Come, children,' she called from the door towards the
stable-yard. 'Tea will be ready this directly
minute.' And then to Stephen, 'Which he
sent a young gentleman on a pony to tell
Mrs. Aubrey he was quite well and should
be home tornorrow.' She hurried into the
kitchen, where she could be heard telling
the maids, 'And the Doctor says to me "I
have just run down to see whether you
have any news of *Surprise* and Captain
Aubrey", and I says to him . . .'

Stephen walked out on to the familiar
strand: news of his arrival had spread, and
several of his former shipmates, particularly those he had treated, came to shake
his hand, give him good day, and say how
well the barky looked, in spite of her
wounded bows; but some, even most, were
shy of doing so, which puzzled him. Presently he invited five or six men he knew

particularly well to come and take a pot of ale with him; and when they had sat down in the parlour he said to the eldest, a former quartermaster, 'What is amiss here in Shelmerston? Why do some of my old shipmates seem uneasy in their minds?'

'Well, sir,' said Proctor, 'it is like this: with the end of the war — with the *two* ends of the war, the one when you was in *Bellona* and this one just now, with Waterloo — well, at the end of the war, for most of the people here it was the end of all peace. I mean the peace of being sure of your victuals, however rough, and a little money to send home. We were turned ashore; paid off. Ordinarily, for a sailor-man, living in the usual sort of port, that means finding another ship — not very hard, when trade is brisk. But this ain't the usual sort of port. With our damned bar and our damned rocks, there is hardly any coastwise trade. This was first a fishing-village: but the fishing fell off — would not keep above a score of boats. So presently we became a kind of privateering port; and we did pretty well, sir, as you know, so long as there were enemies to privateer upon — French, Spanish, Portuguese, Americans some of the time, the Dutch and the northern ports like Papenburg and so on.

123

But where are they now? All at peace.'

'Was there not a little running of uncustomed goods?'

'Well, sir, I must admit that some people — I name no names, mark you — did not object to occasional smuggling. You had to be a damned good seaman with a right weatherly craft to prosper; yet as I think you know very well, sir, brandy was what you might call the life-blood of Shelmerston.'

'Well?'

'Well, sir: just lean over and look out of the window, a little south of east.'

'Cutters?'

'Yes, sir. The new sharp-built revenue cutters, very well-manned and very well built — just up the way, and how young Mr. Seppings found it in his heart to do so, I do not know. They can eat the wind out of any of ours. And right high on the cliff they have a look-out post. The wicked dogs get half the fine and half the goods. It is enough to make your heart bleed, to see their zeal.'

'I can well believe it.'

'So, do you see, when we saw *Surprise* come in this morning it was like — well, I must not be irreverent, but it was a wonderful sight. And when his honour took a dozen of us aboard to run her up to the yard, oh we were right glad that she was to make a voyage, after repairs.'

'Did Captain Aubrey tell you about his intention?'

'Oh yes, sir. He said it was just for surveying the Horn, the Straits and the Chile coast — little chance of any prize, unless we happened to run into a pirate. Hard-lying guaranteed, but nothing much in the way of hard-lying money. But those he picked, oh, was they glad to have a berth with him! They knew something about Captain Aubrey's luck — we all know something about Captain Aubrey's luck: and if you could put in a word for any of us, sir, we should be right grateful.'

Although the children were very urgent to push on to Seppings' yard, Stephen would have none of it, and presently the dog-cart was creeping up the rocky hill-road out of Shelmerston. 'There is the Sethians' chapel,' he said, nodding in the direction of a white building with enormous brilliant letters of brass on its face. 'Seth,' they read. 'What is Seth? Who is Seth?'

'He was one of Adam's sons, brother to Cain and Abel.'

'Oh look!' cried Brigid. 'Just over the horizon! There is *Ringle* fairly tearing in.'

'We shall see them all tomorrow,' said Stephen. 'What joy!'

Yet they had first to pick up *Surprise*'s young gentleman, Mr. Wells, whose pony had tossed him into a deep ditch lined with stones and surrounded by brambles, and had then run away. Fortunately he was rather dwarvish even for a first-voyager, and they were able to cram him into the dog-cart, although at the cost of blood-stains all round.

Home, and frocks had to be changed, Mr. Wells stripped, daubed with balm, hog's lard and court-plaster — even a few stitches here and there — and then everyone, including Mr. and Mrs. Andrews, had to be fed. Stephen had known battles more wearing, and he retired to his own room quite early.

Dr. Maturin had certain practices that he would have condemned in others as unhealthy, self-indulgent and even immoral, such as the smoking of tobacco and Indian hemp (or bhang), the drinking of alcohol in all its forms from mild ale to brandy, the taking of opium and coca, and the frequent inhalation of nitrous oxide; but in his own case he had nothing to say against any of them. Indeed, he judged their effects wholly beneficial: and this was because he never (or very rarely) countenanced the least excess. Yet there was still another practice that he had often abandoned as improper, and had as often taken up again in spite of the pricks of conscience: this was the keeping of a diary — harmless enough in almost all cases and even benign; but not in that of an intelligence-agent. As he knew very well, it might be captured, explanations might be demanded, the code might even be broken, exposing his colleagues, his allies and informers. This was an extremely unlikely event, since he knew many languages and used them all; yet even so it was with a feeling of guilt that he now opened his bag and drew out a very small book — the volumes had grown smaller, more rapidly disposable, with the years, and the writing so minute that few ordinary eyes could read it at all, while Stephen himself had to wear powerful spectacles.

'After long consideration,' he wrote, 'I think I must treat the whole of Blaine's remarks about Horatio and his inferences as confidential.' And having written this, together with an outline of what was permissible, with his crow-quill he leant back and reflected upon the manner in which he should keep the whole transaction on a purely naval basis. He reflected long upon Jack's character, its curiously unworldly aspects, its frankness; and having walked up and down for some time, scratching himself, he said, 'I think it can be done,' and went to bed.

The next day — such a pretty day, with dew sparkling on the lawn — William Reade came over, with most encouraging news from the yard. Young Mr. Seppings was delighted that his father's diagonal bracing had stood up so well; her bottom, inspected very closely in the slip at low tide, was as sound as a bell; and he would undertake to make her bows sounder than a whole chime of them in ten working days. But he must insist that no officer, no carpenter or carpenter's mate, and no bosun or bosun's mate should come aboard. He would undertake to find perfectly suitable food and lodging for all hands — in Pompey itself for the officers if need be — but he and his shipwrights must be left to work without advice, however kindly meant. And if Captain Aubrey agreed, he had but to send word by the fishmonger's cart and they would start tomorrow.

★ ★ ★

There was no hunting or real shooting at this time of year, but there was cricket and there was fishing, and some very beautiful days they had at both, for Stephen, having at last grasped the principles of the complex game, turned his old skill at hurling to great account, striking the ball all round the field and running between the wickets like a man demented, shrieking to Padeen (his frequent partner) as he went.

Yet on an unlucky Friday a messenger came over from Portsmouth, where the semaphore had received a signal to the effect that Captain Aubrey's presence was required in London forthwith. His officers, most of whom were now staying in the house, together with some of the midshipmen far from home and Jack's half-brother Philip, sympathised with him very much indeed as he and Stephen left in a post-chaise, and assured him that they would do their very best to crush the village eleven in tomorrow's match.

But this was not the war-time Admiralty: there were night-porters on duty, to be sure, and a junior officer was summoned to receive them: but he very much regretted that Sir Joseph was not expected until Monday, and most unfortunately he was gone into the country. The official could not absolutely assert it but he thought there was some question of very recent charts becoming available.

'Well,' said Jack, as they walked out, 'in a world as unsteady on its feet as this, let us hope that Black's will at least give us supper and a bed. Wilson,' — this to the porter — 'be a good fellow and hail us a coach, will you? And put our bags aboard.'

'Where to, sir?'

'Oh, Black's, in St. James's Street.'

Here indeed they were properly received: beds were promised, and they hurried upstairs to drink a glass of wine while their supper was preparing. Although the club was fairly empty, this being Friday, there were several people they knew, and it was some time before they were called away to their table.

'Lord, that went down well,' said Jack, gazing upon a rigorously empty plate: and to the waiter, 'Charles, would you get me some toasted cheese? I know the Doctor will eat sherry-trifle, but I should like *toasted cheese*, done to the very point of perfection.'

'Point of perfection it is, sir,' said Charles.

Charles had not been gone three or four minutes and Jack was considering his decanter — were two full glasses there? — when he became aware of a tall, bulky form in the candlelight: a man who had stopped just short of their table. Glancing up, he saw the Garter ribbon, recognised the Hanoverian face, and stood up; Stephen with him.

'Captain Aubrey, good evening to you, sir. Doctor, good evening.' Turning to Jack, he went on, 'My name is Clarence, sir. You may not remember me, but I had the honour of meeting you just after your magnificent cutting-out of the *Diane*.'

'I remember it perfectly, Your Highness.'

Prince William laughed in a rather confused manner as Charles edged round him with the trifle and the toasted cheese. 'The odd thing is that I was thinking of you just this very afternoon — and now here you are! Ha, ha! Some little while ago an Admiralty friend told Dr. Maturin that I took an interest in a deceased shipmate's boy. I do not know whether the Doctor has mentioned him to you? His name is Horatio . . .'

'He could not have a better, sir,' said Jack, looking rather sternly at his toasted cheese, rapidly losing its perfect crust.

'Horatio Hanson: Hanson was lost in *Serapis* . . .' Prince William went on at some length about that particular storm and his service with Nelson in the West Indies. Then recollecting himself he said, 'But I am keeping you from your dinner — keeping you standing — a shocking thing to do to an officer of your distinction — forgive me. Would you do me the honour of taking coffee with me when you have finished? There is no sort of hurry.'

They said they should be very happy, and when he had gone the necessary three or four yards they sat down again. When Jack had picked at his ruined cheese for a while he drank the rest of his wine and said, 'There is something very amiable in taking care of a former shipmate's son.'

'Certainly there is.'

'You did not tell me he formed part of the Admiralty?'

'Did I not?'

'Well, it don't greatly signify: I shall tell him just what I told you between Haslemere and Guildford — that I cannot take sucklings on such a voyage. Come to think of it,' said Jack after a pause, 'I have heard that he is very good to his old ratings in Greenwich. Shall we go?'

The Duke had taken a discreet place in the far corner, and although his voice was naturally loud, as became a sailor, the room could have had many more people in it without inconvenience. He was clearly nervous; and since with fat men anxiety is often turned into sweat, his large face glistened. 'Roger, you whoreson bugger, where is that fucking coffee?' he called to a waiter as they approached: then 'Gentlemen,' making a half motion as if to rise, 'let me beg you to take some brandy. Pray sit down. Roger, you swab, the best old Nantz.'

The coffee arrived, the brandy immediately after, and there was an awkward pause. Jack, having sipped his coffee, broke it by saying, 'Your Highness, Dr. Maturin did speak to me about Horatio and your wish that he should go to sea in the midshipmen's berth of *Surprise*.'

'Yes. I should like to give him the very best start, under a captain for whom I have the greatest respect — a right seaman.'

'You are altogether too kind, sir. But as far as seamanship is concerned, I do not believe I could tell you anything about ship-handling.' The Duke looked extremely pleased, and took a great draught of brandy. Jack went on, 'But, sir, I told the Doctor just what I shall tell you now, if I may — plain frankness is best between sailors —'

'Hear him, hear him,' said Clarence.

'I told him that the contemplated voyage is long and of its nature perilous — fifty and even sixty degrees of south latitude, sir, apart from anything else — and that my midshipmen's berth must necessarily be a hard berth. There are some youngsters aboard at present whom I shall send home, as too tender. A hard berth, with no favours. And of course I must have a good look at him first, to see whether we suit one another or not: there must be good feeling on both sides where a very long voyage is concerned. So since you, sir, who are a sailor, take so respectable an interest in this boy, and if what I have said does not disturb you, may I suggest that you should send him with a servant to the Grapes, an inn where Maturin and I often stay in the Liberties of the Savoy —'

'Why not here?'

'Because, sir,' said Jack, looking him full in the face, 'this is a place frequented by public men — I dare say we have at least half the Opposition, or more, and several ministers — and I do not wish it to be supposed that I am in any way currying favour with the Court. With the utmost respect, Your Highness, I am not, most emphatically *not* doing so. If Horatio and I like one another, and if I think him fit to make the voyage and fit to be a sea-officer eventually, I shall take him. Otherwise I shall not.'

'Well, sir, that is frankness indeed,' said Clarence, looking from one to the other, somewhat taken aback. He wiped his nose with the back of his forefinger — a gesture familiar to Stephen — then after a short silence, he said, 'And I thank you for it. When should you like to see the boy?'

'At half-past two o'clock on Monday, sir, if you please.'

At twenty-nine minutes past two on Monday, Lucy tapped at their sitting-room door and said, 'If you please, sir, there is a man in black downstairs with a young gentleman. Shall I show them up? And Doctor, the apothecary asks if you could do with another bottled asp.'

Jack said, 'Pray show them up.' Stephen said, 'By all means: let him send it round.'

The visitors walked in. Jack said, 'Mr. Hanson, pray take a seat,' and to the other, a discreet upper servant, 'I shall probably be about an hour with Mr. Hanson: do you choose to wait in the snug, or shall I send him home in a chaise or a hackney?'

'I had rather wait, sir, if you please.'

The boy, a slim, fair, rather good-looking youth of about fifteen, was pitifully nervous — he also seemed to have at least the beginning of a cold — and he watched the disappearance of his only ally with a barely-concealed anguish: but he gathered his courage and addressing Jack he said, 'Sir, my Uncle William sends you his good-day: he told me that you had very, very kindly agreed to receive me, to judge . . .' he faltered, but then began again, '. . . to judge whether I might be admitted to your midshipmen's berth.'

'So I did,' said Jack, as kindly as he could. 'And first I should like to ask you some questions to get an idea of how far you have advanced. Since you have not yet been to sea I shall not trouble you with sails and rigging, but I dare say you already know that the mathematics are of the first importance to a sea-officer?'

'Yes, sir.'

'You know the elements of arithmetic, I am sure; but have you learnt any algebra and geometry?'

'A little, sir. I can manage the quadratic equation fairly well, and I am tolerably forward in Euclid.'

'Could you define a hypotenuse off-hand?'

'Oh yes, sir,' said Horatio, smiling for the first time.

Jack drew the familiar figure and said, 'Now tell me how it can be shown that the square on the hypotenuse is equal to the sum of the squares on the other two sides, will you?'

Horatio did so, his voice growing clearer and more confident; and Stephen's attention wandered. Remotely he heard the boy tell the nature of a secant, a cosecant, a tangent and cotangent, a sine and its fellow; and when next he took notice they were talking with real animation about such astronomy as Horatio and his grandfather's curate, Mr. Walker, had managed to accomplish with a homemade refracting instrument just powerful enough for the moons of Jupiter, the delightful moons of Jupiter, on a clear and moonless night. Stephen let his eyelids droop.

'Sir,' said Horatio gently in Stephen's ear, laying a hand upon his arm. 'I believe the Captain is speaking to you.'

Stephen was not much given to lying, but he was as reluctant as any other man to admit that he had been asleep: he now strongly affirmed 'that he had been meditating on some of the Pythagoreans' wilder statements.'

'Doctor,' said Jack, 'may I beg you to address Mr. Hanson in French and Latin? Perhaps Greek would be coming it rather high, for a sea-officer. Do you know any Greek, Mr. Hanson?'

'No, sir,' said Mr. Hanson, with a particularly charming and happy smile. 'Only the alphabet: but I was going to start next year with Mr. Walker. Greek, and even Hebrew.'

While Stephen and Hanson were prosing away in French and Latin according to the curious English pronunciation, Jack made a rough draft of his promised letter. He had almost finished it when he heard the sounds of a good-natured conclusion on the other side of the room. 'There,' he said, standing up, 'I have almost reached the end, and I shall finish when the Doctor has told me what he thinks: so if you would like to walk about for half an hour — the river and its shipping is just down the way — I shall put my draft into proper shape for your Uncle William — what is that infernal row?'

It was Sarah and Emily, back from school and over-excited by their new boots: they burst in, kissed Stephen, kissed Jack, and then gazed at the wholly unexpected Horatio, who gazed back with at least equal surprise.

'My dears,' said Stephen, 'this is Mr. Hanson, who may be going to sea: Mr. Hanson, these are my god-daughters, Sarah and Emily. And since you have half an hour to spare, I am sure they would show you the delights of the river, which they know intimately well.'

'How they have shot up,' said Jack, as the boots went clattering down. 'Dear little souls: I remember them as poor puling little objects, fit only for bait. Now I must hurry with my fair copy — but first tell me what you think of the boy.'

'He seems to me an agreeable, ingenuous, well-bred youth: his French is well above the English average, and his Latin is acceptable.'

'I am very glad of that. I tell his uncle that he has a surprising grasp of mathematics, particularly those applied to navigation and astronomy. He already has the basis of a sea-officer. He takes a real pleasure — more than pleasure — in those studies, and I say that subject to the ordinary allowance of a hundred a year and a proper outfit, I should be happy to take him, all the more since you have said that his French is quite good and his Latin passable. But before binding myself fully I feel that a few words with His Highness are called for: so since I am cruelly pressed for time, I beg for an early interview tomorrow morning. Do you think that covers the ground?'

'Admirably, my dear. While you write it fair I shall see what we are to have for dinner.'

It was a pair of fowls. But before they could be put down to the fine bright fire, Horatio and the little girls came back, obviously great friends. Horatio hurried upstairs. 'I do hope, sir, that I am neither early nor late? My Uncle has always said that the Navy absolutely insisted upon punctuality.'

'No,' said Jack, 'you are to the minute. Now here is a letter for your Uncle: in it I say that as far as I am concerned I should be happy to have you aboard.' The boy flushed, and his chin trembled. 'But of course, the final decision rests with him. If he agrees with my conditions, I have suggested an appointment for the Portsmouth coach on Saturday. Here is the letter: it also says that I should like to wait on him early tomorrow morning. Perhaps he would send a servant to appoint the time? Now cut along — you must not keep him from his dinner.'

★ ★ ★

Early the next morning at Fladong's hotel Clarence was waiting at the top of the stairs, and he saw with some concern that Captain Aubrey's face, usually brown from the wind and the sun, was now a disagreeable yellow, his eyes dark-rimmed, and his expression, though properly deferential, by no means as amiable as it had been yesterday: this was the result of a late leave-taking feast with old shipmates and measureless wine, but the cause did not occur to the Duke, for whom Jack Aubrey was not only one of the most successful fighting captains but also the very type of virtue. 'Pray come in and take a seat,' he said; and then, after a pause, 'I cannot tell you how your letter pleased me: but may I ask whether you choose to take him?'

'Well, sir, he seems to me a thoroughly good boy, and I should be happy to take him: but on condition that he is treated as an ordinary reefer. I should deplore the presence of any senior officer when he comes aboard.' (Clarence had long since reached flag-rank.) 'It might have an appearance of favouritism, which is very much disliked in a company of young men who usually have little influence and less money, and who are likely to lead the favoured youth — particularly a first-voyager — a miserable time of it. And although there are some eminent exceptions' — with a bow — 'I have very rarely known a privileged midshipman of that kind make a good officer. And in passing I may say that I shall warn him very strongly against the least hint of influential friends or connexions.'

'I entirely agree with you, sir,' said Clarence. 'I myself felt the weight of influence very strongly, and many, many a time did I tell myself that I should never have been made post without I was King George's son.'

'Oh, sir, I am sure you should,' said Jack, in answer to a singularly touching look. 'At one time we were alongside *Pegasus* in the West Indies, and I never beheld a frigate in better order.'

'Why, to be sure,' said Clarence, positively bridling, 'that is very kind of you to say so, upon my word it is. May I call for a pot of coffee?'

'Not for me, sir, I thank you.'

Clarence raised his head, listening. 'I think that is the boy on the landing,' he said. 'If that is your only condition, I accept it fully, with all my heart.' He shook Jack's hand and then opened the door.

'Come in, Horatio,' he called. 'We are quite agreed, and in his great goodness Captain Aubrey will take you aboard *Surprise*.'

'Oh thank you, sir: thank you very much indeed,' cried the boy, intensely moved. 'I am sure my dear Uncle must have been very happy to hear it.'

He certainly looked very happy, though strangely moved, when he brought Horatio to the White Horse, with a bowed porter carrying the new sea-chest. 'I am so very glad to see you, Aubrey,' he called. 'So very glad to have read your letter over again — admirably well put — and of course I agree to all you have said: admirably well put. Your servant, Doctor. And I assure you, I am most uncommonly obliged . . . but forgive me, I beg, if I run away. There is Mornington waiting for me on the other side, and I absolutely cannot bear partings.' With this, having wrung Jack's hand yet again, he did in fact literally run, moving heavily and thrusting his way through the crowd.

Horatio looked a little nonplussed: but at this moment Jack called out, 'Mr. Daniel! There you are: good morning to you. I have four insides, so heave your chest into the boot and get aboard. But first let me introduce Mr. Hanson, who is joining your berth.' The young men shook hands. 'He is only a first-voyager, but he already has a pretty sense of number, and I hope you will agree very well.'

People were getting in, crawling like spiders on to the roof; friends pressed closer, some calling out farewells; and a much louder voice cried 'Get out of my fucking way, you bloody cuckolds,' and Clarence heaved through the throng, mounted the steps, said 'God bless you, Horatio,' bent over him, pressed something into his hand and backed out, stammering something to Jack about '. . . present . . . forgotten . . . thank . . .' And painful it was to see that large pale glabrous face fairly aswim with tears.

'Let go,' called the coachman, and in a moment the whole massive affair was under way, contributing to the general roar of Saturday's traffic — an exceptionally noisy and crowded Saturday, so that it was not until the coach was running over the newly-smoothed and comparatively silent road across Putney Heath that there was any real conversation — Horatio, much moved, had said nothing at all but 'Yes, sir,' or 'No, sir.' But now, during this quiet

144

running, and during a lull in what little talk there was, a clear small bell struck eleven, and Horatio gazed with amazement at the packet Uncle William had thrust into his hand. In the listening silence Stephen's own repeater uttered the faintest echo of the chime from his fob. 'I believe, sir,' he said, taking out the watch, 'that you have much the same machine as I. May we compare them?'

They were both indeed Breguet repeating watches, wonderfully accurate, wonderfully resistant — Stephen's had been with him (sometimes captured, sometimes restored) years without number and its minute voice had accompanied him through many a sleepless night. 'When we sit down to our dinner,' he said, 'which, with the blessing, will be at Guildford, I will show you how mine can be adjusted for fast and slow, loud or soft for chime, repetition and alarm. They are truly wonderful little machines.'

'Yes, indeed, sir,' said Horatio, and he gazed at its elegant dial, its creeping hands, almost all the way to Guildford, only pausing now and then to ask Daniel, whose kindness he sensed at once, questions about naval life. 'So I am not really a midshipman at all?' he asked, when the others were busy talking.

'No. Seeing you are joining a frigate, where there is not much room, you will be a member of the midshipmen's berth, and seeing that you are quite old, you will not be treated as a youngster, although this is your first voyage: but on *Surprise*'s books you will be a first-class volunteer — a volunteer of the first class — and you will not be a full-blown mid until the Captain promotes you. Still, you wear a mid's uniform, and you walk the quarterdeck: you are only the first term in a progression, to be sure, but you do belong to it; and that is the great thing.'

Progressions, arithmetic, geometric, or just plain physical tend to be very long; and as far as the emotionally worn-out Horatio Hanson was concerned, this first term in his particular sequence would have seemed almost eternal, but for the successive reassuring chimes in his bosom. Jack had asked the coachman to stop at the Hind, where they had a little more to eat and then piled into two local post-chaises with their sea-chests and night-bags for the last leg to Woolcombe.

It had indeed been a long and weary journey for Horatio, with much nervous strain before, during and after it, when he was presented to the Captain's family and a large assortment of his future shipmates, some of them, like the master, almost unbelievably old, others belonging to the berth. The supper and the trial of long corridors unknown, a vast strange bedroom and uncertainty whether he might use the chamber-pot.

But what wonders a long night can work: and a huge breakfast in the company of primarily naval people, none of them at all forbidding, most of them benign. The ease and calm authority of the Captain's daughters and the casual way in which young George wandered to and from the sideboard, helping himself to an improbable number of things, impressed him deeply, but not so much as Mr. Whewell's play-by-play history of how the house team had indeed crushed the village, in spite of their parson, by eighteen runs.

But this satisfactory account was wholly set aside by Harding's arrival, with the words 'Sir, we float!' which were instantly understood by Captain Aubrey and all his officers to mean that Mr. Seppings had finished well before his promised time, that the frigate was moored in the fairway, with the sheer-hulks standing by to restore her masts and the bosun on hot coals to get back to rigging her.

They were words that released an extraordinary amount of energy among the sailors, a decently-restrained grief in Sophie, less decently in her children, and not at all in Brigid, who had to be led from the room. All this distressed the men: it did not interrupt their extremely rapid movement — co-ordinated movement, some going almost by instinct rather than order to their various stations with what speed horses, wheeled vehicles or plain feet could command; some, the best-mounted, to Portsmouth to prepare those ordinarily slow-moving local minds for the laying-in of stores: powder and shot, salt beef, salt pork, beer, biscuit, rum, the necessary water, some linear miles of ropes and cordage and square miles of sailcloth; carpenter's stores, bosun's stores — all those innumerable objects that even a modest man-of-war required for a voyage of enormous length: even the common rhubarb purgative amounted to seven casks.

Chapter Four

At four bells in the morning watch, Captain Aubrey, in a tarpaulin jacket, his long fair hair, as yet unplaited, streaming over the frigate's larboard quarter, came on deck, glanced at the grey, rainfilled sky, saw a tall curling wave break over the starboard bow, dodged at least some of the water that came racing aft along the gangway, and said, 'Good morning, Mr. Somers: I think we may omit the ceremony of washing the decks today. The heavens seem to be looking after it for us.'

'Good morning, sir,' said the second lieutenant. 'Yes, sir.' And directing his powerful voice forward, 'Stow swabs, there.'

Turning, Jack saw a slim, smiling, soaked figure saluting him. 'Why, Mr. Hanson, how are you? Put your hat on again. And are you recovered?'

'Yes, sir, I thank you: quite well again.'

'I am very glad of it. I think we are through the worst of the blow — you see the lightening sky two points on the starboard bow? And if you feel quite well before division we might make an attempt on the mizzen masthead.'

'Oh yes, sir, if you please.'

Jack, having towelled himself moderately dry, returned to his still-warm cot and lay there comfortably, rocked by the measured crash and sweep of the tons of water that broke on the starboard bow. *Surprise* was now heading south-by-west, almost close-hauled under reefed topsails, on a strong but irregular and probably dying west wind: they had cleared the Channel at last, after many days of wearisome beating — they no longer had Ushant and the dreadful reefs he had known so well during the Brest blockade urider their lee; and apart from being struck by lightning or by some demented merchantman they had nothing much to fear until they were off Cape Ortegal, which had very nearly drowned him as a midshipman in *Latona*, 38. However, there were still some hundreds of miles to leeward, and with that comforting reflection and the beat and tremble of the waves he drifted off again until seven bells, when he woke entirely, to bright daylight, a diminished sea, and the disagreeable face of Killick, his steward, bringing hot water for shaving. For once

Killick had no bad news of any kind to report, which probably accounted for his more than usually surly mutter in reply to Jack's greeting; though on reflection he did recall that the Doctor had fallen out of his cot at some time in the middle watch and had been lashed in so tight by Mr. Wantage that he would certainly be late for breakfast.

Breakfast, whose delectable scents were wafting into the great cabin as Jack shaved in the quarter-gallery just at hand, was a good hearty meal to which he often invited one of the officers who had stood the morning watch: but today, in view of the very rough night they had had, and in view of Stephen's cursed snappishness at having been so bitterly constrained — seven double turns and scarcely a breath a minute — he thought they should eat alone.

This they did; and the customary eggs and bacon, toast with Sophie's marmalade, and above all pot after pot of coffee, had their civilising influence, and Dr. Maturin even said, 'Before I make my rounds, I may well shave.'

Several witty replies occurred to Captain Aubrey, but in his friend's precarious state of temper he risked none of them, only replying, 'What do you think of young Hanson's state at present? He stood his watch perfectly well last night.'

'Hanson? Oh yes, Hanson: he made a very quick recovery, as the young so often do. I attribute it largely to my Vera Cruz jalap: most of the others in the sick-bay were on the various kinds of rhubarb, Aleppo and Smyrna Turkey roots, and the best Russian, with some from Banbury: and perhaps half a dozen of them are still in a sad state of flux.'

'Surely you do not experiment on your patients, Stephen?' cried Jack.

'In course I do, just as you experiment with various sails or arrangements of sails, to see what suits a boat best. A boat does not have *three mizzen topsails and a gaff* written on its prow; and my patients do not have *ipecacuanha* tattooed on their foreheads. Of course I experiment. Experiment, forsooth.'

He had indeed experimented, different constitutions requiring different remedies, but always, in this violent outbreak of dysentery (some of the salt pork served on the first day had already crossed the Atlantic four times, with a long pause in Kingston, Jamaica) on the general basis of similia similibus, carefully noting the various results: and watching, with an anxious eye, the frightful diminution of his stores — at one time, before they were clear of soundings, three-quarters of the Surprises had been helpless, incapable of duty, but eager and willing to take enormous doses of rhubarb.

'But as for young Hanson — for whom, I may say, I feel a certain responsibility, as well as an affection — he was fit for duty three days ago.'

'I am glad to hear it,' said Jack; and later that day, after a morning of paperwork with his clerk and the purser, and after dinner, he walked the quarterdeck with a coffee-cup in his hand. The day was brighter now by far, and warm: clouds were still scudding from the west, but the breeze had dropped, so that *Surprise* was now wearing her courses.

At five bells they heaved the log. 'Eight knots and one fathom, sir, if you please,' said Mr. Midshipman Shepherd to Whewell, the officer of the watch. Whewell turned to Jack, took off his hat, and said, 'Eight knots and one fathom, sir, if you please.'

'Thank you, Mr. Whewell,' said Jack, gazing up at the masts' pronounced lee-ward angle, 'I believe we may come up a point and a half.'

'A point and a half it is, sir,' said Whewell, and he repeated the order to the quartermaster at the con.

Jack moved forward to the rail and loooked down into the waist of the ship. There he saw what he expected to see, some of the younger midshipmen learning the fine points of their craft — long-splicing to leeward, a complex system of pointing to windward, and just beneath him Horatio Hanson was being shown some elementary skills such as sheet-bend, bowline, clove-hitch and rolling hitch by Joe Plaice, his recently-appointed sea-daddy, already horribly loquacious and didactic, though good-natured with it all.

'Mr. Hanson,' he called.

'Sir?' cried Horatio, dropping his fid and running up the ladder.

'How do you feel at present?' asked Jack, looking at him attentively.

'Very well, sir, I thank you. Prime,' he said, standing straight, his hands behind his back.

In a private tone Jack went on, 'You do mind my words about a first-voyager being meek and mute in the berth, I trust?'

'Oh yes, sir,' said Horatio, blushing. 'But, sir, you did say that I did not have to put up with everything, however gross.'

'Perhaps I did.'

'So when a — a shipmate — called me a pragmatical son of a bitch, I thought I had to resent it.'

'Not a superior officer? Just a member of the berth?'

'Yes, sir.'

'Then of course you had to resent it. Show me your hands. Turn them over.' It must have been a heavy left-handed blow to split the skin to that extent. Jack shook his head. 'No, no: it will not do. I doubt anyone else in the berth will speak to you like that again — a gentlemanly lot, upon the whole: but if it should happen you must say, "Blackguard me as much as ever you choose: the Captain has tied my hands." '

'Yes, sir,' said the boy, with proper deference and a total want of conviction.

'Well, now: since she is not what you would call lively' — the mastheads swept out an arc of no more than forty degrees at present — 'perhaps we might try the mizzen crosstrees. You remember what I said about both hands and never looking down?'

'Oh yes, sir.'

'Then away aloft, and I shall follow you.'

Hanson ran aft, nipped on to the rail, and leaning out he seized the third and fourth mizzen shrouds as they rose from the channel, writhed between them, setting himself on the outward side, grasped the ratlines that ran horizontally across the shrouds and climbed a step or two of the ladder they formed, and waited.

A moment later he felt the whole mass of rigging tighten as it took the captain's weight: then the captain's powerful hands on his ankles, shifting his feet in turn up and up and up. 'Do not look down,' said Jack presently, 'but just about level, at the mast. Just forward of the gaff there is a block.'

'I see it, sir.'

'It leads the starboard main-topsail-brace straight down on deck: give it a gentle pull when it is in reach and you will see the brace respond.'

So it did: a most gratifying sweep. But now they were close to the lower side of the top, that broad platform at the head of the lower mast that bore the topmast and its matching array of shrouds, spread by the crosstrees and towering up to the topgallantmast and the upper crosstrees. From immediately under the top Jack threaded Hanson up through the lubber's hole, himself taking the backward-leaning futtock-shrouds and dropping from the rail to join him. 'You must always come up through the hole for the first seven times,' he said. 'To be sure, it looks lubberly, but seven times is the law. You will very soon get used to laying aloft, and after those holy seven times you will use the futtock-shrouds without thinking about it. Now let me show you the things in the top . . .' This he did from the top-maul to the fid, fid-plate, bolster and chock.

Jack's voyages were rarely of a kind in which a first-voyager would be either proposed or accepted; yet some did come aboard, propelled by very high authority or the plea of old shipmates, and it was Jack's habit to take them aloft himself, at first. It established a particular contact, and it told him a great deal about the boy. Apart from anything else it made ordinary human conversation possible, a very rare thing between the extremes of rank.

They sat in the top for a while sitting on folded studdingsails while Jack explained various points in the running rigging and Horatio gazed out with open wonder and admiration at the immense, ordered intricacy of a man-of-war, its extraordinary beauty and the even greater beauty of its surroundings.

'I am afraid your knuckles are bleeding on your trousers,' Jack observed, after a pause.

'Oh, I am so sorry, sir,' cried the boy, in horror. 'I am afraid they are. I beg pardon, sir. I shall wrap them in my handkerchief.'

'The great thing for *blood*,' said Jack, speaking with some authority, 'is cold water. Just soak whatever it is in *cold* water overnight and in the morning it will be gone. But tell me about boxing, will you? Have you done much?'

'Oh no sir. I hardly went to school: but the boys who came to be prepared for first communion by Mr. Walker or my grandfather and I used to mill in the barn afterwards.'

'Did you use gloves?'

'No, sir: just muffles. But then there was the coachman's boy whose uncle, a real prize-fighter who kept the inn at Clumpton and who taught him a great deal — he had gloves, and he taught me.'

'So much the better,' said Jack. 'When I was a reefer in a ship of the line with a lot of others in the berth, we used to have set matches, and we challenged other ships in the squadron. So did the ratings.'

'That must have been capital fun.'

'So it was, indeed. Perhaps we might do

something . . . what do you weigh?'

'Almost nine stone, sir.'

'We must see what can be done. Are you puffed with your climb?'

'Not in the least, sir.'

'Then let us go up to the crosstrees. You do not mind the height?'

'Oh no, sir, I do not mind it.'

Jack turned him round, set him in position, both hands firm, and once again he called, 'Away aloft.' They moved briskly up the narrowing ladder, the shrouds so close at the top that Jack swung round to the larboard set, swung up to the larboard crosstree and gave the boy a hand to heave him up to the other. There they sat, one each side of the mast, each with an arm around it. They seemed incomparably higher up here, the sea stretching almost to infinity, the sky unimaginably vast: Horatio had opened his mouth to exclaim at the ethereal beauty of the ship and her setting when he remembered the words 'mute and meek' and shut it again. Jack said, 'If the breeze comes a trifle more aft, you may see stunsails set. Now cling to the crosstree with both hands once I am under you, dangle your legs and let me place your feet.'

Down and down again: and on deck Jack

said, 'You did pretty well. Next time you must lay aloft with one of your mates — Mr. Daniel, say — and in a week you will find it as easy as kiss-my-hand.'

'Sir, thank you very much indeed for taking me: I have never seen anything so beautiful in my whole life. I wish it could go on for ever.'

He regretted these last words as being enthusiastic, out of place to a post-captain: but they had barely been uttered before they were drowned by a prodigious bellowing from the look-out on the foretopsail yard, a former (and most passionate) whaler. 'There she blows! Oh there she blows! Three points on the starboard bow. Pardon me, sir,' he added in a lower tone, for this was not a Royal Naval cry.

There she blew indeed — a great dark heave in the smooth sea and then the jet — and not only she but her six companions, one after another, heaving up enormous, blowing and smoothly diving each in turn, and each heartily cheered by the Surprises. 'What kind, Reynolds?' called Jack.

'Oh right whales, sir, as right as right could be, ha, ha, ha!'

'Why do they say *right* whales?' asked William Salmon, a master's mate, when the berth had settled down to dinner — a diminished berth, now that Jack had dispensed with some of the more indifferent midshipmen.

'Why, because they are *right* in every respect,' said Adams, Captain Aubrey's clerk. 'They are in the right place — off Greenland or in the Bay — they have the right whalebone, by far the best in the market — and the right amount of oil, six or seven tons of it. And the right temperament: they move slow, not dashing about like your finwhale, or turning spiteful and crushing your boat like a sperm. You cannot say fairer.'

'No, to be sure,' said the berth, looking eagerly at the pudding as it came through the door, a fine massive plumduff. Officially, and actually in time of dearth, the midshipmen ate the same food as the other ratings, but since their captain insisted upon quite a considerable allowance those in *Surprise* did very much better, having laid in stores, livestock and even a moderate quantity of wine, some of which they drank at the end of the meal.

'Here's to a sweet and prosperous voyage,' said Daniel, raising his glass.

'A sweet and prosperous voyage,' they echoed.

Sweet and prosperous it was, in a way, for although the breeze was now so faint the ship could hardly log more than a hundred miles from one noon to the next (a distance very accurately measured by Daniel and Hanson) it was wholly favourable, while the calmness of the sea, the almost unmoving deck, made gunnery a rare delight, and with his wealth of powder and shot (all to be renewed in Madeira) Jack exercised his crew with live ammunition, once they had loosened their muscles by running the guns in and out half a dozen times, and now each crew had the lively satisfaction of destroying a number of empty casks, towed out sometimes to a considerable distance. Then came the repeated broadsides: this was not the dumb-show of usual practice at divisions, but the shattering din of battle, the flashing stabs of fire, the shriek of each gun's very dangerous recoil, the heady scent of powder-smoke along the decks; and there was the frigate, under her fighting topsails, in the midst of her own cloud as the breeze swept the smoke back across her — smoke lit from within, and an enormous, almost continuous roar as the firing started with the foremost starboard gun and ran right down the broadside. It was as though *Surprise* was fighting a dreadful battle of her own, the hands stripped to the waist, handkerchiefs round their heads, deadly serious, extremely active, checking the recoil, sponging, loading, ramming home the charge and running the ton of metal up against its port with a bang while the gun's captain aimed it and the powder-boys ran at full speed with their cartridges from the magazine, while the deck trembled and the taut shrouds vibrated.

' 'Vast firing,' called Jack as the aftermost gun shot inboard. 'Swab and load and run them up. Now take breath while the target is towed out, and then let us have three brisk ones.'

Men straightened, grinned at one another, wiped their foreheads — their pale bodies gleamed with sweat — and most went to the scuttle-butt for a long and gasping drink.

When all was ready, guns loaded and run out, Jack said, in a voice suited to the battle-deafness of all hands, 'Target's away. From forward aft, as they bear.' He spoke with a watch in his hand: most of the people knew what that meant, and the foremost gun was wonderfully prompt, followed by the rest of the broadside — a scene of extraordinary activity, since all his old shipmates were aware of the value he attached to very rapid accurate fire. 'If a ship can manage three broadsides in five minutes, there is no enemy can stand against her,' he had repeated many and many a time: and in the past he had proved it.

The target vanished in foam before the end of the first, but with undiminished zeal, toiling like devils, the other two broadsides pounded the wreckage until the last gun bawled out and a shocked silence fell over the sea.

'Well, shipmates,' said Jack, 'it was pretty good: I do not think there are a great many afloat that could call us slow-bellies; but by the time we reach Freetown, I think we may do better.'

The Surprises looked a little disappointed, but none of the really expert gun-captains expected anything else; and even the heaviest of the few new hands had seen that guns three and five had checked the pure, even sequence of the broadsides.

'It was pretty good, however, for a somewhat mixed ship's company,' said Jack as he walked into the great cabin. 'But I tell you what, Stephen: the wind is about to change.' He tapped the barometer. 'Yes:

and before nightfall, too. Come in.'

'I beg pardon, sir,' said Wells, the dwarfish midshipman, 'but Mr. Harding says, with his duty, that *Ringle* is in sight, under a press of sail, bearing east-north-east.'

'Thank you, Mr. Wells. Now, Mr. Adams, what have you there?'

'Sir, the young gentlemen's workings, if you please. The master begged me to carry them to you, as I was on my way aft. He has to go to the seat of ease again.'

Stephen shook his head: Mr. Woodbine was one of his most obstinate cases. Was there perhaps some hidden or at least contributory cause? Patients were either intolerably garrulous about their symptoms or obscure, taciturn, even secretive, as though they suspected the medical man of trying to entrap them — perhaps even to lead them to surgery. When he had finished with these reflections, his eye caught the score of a prelude and fugue in D minor for violin and 'cello that he had composed some time ago and that he had now copied fair, profiting by the calm.

Jack, sorting through the young gentlemen's workings — their reckoning of the ship's position by noon observation of the sun and a variety of other calculations —

caught Stephen's glance and said, 'I have been making attempts on the opening page of the prelude: but Lord, Stephen, I am grown so thumb-fisted! I have scarcely had my fiddle out of its case since we sank the land, and now most of my notes are false and my bowing all astray.'

'No. We have not played at all, these many days and more.'

Jack agreed: then he said, 'But here is something that will give you pleasure,' and he passed two slips, both with figures neatly ranged and a resulting position that agreed within a few seconds. 'The one is John Daniel's, as you would expect from a capital hand at the mathematics; but the other is young Hanson's, and I am sure there was no copying. What a pearl Mr. Walker must have been, the boy's tutor, to have shown him how to take such a pretty altitude: though to be sure the Duke did treat him to as fine an instrument as I have seen. The two of them agree in setting us within a week's sail of Madeira, and if this breeze holds, as I believe it will — or rather,' he said, touching the wooden arm of his chair, '— as I hope it will, we shall be able to say that we have done the first leg in reasonably good time, in spite of a most unpromising start.'

★ ★ ★

The breeze did indeed hold fair, usually coming in over the starboard quarter as steadily as a trade-wind, which allowed the *Surprise* to spread a glorious array of royals and studding-sails that sent the water racing down her side, filling her people with such high spirits that when they were turned up in the last dog-watch they sang and danced on the forecastle to the sound of a fife and a drum and a small knee-harp with such spirit that it sounded like Bartholomew Fair, only more harmonious.

It was on just such an evening, when they were within a day or two of Madeira, that Jack Aubrey squared to his desk to continue his letter to Sophie and perhaps finish it so that all his papers of every kind might go with the next packet. 'This is sailing indeed,' he wrote, 'sailing with the kindliest wind in a ship one loves and a crew most of whom one has known for years, and nearly all of them right seamen.' Here he took a new sheet and continued, 'It seems wickedly ungrateful to say so, but some of us miss that perpetual vigilance, that hawk-like scanning of the leeward horizon for a sail that may be an enemy or, praise be, a lawful prize. Yet of course this is peace-time, and peace-time in mild, favourable weather can, to a thankless mind, seem rather flat on occasion.' But having paused to sharpen his pen — he had a razor-sharp little penknife that also split quills — he looked over these last words with a more critical eye, balled up the paper and took another sheet. 'It is true that even some of our quite old shipmates can be a little difficult on occasion,' he continued. 'Your favourite Awkward Davies can be positively dogged, if crossed by a new hand: but in a boarding-party, or storming a shore-position, he is worth his weight in gold, heavy though he is. His huge bulk, his terrifying strength and activity, the awful pallor of his face and his way of foaming at the mouth when he is stirred, all make him a most dreadful opponent. What Stephen calls his berserker rage fairly clears the enemy's decks before him. He also howls. But he has other sides: not only is he very useful when you must sway up the mast short-handed, but in sudden emergencies too. Do you remember the pitifully shy boy Horatio Hanson you were so kind to at Woolcombe? He shows remarkable promise as a navigator, but he is not much of a topman yet — how could he be? — and he got himself sadly entangled coming down from some improbable height — the fore-royal truck or something like that. Davies saw him, and shoving Joe Plaice aside — Joe is the boy's sea-daddy — he fairly swarmed aloft, seized the young fellow's shin and absolutely carried him by brute-force upside-down to the top, where he was safe, and so left him with an angry mutter . . .' He broke off. 'Now, Stephen,' he said rather pettishly, 'what are you pottering about for?'

'Pottering, is it? Have I not been searching every nook and cranny in this vile tub and the Dear knows she has a thousand of both systematically searching for my rosin, my only piece of rosin since an ill-conditioned rat ate the others. May I ask you to look in your pocket?'

'Oh, Stephen,' cried Jack, his look of righteous indignation changing to a flush as he brought the rosin out with his handkerchief. 'I am so sorry — so very sorry. I do beg your pardon.'

'Was you playing?' asked Stephen as he picked fluff and hairs off the ball.

'I had thought of it — took my fiddle out of its case, indeed, but then reflecting on all the paper-work Adams and I must have ready in Funchal, it appeared that I should get Sophie's letter sealed up first.'

'Give her my love, if you please,' said Stephen; and pausing in the doorway he added, 'I dare say you know the *Ringle* is coming up hand over fist?'

'She has been reported from the masthead every watch since the horizon cleared; and with the glass quite steady I hope to reduce sail in an hour or two so that we may enter Funchal together before the evening gun.'

At first sight poor ravaged Funchal still had a blackened, desolate appearance, but from the maintop a closer view, helped by a telescope, saw that a great deal of repair had in fact been carried out, that Coelho's famous yard though not busy, was working again, with piles of fresh timber clearly apparent, and that the Royal Navy's depot was reasonably trim, with a store-ship lying off the wharf and lighters plying to and fro, while a Spanish packet rode at single anchor a cable's length astern. The *Surprise* saluted the castle and took up her familiar moorings, with the *Ringle* under her lee. The castle returned as briskly as could be expected; and Stephen said privately to Jack, 'Pray, my dear, let me be put on the strand in a small boat once darkness has fallen, to be taken off just one hour later.'

Darkness fell, helped by a run of clouds from the southwest and a small rain. Stephen was handed down the side as though he were a basket of singularly fragile china by seamen and officers who were accustomed, long accustomed, to his wild capers when going ashore in the mildest of swells, and he found himself sitting in the stern-sheets next to Horatio Hanson, who had taken to seafaring so thoroughly and naturally that he could be entrusted with the captain's valuable gig and even more valuable crew of right seamen. 'I forget, Mr. Hanson,' he said, 'whether you were aboard on the way north from Gibraltar or not?'

'No, sir: I am afraid I was not so fortunate.'

'Ah, indeed? Yet you seem to fit in quite naturally.'

'Perhaps, sir, because my father was a sailor.' And raising his voice, 'Give way, there, give way,' running the boat well up the pebbles, while bow-oar and his mate handed Stephen dry-foot clear of the next wave. 'Thank you, Evans; thank you, Richardson,' he said; and louder, 'Mr. Hanson, in just an hour's time, if you please: I know our watches are in agreement to the second. And if you choose to return to the ship, I shall wait here a good seven minutes.'

He walked up and into the town, pausing under a reed awning that shed the rain for a cup of really powerful coffee and then following the carefully remembered turnings to a modest establishment in an indifferent, mercantile part of the town; modest, but remarkably well-guarded by the local equivalent of English pugilists, since it was frequented by dealers in precious stones who could be seen passing their wares wrapped in tissue paper from hand to hand, whispering to one another. And as Stephen had noticed before, those to whom the little parcels were handed seemed to divine their contents by some supernatural power since as far as he could make out they never opened the wrapping: nor did their conversation ever vary from a low (but not evidently secretive) monotonous discretion. Another thing that he noticed, and noticed with a galvanic shock which he only just managed to control, was the presence of his friend, colleague and ally, Amos Jacob, for whom he had intended to leave a message, hoping that it might be collected in a month or so.

They exchanged a fleeting, meaningless glance, and when Stephen had drunk up his glass of wine and paid his reckoning he walked out into the wet, deserted street: the drizzle had stopped but the cloud still hung low and he was glad when Jacob caught up with him, carrying an umbrella. They at once embraced patting one another on the back in the Spanish manner and continuing in that language, perfectly familiar to both but so usual in Funchal to excite no comment. 'Sir Blaine sends you his kindest greetings,' said Jacob, 'and I am to tell you that Sir Lindsay will probably sail on the twenty-seventh of this month, calling at Funchal (where his agents, a precious set of boobies, are buying war-surplus arms) and then at Rio. He has received no countenance from the Admiralty, nor of course from the Hydrographical Office, and he comes as a private person invited by a private committee, the Chilean declarations having been neither officially recognised nor even acknowledged. He has acquired a moderate ship-sloop, sold out of the service; and another, called the *Asp*, is being repaired for him in Rio: his function is to train the Chilean authorities — if such a name can be applied to a disparate, self-elected committee or collection of committees that is likely to split at any moment . . .'

'Dear friend, you are in danger of losing yourself.'

'I ask pardon . . . to train the infant Chilean navy, since Spain still holds the great Chiloé archipelago in the south; so that the smaller Spanish men-of-war and privateers haunt the Chilean coast; while in the north, just at hand, in the great Peruvian naval base at Callao, they have some quite important vessels.'

Stephen reflected, and then said, 'It is some considerable time since we have been able to speak confidentially: tell me, have you any recent local information that I should know? Anything about the nature of the split?'

'Indeed I have. I was talking to an intelligent Chilean business connection, a jewel-merchant specialising in emeralds, Muzo emeralds — I even bought a small parcel from him — and he told me that the split was imminent. The two main sides live at some distance from one another: Bernardo O'Higgins and his friend San Martín, who beat the Royalists at Chacabuco, as you will remember, and whose associates invited Captain Aubrey in the first place, lead the northern group; while it was those in the south who invited Captain Lindsay.'

'Could you briefly outline their views?'

'Not briefly: there are so many of them with such different aims, and they are all so very talkative. But I might hazard the rash generalisation that the southern gentlemen are more idealist, their feet well off the ground, whereas the northerners under O'Higgins and San Martín, with much more limited aims, are very much more efficient. And although they have some lamentable friends I think they are upon the whole very much less self-seeking.'

Stephen sighed. 'Clearly, it is a deeply complicated situation,' he said, 'with infinite possibilities of making grave mistakes. How I wish you could be there well ahead of Lindsay and of us, so that, with no ostensible connection between you and me, the *Surprise* could sail into a wealth of intelligence. Let us search for some kind of timely packet or returning merchantman . . .'

'My dear sir, I believe it can be done without packets or merchantmen. Did Sir Blaine never speak to you of our man in Buenos Aires?'

'The invaluable Mr. Bridges, of the chancery? He did: but as I recall chiefly with regard to his encyclopaedic knowledge of early music . . . However, Sir

Joseph sometimes speaks very low, for emphasis, and I do not always catch what he says: nor do I like to cry "Eh?", or "What?" '

'Well, the gentleman is also a most eminent mountaineer — has climbed some astonishing Andean peaks — and with some chosen friends, Auracanians I believe, of the most ferocious kind, he has rapidly traversed the whole range by unknown or long-deserted passes; and with his help and his guides I could be in Chile long before you have threaded those tedious Straits or rounded a frozen Horn.'

'Are you serious, Amos?'

'I am. The mountain is my only mistress: I climb with infinite joy. There is not a peak in the Djebel Druse I do not know.'

'Have you any luggage . . . my boat is on its way.' Jacob nodded. 'Then pray bring it to the naval depot as discreetly as possible in the morning: say that you belong to *Surprise* and desire them to roll out seven casks of rhubarb purgative, and I shall have the pleasure of seeing you there when I come with other demands for medical supplies. God bless, now.'

'Jack,' he cried, bursting into the cabin. 'Oh, I beg your pardon.'

'Not at all, brother,' said Captain Aubrey: he closed his book. 'I was only reading a most uncomfortable piece in Galatians: damned, whatever you do, almost. I am afraid you have torn your stockings.'

'It was one of those upright things that caught me as I tried to come over the side in a seamanlike manner. Jack, I went ashore, as you know, in the hope of leaving a message for Amos Jacob, in the event of his joining us eventually as Sir Joseph wished. And *there he was in the flesh*, sitting not ten yards from me! So we met discreetly on the strand. He had already gathered a great deal of prime intelligence, and as my memory is by no means all I could wish I begged him to come aboard and give you all the main points. He will accompany us as far as Rio — and then with the blessing join us overland in Chile. But not to torment you, let me say at once that Sir David does not set out until the twenty-seventh: that he has a "moderate ship-sloop" sold out of the service, with another, called the *Asp*, being repaired for him in Rio, where he must call, before attempting — if my memory serves — to pass into the Pacific by the Strait. But Jacob will tell it more accurately, together with his detailed information about the various parties in Chile. Lindsay, by the way, already has agents here, buying used weapons against his arrival. To avoid any hint of collusion, I have begged Dr. Jacob to repair to the depot with his chest early in the morning, to present himself as one belonging to the *Surprise* and to ask the people there to have seven barrels of the rhubarb purgative ready to trundle down into the boat that will bring him out to the ship.'

'God love us all,' said Jack. 'Stephen, you quite astonish me with all your tidings — astonish and delight me. I do not know about dear Jacob's "moderate ship-sloop", but I do remember the poor tottering old *Asp*, when I was a boy; and I doubt she could withstand a single one of our broadsides. In any event, we have plenty of time, plenty of time for making a long southern sweep and steering north and west when the Antarctic weather, the Antarctic ice, are a little less horrible at the beginning of their summer, keeping the Horn way, way to leeward and so to the height of Valparaiso. Unless we have uncommon bad luck in the doldrums, we have time and to spare — just touch at Freetown to refresh, touch and away . . .'

'Touch and away, Jack?' asked Stephen. 'Touch and away? Do you not recall that I have important business there? Enquiries of the very first interest?'

'To do with our enterprise? To do with this voyage?'

'Perhaps not quite directly.'

'I do remember that at one time you did make a particular point of Freetown. You had hoped that we should "slope away for the Guinea Coast" directly from Gibraltar; and at that time I represented to you that the patching we had received in the yard did not prepare the barky for the Chile voyage — that Madeira was essential. Then we found Madeira town and above all Coelho's yard burnt to a cinder, so we had to go home, where she was thoroughly repaired and manned. But if you still feel strongly about the Guinea Coast and its pottoes, about Sierra Leone and Freetown, it could certainly be more than touch and away. What would you consider an adequate stay?'

After a hesitation Stephen said, 'Jack, we are very old friends and I do not scruple to tell you, in confidence, that I mean to beg Christine Wood to marry me.'

Aubrey was perfectly taken aback, dumbfounded: he blushed. Yet quite soon his good nature and good breeding enabled him to say 'that he wished dear Stephen every success — a most capital plan, he was sure — and that *Surprise* should lie there until she grounded on her beef-bones, if Stephen so desired.'

'No, my dear,' said Stephen. 'In such a case, and with such a person, I think it would be a plain yes or no. In the event of the first, I believe I should like to stay a week, if a week can be allowed. Otherwise we may sail away that same day, as far as I am concerned.'

They parted for the night with expressioins of the utmost good will on either side; and early in the morning Dr. Jacob's rather frowzy appearance in the great cabin changed the atmosphere quite remarkably. He explained the situation in Chile with a wealth of details (many of which Stephen had forgotten, his mind being elsewhere) which Adams, the captain's clerk, took down in a shorthand of his own.

The explanation was interrupted by the arrival of the casks of rhubarb: then by important quantities of round shot and a little chain; and then by the necessity of hauling off into the fairway, so that once the galley fires were doused and every living spark aboard extinguished, the powder-hoy could come alongside and deliver her deadly little copper-ringed barrels to the gunner and his mates.

With a fair wind and a flowing sheet the *Surprise*, stores and water all completed — no stragglers, no drunken hands taken up by the Funchal police — bore away a little east of south; and by the time stern-lanterns and top-lights were lit, those hands who were inclined to smoke their tobacco rather than chew it gathered in and about the galley, where in addition to the pleasure of their pipes they had the much-appreciated company of women, perfectly respectable women, Poll Skeeping, Stephen's loblolly-girl, and her friend Maggie, the bosun's wife's sister.

'So it seems the Doctor's mate has come aboard again,' said Dawson, the captain of the head, who knew it perfectly well but who liked to hear the fact confirmed.

'Was he carrying another Hand of Glory? How I hope he was carrying another Hand of Glory, God bless him, ha, ha, ha!'

'No, nor another unicorn's horn; that will be for next time.'

All those who had shared in the *Sur-*

prise's most recent and most glorious prize laughed aloud; and a Shelmerstonian, who had not been there of course, said, 'Tell us about it again.'

They told him about it again, about those splendid barrels brim-full of prize-money, with such vehemence and conviction, most of them speaking at once, that the blazing gold seemed almost to be there before them.

'Ah,' said one, in the ensuing silence, 'we'll never see days like that again.' A pause, and a general sigh of agreement; though many spoke with very strong approval of the doctors and the luck they brought.

'So we are bound for Freetown,' observed Poll Skeeping.

'Yes,' said Joe Plaice, one of Killick's friends and a fairly reliable source of information. 'Which the Doctor — our doctor — is sweet on the Governor's lady: or, as you might say, his widow. She lives there still, in a house.'

'What, an ugly little bugger like him, and that lovely piece?' cried Ebenezer Pierce, foretopman, starboard watch.

'For shame, Ebenezer,' said Poll. 'Think of your arm he saved.'

'Still,' said Ebenezer, 'you can be a very

clever doctor and still no great beauty.'
And in the inimical silence he walked aft,
affecting unconcern, and tripped over a
bucket.

'I wish the Doctor well, by God,' said a
carpenter's mate. 'He's had it cruel hard.'

Chapter Five

' "Governor welcomes *Surprise*: should be happy to see Captain, gunroom and midshipmen's berth at half-past four o'clock",' called the signal midshipman to the first lieutenant, who relayed the message to Captain Aubrey, three feet from its source.

'Very kind in him, I am sure,' said Jack. 'Please reply "Many thanks: accept with pleasure: *Surprise*." No: scrub that. "With greatest pleasure: *Surprise*." You know the moorings as well as I do, Mr. Harding: carry on, if you please, bearing the surf and our number one uniforms in mind.'

The captain and the officers of the frigate had done pretty well — even very, very well — out of their Barbary prize, but from the depths of their beings rose an anxious care for the outward marks of their rank, insignificant in comparison with those of their fellows in the army (often well-to-do), but of the first importance to a sailor living or attempting to live on his pay. Another fact that tempered their delight in the invitation was the Royal

Navy's custom of feeding its midshipmen (as much as it fed them at all, apart from their private stock, stores, and family pots of jam) at noon; the officers rather later; and the captain whenever he chose, usually at about one or half-past. So as usual, in response to an official, land-borne invitation, the Surprises approached Government House, groomed to the highest state of cleanliness and polish, but slavering with greed or with appetites wholly extinguished. Yet at least this time their precious uniforms, thanks to a little new jetty or pier, were still immaculate; and as soon as they had been properly introduced to Sir Henry, given their glass of sherry and seated, the officers with a female partner and the midshipmen promiscuously, their spirits began to revive.

Jack's partner was of course Lady Morris: Stephen's, apparently without any regard for his humble service rank, was Christine Wood. This was obviously the result of a deliberate manoeuvre on Lady Morris's part — she said something about 'common interest in birds' as Christine made her curtsey and Stephen his bow, and was sure that dear Mr. Harding would forgive her when she introduced him to the ADC's ravishing young wife — would forgive her on the grounds of a previous acquaintance, in spite of his seniority.

Previous acquaintance or not, they were painfully embarrassed, tongue-tied and awkward as they sat there, crumbling bread and responding to the usual civilities from their other neighbours. It was only when a plantain-eater uttered its horrible screech that Stephen cried, 'Surely it is too far north for that creature?' and she replied almost sharply that in spite of Hudson, Dumesnil and others Sierra Leone was by no means the northern limit of the plantain-eaters — two pairs had bred in her garden this year and there were reports of others well beyond the river, even. This re-established them on their former basis of scientific candour, and he told her of his anomalous nuthatch in the Atlas, of the numerous bodies of lions that would gather to roar at one another from either side of a river in those parts, of the extraordinary wealth of flamingos: presently their earlier friendship, affection and more than affection flowed back like a making tide on an open strand, flowed imperceptibly but without the least question. Like civilised creatures they paid proper attention to their other neighbours; but to the observant part of the company in general their particularity was so evident that a Mrs. Wilson, whose daughter was on Stephen's left, was heard to say, 'Really, the gentleman seems quite besotted with that Mrs. Wood.' Her friends replied that a rich widow would naturally seem very desirable to a penniless naval surgeon.

When they parted he said, 'I am so very glad to have seen you again. I am a most indifferent writer and I am only too painfully aware that my answers to your dear letters — to one above all — have been painfully inadequate. May I presume to call upon you tomorrow? I long to see your latest remarks on Adanson: and then again there is all the northern shore of the marsh that we had to leave unexplored — did you in the end fix our porphyria as a breeding species?'

'I should be very happy to see you,' she said, a little nervously. 'Shall we say at about ten, if your duty allows? You know where I live, I presume?'

'I do not.'

'It is the rather brutal square building below Government House, perhaps half a mile to the north, almost at the edge of the water: I bought it myself as a holiday place — in no way official, and as I said, near the shore. I shall send Jenny, in case you

187

should miss the way.'

Well before ten Jenny came alongside in a skiff expertly rowed by Square, a beaming Kruman who had accompanied Stephen on his earlier visit, and who now hailed the ship with such pleasure that all who heard him smiled.

'Dear Square, how happy I am to see you again,' said Stephen, descending with his usual grace, saved at the last minute by a powerful hand.

'The lady said I was to see you safe aboard, oh mind them thole-pins.' Square seized him again, and somehow balancing the frail craft while Jenny slid forward, set him down in the stern.

'Easy does it, Square,' called Jack, voicing the anxiety of all aboard.

And in fact easy did it: in time they saw Dr. Maturin creep up the few remaining steps of a solid, unmoving ladder (the tide was almost full) and walk firmly away into the town. 'What possessed me not to lay on my own barge I cannot imagine,' said Jack to his first lieutenant, who shook his head, unable to offer any comfort.

'Should you like a hammock, sir?' asked Square, meaning one of those drooping cushioned nets, extended by poles and a yoke, which served as sedan chairs or hackney coaches in Freetown.

'I had as soon walk,' said Stephen. 'But let us skirt the market-place, and perhaps Jenny will buy us each a length of sugar-cane.'

This they did, gazing over the great crowded, immensely vociferous square on the right hand, piled with glorious fruit, fish-slabs with half the wealth of the Atlantic, decently shrouded booths beyond, holding dark, nameless flesh; while away on the left, spotted with disconsolate camels and asses, an anonymous pasture stretched beyond the walls right down to the water's edge — varying waters, salt, fresh, and semi-liquid mud among the mangroves, with the brutal square building in its garden a great way off but quite distinct.

At the first heap of sugar-cane Stephen gave Jenny a small silver piece and they turned off to the left, threading their way down through as surprising a mixture of African and European nations as can well be imagined, with a plentiful sprinkling of Arabs and Moors and Syrians, and crosses of almost every shade including some with naturally rather than henna'ed red hair. But as soon as they were clear of the town the easy downward slope had almost no one on it and Stephen walked with his gaze well above the horizon, indeed half-way up the sky, for already the rising currents of air had carried many a soaring bird aloft.

He was intent upon one of them: a vulture, of course; but what vulture? Griffon? Lappet-faced? Hooded? Possibly Rüppell's griffon? The light, though strong, was awkwardly placed for the distinguishing marks of a very high bird planing on the southwest breeze.

'Sir,' said Square, stopping on the edge of a small freshwater stream that ran down from the right. And following the pointed finger, Stephen saw an exactly defined print in the mud, a leopard's left fore-paw, perfect even to the slight claw-mark, and strikingly recent.

'They come for dogs,' said Jenny. It was perfectly true, but neither of the men thought it her place to say so; and the word 'spots' died in her mouth.

'This is much more promising,' observed Stephen, his small telescope having shown him the surface of the bay dotted with water-fowl and perhaps some few waders far over. The minute 'ping' of his watch — it could hardly be called a chime — interrupted his close examination of the flamingos, and he said, 'Come, Square, come, Jenny. We must not be late.'

In through a massive gate to a stable-yard with an assembly of bristling, suspicious dogs, kept in order only by Jenny's presence and firm admonition, and so round to the front, where Mrs. Wood had just finished thrusting her puttee'd legs into riding-boots. 'Oh,' cried she, "I do beg pardon for not having come out to meet you — we had a roaring, bellowing night of it with that damned leopard, and the dogs are still very cross — what she hopes to gain by it, I cannot imagine. Should you like some canvas-topped boots? I can almost promise a tolerable bird, if we go almost at once: but we should have to paddle or even wade a little by the mangrove and the leeches are such a nuisance.' She sounded so very like her brother Edward when she said this that Stephen replied, 'Dear Miss Christine, how kind you are: I truly detest a leech.' But collecting himself as she laced the sailcloth tops he went on, 'Forgive my familiarity, I beg: that is what Edward and I used to call you.'

'And he called you Stephen, as I did when speaking of you to him: so if I may, I shall go on. It comes so naturally.'

Perfectly naturally, by the time they

reached the water and she was explaining its very curious nature. 'Now look, Stephen, beyond the pygmy geese but before the flamingos . . .'

'Christine, can you make out whether the nearer bird is a greater flamingo or the slightly smaller kind?'

'A lesser, I do believe. But we shall see better when we are a little farther round and he brings his head up, showing his bill more clearly. Well, between the pygmy geese and those sparse dubious flamingos, there is a sandbank that will show in an hour or so: the water on the far side is brackish and on our side fresh: well, fairly fresh except at huge great high tides. But if you look along the shore to the right you will see a fair-sized fresh-water stream coming down through the tall reeds: beyond that a dark bank of mangroves with their feet in the brackish mud, because there the sandbank curls in to the shore. Then farther on, though you can hardly see it from here except for the trees growing on its banks, another stream — a small river, indeed, where Jenny and I go and swim.' Stephen nodded. 'And there is an inlet beyond its mouth where I hope to show you a splendid bird. Oh, and thank you very much for the hermaphrodite crab:

there is something like him or her in that small bay. Shall we sit down on the bank here — this dear little northerly breeze keeps the mosquitoes off — and look at the birds? If there are any uncommon stragglers we may be able to make them out between us, or at least take notes.'

There was indeed a splendid wealth of birds on the water, including some very, very old friends such as wigeon, tufted duck, mallard and shoveller, perfectly at home among the neat little pygmy geese, knob-billed and spur-winged geese, white-faced tree-duck and the odd anhingas, to say nothing of the blue-breasted kingfisher that darted overhead and the steady patrol of vultures in the upper sky.

'Shall we go on?' asked Christine at last. 'You do not dislike mangroves?'

'Not at all,' he replied. 'I cannot say that I should ever deliberately cultivate one, but I am accustomed to their presence — have crept some miles among them and their loathsome flies further down the coast.'

'These are only a sickly little patch: they have too much sweet water, and they cannot thrive. Yet at least it is oh so much quicker and less painful than struggling through those cruel thorns higher up the slope behind them. I find the best way is to cling to the aerial roots as well as anything else that comes to hand. Undignified, if you like; but better than falling plump into that vile stinking black mud. And we must get along fairly quick. He begins to move when the sun is about this height.'

Stephen understood that 'he' was some particular creature — bird, reptile, possibly mammal, of a rarity that would delight him. He asked no questions and soon he had no time to ask any that might arise as he concentrated on following her practised steps through this slimy shade.

Yet most unhappily, as both sun and tide mounted, Christine moved faster, just too fast for her mud-clogged boots. The aerial roots, pale wands hanging plumb-straight down from the upper tree, betrayed her, and she did indeed fall plump into that vile black stinking mud, angering the small fishes that skipped on its surface, the many kinds of crab, and the little mud-tortoises that preyed on both. Stephen lurched forward to heave her out — met with the same fate — and they wallowed painfully, slowly, on all fours to the extreme edge of the mangrove trees, where clean water and a fairly clean bottom allowed them to crawl ashore in a very distressing state of filth.

She gasped, begged his pardon, said,

'How I hope we did not disturb him — probably not — there is two hundred yards to go. Does nakedness worry you?'

'Not in the least. After all, we are both anatomists.'

'Very well,' said she. 'There is nothing for it. We must both strip and rid our clothes of mud, our bodies of leeches. We have clean water here, thanks be: and in my pocket there is salt for the leeches, in a corked bottle. May I give you a hand with your boots?' She did so; he did the same for her; and they stripped off their clothes without the least ceremony, floating the mud out of them, weighing them down with stones; and then they attended to the astonishingly numerous and avid leeches, each dealing with the other's back in a wholly impersonal manner.

Apart from some artists' models and nations that possessed no clothes at all, Stephen had never seen anyone so unconcerned with nudity: and on reflection he remembered her brother Edward, his intimate friend, telling him that he and she had bathed, naturalised and fished, wearing nothing at all, from small childhood to maturity, in the isolated lake that formed part of their family's park. Well before this, during his first visit, she and her black companion had wandered into his field of vision as he searched the farther shore of a mere for birds and he had admired not only their freedom but also the combination of green, black, white, and the whiter than white of an egret, yet as objectively as he watched duck and cormorants. But now her tall, graceful, willowy shape was emphasised by the thin vermilion streams that flowed from the leech-bites (it did not coagulate, the creatures injecting a substance that thinned the blood, turned it a fine vermilion and allowed them a much longer period of feeding) and these outlined the curve of her long, long legs with an extraordinarily pleasing effect; and now something of the scientist, something of the pure anatomist, began to leave him.

'Presently the flies will grow intolerable,' she said. 'It would be better to put on damp clothes than to have them crawling about all over one.' Still, she did spread some of the wettest on sun-warmed rocks: they dried quite soon, but even sooner the mounting sun made her uneasy. They put the garments on, as well as they could, and she led the way, murmuring, 'Oh that he may not have gone.'

She reached a last screen of rushes

before a small, secluded inlet, and as she did so there leapt into the air a perfectly enormous bird of the heron kind, blueish on top, chestnut below, with immense green legs and a deep, furious baying cry — he filled the narrow space of sky before vanishing seawards, leaving Stephen perfectly amazed. He kissed Christine quite ardently, thanking her with the most profound gratitude. She blushed, and said, 'Oh how glad I am we had not flushed him. He is as touchy as a Roman emperor.'

'Lord,' said Stephen, 'that such a bird can fly! Can take to the air!'

When he had recovered from his amazement, which was not soon, and when their clothes were moderately dry, he observed with pleasure that in spite of the fact that they had stalked about together stark naked she had a certain coquetry in arranging the fall of her principal garment. 'Now, should you like to go to the house and have tea and then come down to the hides out there' — nodding to some reed shelters on or just off the true shore — 'so that when the sun is gone I hope to be able to show you a most prodigious wonder. You do not have to go back to the ship directly, I trust?'

'Oh no. If there is any urgency aboard

they will send for me; but with my colleague already there, it is scarcely possible.'

'To tea, then; and at least we have a Christian path to the house. Coming down it again, we should be wise to carry a gun. The poor leopard is growing desperate, I fear — so many insatiable cubs.'

'Have you ever seen them?'

'Yes: she keeps them in a tumble of rocks on the hillside, and if you climb an oil-palm about two hundred yards along, you can see them peeping out just after dawn, waiting for her. I drove tenpenny nails into the trunk, and many a good skirt have they cost me, when I slip.'

'Jenny,' she called, walking into the house with a little cloud of dogs, 'tell N'Gombe that we should like tea, and pray run and fetch a really cool cucumber for sandwiches. Stephen,' she went on, 'should you like a dressing-gown?'

'No, thank you, my dear: I have walked myself dry.'

'Then forgive me for a moment while I put something decent on my back.'

There were some bird-skins on her work-table, with the heaps of notes required for an intelligent commentary on

Adanson, and he looked at them with an interest quite devoid of prying, at the same time revolving one of those curious problems of limit: you may kill a leopard if she assumes a threatening attitude, thus condemning her beautiful cubs to a hideous and lingering death. You may shoot and skin a number of slightly differing green pigeons and wood-doves with no more of a tremor than Sir Joseph Blaine impaling a butterfly. Yet to the question 'You would not destroy the whole litter and be shot of them?' you may reply 'If you had seen a little leopard, I do not think you would ask.'

The door opened. 'Why, my dear,' he said, 'how very fine you look, now you are cleaned and brushed. Pray what is this skin? Clearly a pigeon, but I cannot make out which.'

'He is Gmelin's *Treron thomae*, from the island down in the Gulf. Here comes the tea: what joy. There is nothing like tea for getting rid of the taste of mangrove mud.'

It was brought with proper ceremony by an immense, grave, very black man, and almost immediately after it was followed by the cucumber sandwiches and some little round affairs, not unlike marzipan.

They made a good, serious tea, passing

bird-skins from hand to hand and speaking of their infant greed — muffins, crumpets, buttered toast with anchovy relish, deeply iced fruit cake — in the most companionable way. But towards the end Stephen noticed that she was looking out of the window with something of the anxiety of one who does not wish to miss the evening rise: he refused 'another cup' and rose briskly at her suggestion that they should go down to the hides — lanterns would bring them up again, so they could stay as long as they chose.

'I shall entrust the gun to you, if I may,' she said, rather as though it were an umbrella, and led the way out with a fine elastic step, putting her boots on again in the hall.

Down, with plenty of light and a three-quarter moon rising over Africa: Stephen said, 'Sometimes, you know, I am shockingly careless of the common decencies of life.'

'You mean taking all our clothes off in that abandoned way?'

'Dear me, no: our forbears did that long before us — long before they had any notion of that apron of fig-leaves. No: what grieves me is my never uttering a single word — not the least enquiry after your chanting-goshawks, begging you to tell me how they do?'

'Alas, Stephen, alas: a bateleur killed their mother, and I did not succeed in bringing them up. You have seen a bateleur, I make no doubt?'

'I have, too. The most remarkable of the eagles — if he is an eagle at all, which some naturalists deny.'

'She was out in the yard, on her perch, and he came down with a noise like a stooping peregrine but twice as loud, chased her into the stable and instantly killed her. Hassan took her body away, netted the eagle, and so left him in the dark. He was — and is — a young bird, and terribly fierce at the slightest threat. But quite soon we were on reasonably good terms. He is surprisingly intelligent, and even kind; indeed very good terms. I turned him free, and even now — for this is his territory — he will come racing down on to my shoulder to ask how I do.'

'How I hope I may see him: he at least is a bird one can never mistake — no tail, no tail at all. You would say a scythe, flying at enormous speed; wonderful gyrations. Tell me, what about bats?'

'I must confess that I have not paid as much attention to bats as I should have

done. There are such myriads of birds —
one of them, by the way, lives on bats,
together with the odd evening pipit. He is
a buzzard really, of moderate size but
extraordinary agility, as you may imagine:
they eat their bats straight out of their
talons, in the air. I only know two couples.
Here we are: and here is really quite a
good path and then a little sort of
causeway to the main — well, you can
hardly call it a building — but the place or
hide from which my husband and his
guests used to shoot the flighting duck and
the smaller geese. You can stand there,
seeing and not being seen: a capital place if
you like to watch the waders and many,
many of the little things in the reeds. Take
care on the causeway — here is the rope.'

Inside it was surprisingly light. Their
eyes were already accustomed to the after-
glow — it was no more — and they could
make out geese and duck by the hundred.
'But my dear Stephen,' she said, gently
turning him round to the shore and the
trees, 'this is the way you must look, and
oh how I hope my nine-days' wonder
remembers the appointment. We are rich
in nightjars, as you know — do you hear
the one over to the east?'

'A dear bird. Our homely European

kind, is he not?'

'Certainly; but I meant the deeper croak to the left.'

He listened, caught the sound, and said, 'It is a nightjar of a sort, to be sure: the family voice.' The bird stopped: they stood poised, listening: then suddenly she touched his arm. 'There is my bird,' she whispered. 'Oh, how I hope he comes.'

Stephen caught the shrill, lasting churr: and as a waft of air brought the sound closer it soon dropped in pitch, growing much more present. 'Don't move,' she murmured.

They stood taut, their senses at the stretch, the utmost stretch; and clear against the pale sky, not twenty yards before them, flew a bird with a nightjar's action but extraordinarily modified by two immensely elongated flight-feathers on either side, trailing far behind, more than doubling its length. With an instant change of direction it swooped on a pale moth, captured it and flew off, lost against the darkness of the trees.

She had been gripping his arm: now she released it, saying, 'He *did* come: oh I am so glad. You saw him clear, Stephen?'

'Clear, perfectly clear: and I am amazed, *amazed*. Thank you very much indeed for showing him to me, dear Christine. Lord, such wealth! Such an acquisition! Will you tell me about him?'

'What very little I know. He is Shaw's *Caprimulgus longipennis*, and he is uncommon in these parts, above all in his full mating plumage — I have seen only two all the time I have been here. That perfectly astonishing train, by the way, is just the ninth primary on either side; and how the poor bird manages to get into the air I cannot imagine, above all if he happens to be on the ground: we have another nightjar with enormously exaggerated flight feathers, *Macrodypteryx vexillarius*, but his are only pointed, not bushy at the tips, like ours . . . But in any case I have never been able to make really valuable observations of either, nor of their plain long-tailed cousin.'

'I should not have missed that for anything. On the face of it those primaries destroy the bird's efficiency, just as the peacock's ludicrous train or the lavish display of the birds of paradise may be presumed to cost them a very great deal. Yet they live and even thrive: could it be that our notions, or at least my notions, are fundamentally mistaken?'

'There he is again. And another: the

ordinary long-tailed bird.'

They stood in silence, slowly relaxing. 'There is our scops owl,' said she. Some duck passed over, wigeon by the sound of their wings, and broke the surface a hundred yards away with a surprising noise in this dead-still night.

'Stephen,' she said after a while. 'I am afraid you are uneasy. Shall I go away for a few minutes? You can whistle when you want me back.'

'No, soul,' he said, 'this is really not the usual physical matter but rather a question of throwing my petition into a reasonably acceptable form. In short, it would give me infinite joy if you would marry me: yet before you instantly put me to silence, let me at least say what I can in my own favour. Admittedly, I am very far from being even tolerably good-looking; but from the physician's point of view I am pretty sound, with no grossly evident vices; materially I believe I may say that I am what is ordinarily called well-to-do, with an ancient house and a reasonable estate in Spain — I could without difficulty buy a decent place or set of chambers in London or Dublin: or Paris, for that matter. I stand reasonably well in my profession and in the service. My worst enemies could not truthfully say that I was a loose-liver, addicted to gaming or the bottle. And although in candour I cannot deny that my birth was illegitimate and my church that of Rome, I do not think — I do not like to think — that to a person of your distinguished intelligence, these are total bars to a union, above all since I should make no claims of any kind. Finally I should like to add that as you are aware, I am a widower — your letter touched me to the heart — and that I have a daughter.'

After a while, during which at least three separate nightjars churred and one owl called, she said, 'Stephen, you do me infinite honour, and it grieves me more than I can say to desire you to dismiss the subject from your mind. I have been married, as of course you know, and very unhappily married. I too am pretty sound from the physician's point of view: I too am reasonably wealthy. But — I am speaking of course to an honourable man — my husband was incapable of the physical aspects of marriage and his vain attempts to overcome this defect gave me what I have believed to be an ineradicable disgust for everything to do with that aspect — the whole seemed to me a violent and of course inept desine for possession and physical dominance. And this impression was no doubt reinforced by own fear and reluctance.' And speaking in an entirely different tone after a period of silence she said, 'In your experience as a physician, would you say that this was a usual state of mind in a young married wornan?'

He reflected and said, 'I have very rarely encountered a case in which the circumstances were so extreme as yours: but I do know how often the sorrow and woe that is in marriage arise from want of elementary physical understanding, to say nothing of ineptitude, selfishness, gross ignorance . . .'

'And a kind of hostility, resentment . . .'

'Agreed, agreed. Please wipe my foolish, self-seeking words from your memory as far as ever you can. But do let us go on exchanging notes on Adanson. There are the lanterns coming down through the trees.'

'Oh dear,' she said, taking his hand. 'I am afraid I have wounded you, a man I esteem more than any who have ever addressed me. Stephen, I am so sorry . . .'

The eastern nightjar had begun its song again, its churr, apparently without ever drawing breath; and by way of distracting his mind from the sorrow, Stephen counted the pulse of his heart: he had reached seventy-five before the bird stopped. The lights were on the edge of the wood, and he was aware that Christine had been weeping.

On the way up she took his arm, and in the house they sat down to a curiously delicious supper based on African vegetables that he did not know, and eggs, with a tolerable white wine; then came the almond pudding, followed by a capital madeira.

Pushing the plates aside she showed him the astonishing skin of *Caprimulgus longipennis* and told him about the power of those particular feathers as ju-ju in local belief. 'The longer I live in Africa,' she observed when they were drinking the wretched coffee and some excellent rum, 'and the more I know about Africans, the nearer I come to a sort of diffused pantheism.'

Reverting to this a little later, when her spirits had revived somewhat, she said, 'I know my divinity angers missionaries to a quite surprising degree, and upon the whole I do not care for them either, not very much. But sometimes a missionary is also a naturalist, and if he is far away in the bush he may have wonderful opportunities. I am sure you have heard of the Congo peacock?'

'Indeed, I have often heard tell of him; but I have never known him described by a credible witness.'

'Well,' she said, feeling in a drawer, 'I do not say that this is proof positive,' — holding out a green feather — 'but it was given me by a very old — Franciscan, I think, a Catholic in any event — who died here before he could take ship, and who told me without the least pomp or showing away that he had plucked it from the back of a recently dead peacock in the Congo: I forget the name of the district, but the bird lived in open woodland.'

'Dear me, Christine,' he said, caressing the feather, 'you have amazed and delighted me three times today. The elephantine heron; the wildly eccentric, more than improbable nightjar, and now the fabled Congo peacock, on whose existence I shall now pledge my soul. I am sorry that you do not choose to marry me, but I thoroughly understand your . . . what shall I say? Disinclination.'

A surprising length of time, of emotional time, had passed between their standing in the hide, the space of his declaration, and the present, with its entirely different context. She smiled, drank a little more rum, patted his knee, and said, 'Tell me, Stephen, if I had accepted your dear, dear proposal, how should you have managed the purely material side of the union? You have spoken of your daughter. How old is she?'

'I am ashamed to say I cannot tell. Quite young, sure: nowhere near puberty.'

'Then again you are engaged with your friend on a distant and I presume important voyage?'

'To be sure,' said Stephen, looking wretchedly from side to side. 'Yet I was not entirely thoughtless. Believe me,' he said earnestly, 'I was not entirely selfish. I had a very pretty solution: my idea was that you should go to England, there to stay with Sophie Aubrey, a charming woman and a very old friend, who has two girls and a son, who looks after Brigid, my daughter, and who lives in a large house in Dorset with quantities of friends all round and a most respectable body of servants. And then, it appeared to what I can only diffidently call my mind — in other words the embodiment of my wishes — that I should return from the sea, and that together we should plot the course of our days: England, Ireland, France or Spain, or any combination according to your choice.'

'Dear me, dear me,' she said with a sigh:

and hearing the minute voice of Stephen's watch, 'was that a clock somewhere? Can it be twelve?'

He plucked it from his waistcoat. 'Yes, twelve it is, by the ship's exact noon observation of the sun.'

'Oh what a pretty thing. Will it chime again?'

It chimed again, and Stephen asked, 'Do you like it?'

'I think it is perfectly beautiful. Is it what they call a repeater?'

'Yes, ma'am.'

'I have never seen one before.' She was clearly fascinated.

He put it back into her hand, showed her the buttons to be pressed, and said, 'There, my dear. It is yours: a very slight acknowledgement of the delights you have given me today.'

'Oh, what nonsense, Stephen dear,' she said, repressing a smile. 'Of course I cannot possibly accept such a present: though I return a hundred thousand thanks for the intention.' She put it gently on the table, stood up, and said, 'Come, it is already late. Let me show you to your room.'

It was a fine large airy place and the window framed the declining moon. She drew the curtain and said, 'I am afraid you brought no night-clothes, Stephen. Should you like one of my gowns?'

'Lord, no, my dear: I am perfectly happy to lie in my skin, like Adam before the fall.'

'Well, good night, Stephen. There is water, and a towel. There is soap. I do hope you will sleep well.'

'Good night, my dear. I shall be up before the sun, since I mean to walk up and over to rejoin my ship; so please forgive me if I take my leave now.'

Long he lay on the flat of his back, head supported by both hands and above all by his sense of the weakening of Christine's absolute resistance; he turned the events of a singularly varied day in his mind; and a great way off two, three and even four different nightjars churred at their various pitches.

In spite of their earlier farewell, Christine joined him for breakfast. 'I am so sorry I grieved you,' she said, looking at him uneasily, after the first civilities.

'I had no notion of your far more grievous reasons,' he replied. 'It was deeply impercipient. But before I go, please let me say that as I see it marriage does not neces-

sarily mean possession; far, far less dominance.'

'Stephen, I would not hurt you for the
world. You are going on a long and I hope
very fruitful voyage: may I turn the whole
thing over in my mind while you are away?
And with the blessing I may come round
— come back — to thinking and feeling
like an ordinary woman. But, my dear,'
after a long, long pause, 'you are not to
feel in the slightest degree bound: no, not
the very least degree.' Stephen bowed; and
having poured him more coffee she went
on hesitantly, 'Did you not say that the
Aubreys lived in Dorsetshire? I am going
to cousins next month who live near Bridport; and if I can be of any use in carrying
letters, either of you have but to command.'

'That would be wonderfully kind. I know
that Captain Aubrey has a heap of paper,
written small; and I have not done badly.
But tell me — though this is a personal
question, which I detest — do you find it
easy to travel?'

'Lord, yes. I often go back. I may take
Jenny, but I can perfectly well go alone: I
find that men, particularly seamen, are
particularly kind to women on their own;
and a single trunk does very well. A big,

roomy Portuguese Guineaman touches here next month. She will put me down at the Pool, as usual, and the agents will carry me and my trunk to Grillon's, where I generally stay, and after a day or two of shopping I shall take a post-chaise down: it is as simple as that.'

'Of course. I had always known of women travelling to and from India by themselves, but from some imbecility of mind West Africa seemed infinitely more remote. If I may, I shall send up our packets directly, for tomorrow we shall sail.'

'Good-bye, dear Stephen,' she said in the doorway.

'Good-bye, dear Christine: God bless.'

He walked away from the house a little after sunrise with no more than a dissatisfied or inquisitive look from the dogs in the outer yard: a clear, cool morning, and a little flock of bulbuls flew over him as he sat down half-way up the hill to gaze out over the water: the duck were no longer moving, but the flamingos were busy, and he liked to think that behind the mangrove-belt he could just make out the monstrous form of that improbable great heron, *Ardea goliath*.

Rising, he climbed the hill: but with a rather languid step — even a short time at sea made walking on the unyielding ground quite arduous for a while — but his heart glowed with sanguine hope.

Yet for all his meditations on the possibility of a happy future and his rehearsing of the wonders he had seen the day before, his stomach kept up its peevish cry, above all at the scent of coffee wafting from the southern gate. Christine's servants, though devoted and so trustworthy that she could leave the house without a qualm, lacked one prime virtue: they could not make coffee. The household drank tea, and this morning's thin brownish wash (saved from yesterday) was a special concession to the guest, poor soul. Once he was inside the walls he walked straight to a decent-looking place at the corner of the market-square, called for a pot, and heard Jacob's voice saying 'Dear colleague, I wish you a very good morning indeed. May I join you?'

Stephen replied that nothing would give him more pleasure; and after a few preliminaries Jacob said, 'If you were not my superior officer, I should venture to say that you push discretion much too far in not asking me what I am doing, what I think I am about, why am I here, and who is looking after our patients; but you *are* my superior officer, so without any comment I shall voluntarily tell you that two other men-of-war came in shortly after you left with Square and the girl. Their captains paid their duty-calls early, and in the afternoon we began a three-sided competition — games of cricket, a boxing-match, and races between the various boats: they intend doing the whole dreary thing over again today on an even larger scale, together with bouts of raising and lowering masts and sails and even of gunfire, for God's sake, all against a stop-watch. I cannot bear it, so I escaped at the earliest possible moment. I get in the way, I am pushed and blamed and even cursed: and as for patients, we have no patients, no bed-ridden patients, all the sick having declared themselves whole. No patients, other than a youth from the *Erebus* whom your young friend Hanson struck to the ground with a nnurderous blow. It is only in fact a passing concussion, but his shipmates feign infinite concern and swear that if it prove fatal they will keelhaul the Lion of the Atlas, as they call our champion, with his own intestines. The zeal and animation which fills these three ships, with the various exhibitions of maritime skill, passes all understanding: most of the officers are as deeply concerned as the men;

but I must say that Captain Aubrey seems somewhat oppressed, and if he did not have official business ashore I think he might succumb.' He poured more coffee, plucked off another six inches of soft bread, and looking attentively at his old friend, asked, 'Stephen, are you satisfied with the Captain's health?'

'His physical health?'

'Can the two be separated?'

'On occasion, yes: but to be sure, in general the two are very intimately connected.'

'His light seems to have gone out.'

'His wife has used those very words.'

'Whereas yours, if I may say so, Stephen, glows like a moderately resplendent sun. I hope, my dear, you do not dislike my speaking in this way?' — they had as usual lapsed back into the French of their youth — 'But we have, after all, known one another a great many years.'

'We have indeed, Amos. No: I do not dislike it at all, in you: and I shall try to make the dimming — which I perfectly admit — more comprehensible. As far as the Royal Navy is concerned, I, for one, am attached, loosely attached, to the service: he is literally *of* it, and success or failure in the Navy is and always has been of paramount importance. He has risen high: he is a post-captain near the top of the list. But he is at that stage when some members of the group with approximately the same seniority are selected for flag-rank as rear-admiral of the blue. By no means all can be chosen: those who are *not* chosen, those who are passed over, are colloquially or by way of derision known as *yellow* admirals, admirals of a non-existent squadron. And that is the end of the poor man's hopes: there is no return to eligibility. Merit has something to do with this vital step, yet influence has more — political and family influence have more, sometimes much more; and Jack Aubrey has not always been politically wise. He is very much afraid of picking up the Gazette in the next few months and of seeing men junior to himself being given their flag, a *blue* flag to be hoisted at the mizzen, if my memory serves: a piece of bunting extraordinarily important to a man who has pursued it with such ardour for so many years. And now that we are no longer at war, now that there is virtually no chance of his distinguishing himself, it is understandable that his light should at least grow dim: there is the real possibility that it should go out entirely. And there is nothing that can restore it, nothing but that piece of cloth.

Nothing.' A pause, and he went on, 'The malady, the state of mind, is called flagsickness in the Navy, and it affects almost all ambitious post-captains as they approach the decisive period. I have rarely seen it close at hand, since all my service has been under one commander, but I have often spoken of it to my colleagues, and they agree in saying that those affected — that is to say, all but the few officers whose achievements, family connexions or immediate political influence make their promotion sure — suffer from anxiety, loss of appetite and joie de vivre, while often the essentially masculine functions are disturbed, so that medical men have observed either a virtual impotence or an unwholesome activity. Here there is nothing so extreme; but there is an oppression: little or no music, and he will play chess, cards or backgammon only out of complaisance.'

They returned to their coffee and sat considering for a while. Then Stephen said, 'Amos, at one time there were several Syrians and Armenians here: men of business, agents. Do you know any at present? It is of no vital importance, but I should like to know about a large Portuguese Guineaman bound for England, a vessel in which a lady, a friend of mine, is to take passage.'

'Dear me, yes,' said Amos, amused. 'Is not my own cousin Lloyd's representative in this port? Shall I take you to him?'

Stephen felt for his watch — no watch of course, but a jet of delight: and a church clock told him that it was nine. 'You are very good. But would he, or one of his clerks, undertake so small a commission? I only wish to fill her cabin with flowers, or rather to have it so filled. And since we sail tomorrow and the Guineaman does not touch here for a great while, clearly the flowers must be procured by proxy.'

'I am quite certain that he would be delighted. Another pot?'

'Thank you, but I believe I should go down as soon as we have seen your amiable cousin.'

'I shall come with you, if I may: your seniority, your austere countenance, may be something of a protection against rude mirth; and in any case this morning they mean to renew their pugilism, so we may have serious casualties to attend to.'

The two medicos, their errand happily accomplished, set off from the mole during a lull in the roaring aboard *Surprise*, the calls of 'Break him and tear him, mate', and the dull sound of impassioned blows given and received. Some of their friends gave them a hand up the side. 'Thank you, Mr. Hanson,' said Stephen, safely on deck. 'But,' he went on, looking at the youth, 'I am afraid you have been in the wars.' Certainly he had one eye thoroughly blacked, and there was dried blood on his lower face; while one ear was visibly swelling.

'Oh, sir,' replied Hanson, with a cheerful and full-toothed smile, 'it was only a little sparring.'

'Still, you had better come below and let me put a stitch or two in that eyebrow.'

Sitting there on a stool while the needle was preparing, Hanson explained that his adversary, a master's mate from *Hector*, though heavy and a thoroughly game chicken, had no notion of the long straight left to the throat. Not to the *point*, sir, but to the throat. Nothing settled your cove quicker than a determined blow to the throat.

'I should think not, indeed,' said Stephen. 'Now pray lean over, and do not start away at the prick: there. Well done. Are you to fight again?'

'Not until after dinner, sir: and he is said not to be truly wicked.'

'Yet even so, should he aim a blow at

your head, you would be well advised to avert this eyebrow and face him crabwise. Now I must go and see the Captain. In the cabin, I presume?'

'Yes, sir: and thank you very much for your care of me.'

Captain Aubrey was indeed in the cabin, leaning over some bundles of official papers tied with black tape or red. 'There you are,' he cried, raising his head with a smile; and having looked attentively at Stephen's face he went on, 'I do hope you have had some really prodigious good news?'

'I have, too,' said Stephen. 'Not quite so prodigious as I could have wished, since the lady, not surprisingly, declined my proposal; but she did say she would consider it while we were away. And she did offer to carry our letters back to England. She is going to visit cousins near Bridport: so may I beg you, dear Jack, to write to Sophie urging her to invite Mrs. Wood? I should very much like her to become well-acquainted not only with Sophie and her children but also with my Brigid: it would give me the utmost pleasure if they were to love one another.'

'There is no reason why they should not.

I am quite sure that Sophie, bless her, and Mrs. Wood could not fail to get along famously; while Brigid is a dear, affectionate little creature, and she is grateful for quite a little kindness and attention. My girls, being older, do not regard her as much as they should . . . I have often thought of mentioning it; but as Sophie says, rating has never yet begot tenderness. And they tend to be somewhat jealous . . . it is delicate ground to venture on. A stranger can sometimes do more than either parent. I have no doubt that Brigid and Mrs. Wood will be friends: after all, I do know Mrs. Wood quite well, and I esteem her immensely — admire her too, if I may say so. Should Sophie ask her to stay until we come back? We have quantities of room, now that Clarissa is married and gone.'

'That would be more than kind, but she also means to go up to Northumberland to see her brother Edward, my particular friend, a natural philosopher whom you must have seen from time to time at the meetings of the Royal Society; and I doubt if she would choose to leave her African house for so long. She travels with singular ease, quite alone or with just one or two servants. She means to take the *Gaboon* next month, a comfortable Portuguese Guineaman she has sailed in before, which will take her to London, carrying at least some of our letters: there she will stay a few days and then head south in a post-chaise. Purely between ourselves, I may add that she is rather wealthy.'

'So much the better: it does ease travelling so. Lord, Stephen, I am so pleased with what you tell me. You will take a glass of wine, will you not?'

'If you please. I should be very happy to drink a glass of wine with you, my dear. But first, Jack, let me say that a Government packet is leaving at high tide the day after tomorrow, and if it could carry your letter to Sophie together with one of mine, I should be most singularly obliged.'

Jack touched the bell, and without much surprise he saw the door instantly fly open, showing an ugly, inquisitive face vainly attempting to conceal a grin. 'Killick,' he said, 'what have we got in the net under the counter?'

'Three of hock, sir, and half a dozen of champagne.'

'Rouse out a couple of champagne, will you, and light along my best writing-paper and a fresh ink-pot.'

'Aye-aye, sir: champagne it is. Paper, best. Which Mr. Hanson is now stripping for his fight with that dogged *Polyphemus* reefer.'

'Should you like to watch, Stephen, just for a round or two?' asked Jack.

'Certainly: and you will tell me about the finer points. But do not let us cause the wine to lose what coolness it may have.'

On the fo'c'sle, by a gross abuse of cordage, equipment and stanchions, a tolerable ring had been improvised. Both young men were in their corners, listening to their battered old seconds' advice. Then at the bell they leapt up, toed the imaginary line in the middle, and set about one another with a singular ferocity. This was the light-weight final bout and each burned to win it for his own ship — for himself too, but this was less evident. Polyphemus, burly and thick, liked to close and batter ribs, chest and if possible flanks. Young Surprise, more agile, kept his distance, throwing in some very pretty lefts at Polyphemus' bleeding face. But for three gasping rounds he could not hit the stolid youth's chin hard enough to throw his head back. Jack's and Stephen's whispered prayers and audible advice had no effect until the fifth round, when Polyphemus, with lowered guard, sought to avoid a shocking blow on his nose, jerked back, head and all, exposed his throat and received the final, disabling, choking blow.

Jack congratulated both gasping, exhausted combatants, awarded the minute silver cup; then learnt that *Polyphemus* had crushed *Surprise* in the pulling race for cutters round the port; and all hands cheerfully adjourned for a general feast (provided by *Surprise*) at which Harding presided, the Captain being taken up with paper-work, seeing that they were now to weigh at the height of flood.

Chapter Six

'We therefore commit his body to the deep,' said Captain Aubrey, 'to be turned into corruption, looking for the resurrection of the body (when the Sea shall give up her dead) and the life of the world to come, through Our Lord Jesus Christ; who at His coming shall change our vile body, that it may be like His glorious body, according to the mighty working, whereby He is able to subdue all things to Himself . . .' and Harding, the first lieutenant, gave the watching bosun a barely perceptible nod. As all hats whipped off, the hatch-cover tilted, shooting its burden into the advancing roller, which swallowed it with barely a sign; and Henry Wantage, master's mate, sank instantly, sewn into his hammock with four round shot at his feet.

'I went through those words not ten days out of Freetown,' said Jack in the cabin, 'and I have said them after many an action, God knows: yet they move me every time, so that I am like to stumble towards the end. Particularly for poor Wantage, who had such a wretched time of it in Funchal.'

Stephen poured him more coffee. 'Sure,' he said, 'and I grieved for those two sad, wasted yellow-fever boys: to the end I thought Jacob and I might save them: but it was not to be.'

'Apart from a really uncommon bloody action, I do not remember to have seen a midshipmen's berth so mauled. We have only one master's mate, and at present poor old Mr. Woodbine is scarcely fit to stand a watch.' He pondered, drank more coffee, and rang the bell. 'Pass the word for Mr. Hanson,' he said.

'Mr. Hanson it is, sir,' replied Killick; and the name resounded through the ship.

'Sir?' asked the boy, the very young man, who had obviously been weeping.

'Sit down, Mr. Hanson,' said Jack. 'A little while ago Mr. Adams pointed out to me that you have an uncommon amount of sea-time against your name.'

'Yes, sir. My Uncle was good enough to enter me on the books of *Phoenix* and some other ships before I was breeched.'

'Just so. Many captains do the same: the result is that although you are still quite young you are legally senior to most of the people in the berth. And since your navigation is better than most of theirs I am going to take advantage of your nominal service to appoint you master's mate. Mr. Daniel is older than you, and perhaps more able: but with your sea-time he cannot be promoted over your head, and I am sure he has enough experience of the service to accept the apparent injustice without bearing you any ill-will. You and he will be a great support to Mr. Woodbine. You will take poor Mr. Wantage's place in the last dog watch today.'

'Yes, sir. Thank you very much, sir,' said Horatio, looking confused, embarrassed, far from happy.

'Cut along, then: and tell the berth that I have issued those words as a direct order. You may not like it, and they may not like it: but you will have to give them a feast on the last day of the month. If you choose to invite *Ringle*'s mates, I shall give them a bottle of wine apiece, for the honour of the ship: it is the custom, you know.' When Horatio had gone, Jack said, 'That is a good boy. He don't like it; and they won't like it. But I do not think they will tear him to pieces, now that he has shown what he is made of. In any case John Daniel would not allow it; he has real authority in the berth, although he has not been aboard very long.'

The appointment was indeed received with some murmuring in the berth: but it was greeted with general approval by the lower deck, which set an even higher value on physical courage than on the finer points of seamanship — not that Mr. Hanson was so deficient in them, either.

'My dear Christine,' wrote Stephen on page seventeen of the serial letter that would be sent to Dorset from Rio de Janeiro or by the good offices of the first homeward-bound ship they met, 'I think it would please you to watch the formation of a community so close-packed and eventually so tight-knit as the crew of a ship, above all of a man-of-war, which has so many more people to serve the guns, and a far more rigid hierarchy. Remarkably strong and lasting friendships are formed, particularly on very long voyages; but even in a commission so recent as ours the process is evident. Young Hanson, whom I have mentioned before, is, I understand from Jack, really talented as far as the mathematics are concerned, and Mr. Daniel, a master's mate, has helped him in their practical application to the guidance of the ship's course — even to determining her exact position on the trackless ocean, for all love. They have become close companions, which could scarcely have been the case on land, their origins, nurture, and manner of speech being so very far apart. When we were in Freetown they were inseparable, wandering about together, taking the bearings of capes and headlands, the height of towers, minarets, fortifications and so on, together with depths and tides. And now, since Mr. Woodbine's health failed him two or three weeks from the Guinea coast, the two have been devotedly attentive to the ship's motions — longitude, latitude and the like — throughout the long course of unpredictable, varying winds that torment the mariner in the Gulf — until at last we reached the blessed north-east trade, before which we are now bounding at a rate of I think ten knots in the hour; and now they can draw breath at last.

'There are few things more pleasing to see than that rise and growth of a natural, spontaneous liking, sometimes, indeed often, (as in this case), accompanied by similar tastes, abilities and studies: but by no means always, nor by an equality in age, and it would give me the liveliest pleasure to find you and Brigid friends. A very little notice on your part would overcome her timidity, and I know you would not find her wanting in affection, though it has been somewhat damped: the older girls do not show her much kindness, and although I do not advance this as anything more than a conjecture, I have the impression that they regard her as an intruder. And since infant emotions are rarely disguised with any skill I believe I may say that their mother's attentions and her kindnesses to Brigid quite certainly excite their jealousy, that most corrosive of passions, and the most unhappy. There, my dear, I hear the imperious bell — our life is ruled by bells — that marks the beginning of my rounds, and if I do not go at once I shall have sour disapproving looks — not perhaps from Amos Jacob, but certainly from Poll Skeeping and her mate, from all the patients, straightened in their cots, their sheets smoothed tight, their modest comforts hidden, and their faces washed, and not improbably from the ship's two cats, who came secretly aboard at Freetown, and who have grown wholly accustomed to the rigour of naval life, disliking the slightest variation — worthy, scrupulous cats, who regularly visit their little trays of ashes, set out in the galley by the equally severe and righteous cook. My dear, fare-

232

well for a moment . . .'

'My dear, the moment is passed,' he wrote, squaring up to his desk, braced against the frigate's rhythmic heave and roll, 'and I am happy to tell you of a real improvement in the master's health: he has eaten, and retained, two copious meals, the first of fresh flying-fish, the second of a moderately rich lobscouse. This may be connected with the ship's much more even pace, her greater speed, and the general air of satisfaction aboard — the brisk (though warm) and lively air. But I do not like to mention any of these factors, the master being a through-and-through mariner, choleric, and convinced of his own diagnosis: incipient leprosy, overcome by total abstinence from salt, alcohol, tobacco. I wish I could convey the delight of a well-found, well-handled man-of-war, sailing with all reasonable sail abroad, a steady, urgent wind coming in over her larboard quarter, her prow (or I think I should say cutwater) throwing a fine sheet of spray to leeward with each even measured pitch: there is a generally-diffused happiness aboard; and since this is a make-and-mend day, the front part of the vessel is littered with hands busy, some with shears, many more with needles, cutting out their lengths of duck and sewing the pieces together, making their hot-weather clothes with wonderful dexterity. And each time the log is heaved they pause, ears cocked for the midshipman's report to the officer of the watch. "Nine knots and two fathoms, sir, if you please," croaks little Mr. Wells, whose voice is breaking at last; and a discreet wave of mirth and satisfaction ripples over the forecastle, while ten knots is greeted with such thumping on the deck, such enthu-siasm, that the officer of the watch desires the mate of the watch to attend to "that God-damned bellowing and trampling, like a herd of drunken heifers mad for the bull." '

In the comparative silence that followed (comparative, for the beautifully steady wind, the working of the ship and the voice of the sea itself, did not give a damn for the mate of the watch) Stephen abandoned his desk and walked with a reasonably sea-manlike pace to the taffrail, which he leaned upon, watching the interminable wake stretching away and away in a turbu-lent, right true line, and the ship's steady companion, always there just this side of the turbulence, a blue shark, larger than most: all this with the top of his mind, while the rest of it was concerned with Christine, her West African birds, her grace, her frankness, her singularity; while another part of it took notice of a fiddle being tuned in the cabin immediately below him and then the tentative beginning of an adagio obviously adapted from one of his own 'cello suites, but graver by far. Mixed feeling: pleasure that Jack was playing, and playing so well: sorrow that what he played was so unlike the Jack Aubrey he knew, bold, sanguine, enterprising, with a face made for laughter or at the very least for smiling.

A shadow behind him cut his reflection short, and turning he said, 'Mr. Woodbine, I am happy to see you afoot. How do you do?'

'Tolerable, sir, tolerable. Abstinence, if not carried to superstitious extremes, does it, believe you me. So you are contemplating on that old shark, I presume?'

'Just so, Master: he is not alone, not by any manner of means: yet he keeps his station just under the counter — he has a scar just behind, or abaft, his dorsal fin, that is as clear as a visiting-card; and although I suspect that there are at least half a score of his brethren in the darkness of our hull, they do not presume to make their appearance: nor will they, unless we offer them blood.'

'But tell me, Doctor, how do you suppose they know about blood? For they do, even fish's blood, as I have seen time and again.'

'Why, as you are aware, they have gills: more gills than most of their kind. Immense, *immense* quantities of water enter that vast mouth and shoot out by those gills, which are lined with a tissue not unlike that with which our noses are furnished. There, I believe, lies the explanation.'

'Come, sir, what are you about?' cried Killick. 'Which the gunroom's dinner is almost on table, and you in your ordinary everyday old slops. Captain has been ready and trimmed this last glass, before ever he touched his fiddle.'

With real concern Stephen observed that the master was wearing his best coat, distinguished from the others by the absence of grease. 'So we entertain the Captain?' he cried.

'Which I told you so at breakfast. Sir,' replied Killick, with a very exactly dosed insolence.

'To think that I very nearly forgot,' said Stephen, who, although he often, even usually, ate in the cabin, was ex-officio a member of the gunroom mess and therefore one of the hosts on this occasion. Killick sniffed. 'Now then, what do you think you are about?' he called out angrily, addressing one of the cook's mates, who came staggering aft over the living deck, a bucket in either hand.

'Make a lane there,' cried the cook's mate with equal wrath, 'if you don't want to see the deck a —ing shambles.' And then, deferentially, to Dr. Maturin, proffering a bucket, 'With the cook's respects, sir.'

'On the rise,' called the master, seizing one bucket and emptying it straight over the taffrail: cook's mate did the same, spilling never a drop; and in a split second the white foaming wake was scarlet, a most splendid scarlet for thirty yards astern and in the scarlet sharks raced to the surface, sometimes breaking water, lashing and snapping in a blind frenzy of greed and when it was found that the wounded bleeding prey did not exist they turned on the king shark, the big fellow, and a seething mass of long thin fishes not half his size tore and worried and wrenched him to pieces. It was over in barely a minute.

'God love us,' said the master. 'I never seen the like.'

'Come, sir,' said Killick again, utterly unmoved, twitching Stephen by the sleeve: then sharply to the master, 'Mr. Woodbine, sir, pray lead the way. I shall put the Doctor's coat on in the cabin.'

The lieutenants were entertaining their guest with sherry when Stephen came in, his entrance successfully covered by Candish the purser and Jacob, and presently the dinner began with all due ceremony.

Although Stephen, as he was the first to admit, could boast no masculine beauty, and although he was capable of very wild extravagances of conduct, he had in fact been carefully brought up by his Catalan grandfather, to whom elegant manners, a mastery of both languages and of French, as well as horsemanship and a real ability with pistol and small-sword, were necessary qualifications. And when, as sometimes happened — this being an example — Stephen had committed a very gross blunder, he became sad, mute and oppressed, arousing himself only to make a decent number of harmless remarks to his neighbours.

The ritual bowl of dried-pea soup and a couple of glasses of wine re-established him, however, and when, as obviously the most practised carver in the company, he was called upon to dismember a pair of ducks, he became aware that Mr. Harding, the first lieutenant, was still talking about his blacking, a superb blacking of his own invention that would withstand wind, sun, spray and the noxious influences of the moon indefinitely, retaining its superb gleam until well after the day of doom: it contained dragon's blood, together with some other secret ingredients, and its function was to preserve and above all to beautify the yards. Really well blackened shining yards, exactly squared by lifts and braces, added wonderfully to the air of a handsome ship — gave her an air that the others lacked. He had heard it said that Prince William owed his flag to the perfect order in which he maintained *Pegasus*: and *he* blacked his yards like Billy-Ho — no play on words was intended, ha, ha, ha. And if blacking yards could earn a man promotion, why, perfection in the blacking itself was likely to bring it even sooner . . . He went on about the qualities of his invention, and in his enthusiasm he even went so far as to say that he was impatient for the calm of the doldrums — there was no blacking even of the mainyard in this close-reefed topsail blow. It would fly all over the place, ruining the deck.

Jack's face had assumed a grave, detached expression: and well before this Harding had lost the rest of his audience. Nervously passing the decanter he said, 'I beg pardon, sir: I am afraid I have been talking shop far, far too long — a man's hobby-horse can be a sad bore to others. A glass of wine with you, sir.'

This was the first time that Stephen had seen Harding so affected. It was painful in so able and highly-respected an officer; and he knew that this kind of talk — this freedom — was the kind of rambling that Jack disliked very much indeed. Yet from the casual, off-hand, semi-facetious reference to the Duke of Clarence it was evident that Horatio had taken real notice of the warning against any mention of an influential connection — the connection, let alone the relationship, was wholly unsuspected. This raised the boy high in Stephen's estimation: as a fellow-bastard he was well acquainted with the temptation to prattle, and its remarkable strength.

In all their sea-time together, Jack had virtually never discussed his officers with Stephen, who was, after all, one of their number. But in the gunroom itself the case was altered and although one or two of the members were of a somewhat Whiggish turn of mind, Harding's words about Clarence were openly condemned by the other members. 'It is true,' said Candish, 'that not a very great deal can be said for the royals at present; but after all, they *are* our master's sons; one of them is very likely to succeed him; and a certain reticence seems absolutely called for.'

But what really shocked and grieved the lower deck (to whom the unfortunate outburst was very sioon conveyed by the mess servants — one behind each chair and all provided with a pair of ears) was Mr. Harding's 'longing for the doldrums', an observation very ill-received.

'Ain't he ever been turned round and round in the barky — never no wind, week after week — nor no rain except for ten miles away, and water running cruel short, green and stinking; and that goddarn sun beating down so mortal strong the tar drips off of the rigging and the seams open wide as a coach-house door?'

'Which he was drunk: and I've seen you drunk, Abel Trim — pissed as a kippered herring, and speechless, many a time, in Pompey, Rotherhithe and Hackney Wick.'

'Very well: and the same to you, Joe Plaice. But at least I did not go on in that unlucky way about *longing for the doldrums*. So parse that, you old bugger.'

'My dear,' wrote Stephen, 'I love to think of you at Woolcombe, that kind old house which I know quite well — it forms a kind of tenuous link: and not necessarily so tenuous either, since the dawn may well show us a homeward-bound ship beating up against the trade-wind, willing and able to carry our letters to an English port. So let me beg you to go into the library, there to look into Johnson's or Bailey's dictionary for the etymology of *doldrum*. I cannot make it out at all. The thing, the concept, I know perfectly well, having suffered from it, above all when there was gaol-fever in the ship; but how it has come by such a name I cannot tell. The French call it *le pot au noir*, and pretty black it can be, on occasion, when the two converging trade-winds fill a vast space more or less over the equator with clouds, gloom, thunder and lightning from both hemispheres, north and south — a prodigious space, whose width and borders vary year by year: but a space that we have to traverse, a space that no sailor in his right mind will ever mock or put to scorn. When we shall enter this unhappy region I cannot tell — we must be fairly near its northern limit — but I shall ask Mr. Daniel.'

He found Mr. Daniel and Horatio Hanson in the master's day-cabin, which the pair tended to usurp now that Mr. Woodbine spent so much longer below, abstaining. They were pricking the chart, a solemn undertaking, but they left off at once and leapt to their feet. 'Mr. Daniel,' he said, 'pray be so good as to tell me when we may expect to enter the doldrums.'

'Sir,' said Mr. Daniel, 'we have had reports of very strong and steady southeast trades, while ours has been moderate: furthermore, the glass has been behaving in a very whimsical fashion ever since the last dog yesterday' — he pointed to a series of barometric readings, clear proof of the instrument's wanton conduct — 'and I should not be surprised if we crossed its northern border tomorrow.'

'Dear Lord! So soon?' cried Stephen. 'I am so glad that I asked you. I have some delicate specimens of hydrozoa that must be protected — sometimes these seas are perfectly flat, as though oppressed by the weight of the air above them, and sometimes, with no wind or very little, they lose all rhythm, all reason, and toss you about in the most extraordinary fashion.'

'Oh, sir,' cried Hanson, 'I long to see it!'

'I must bestow my pans of hydrozoa. But you will let me know, I trust, when you are sure of our more near approach.'

Stephen was now so old a sea-dog that the grind of holystones and swabs on the deck immediately above did not disturb him: yet a little after this the gentle but persistent pushing of a hand and the repeated 'Sir, oh sir, if you please', eventually moved him to roll over on to the other side, with an ugly snarl. It did not answer. Rearing up in his cot, he saw young Hanson holding a lantern which showed his delighted face and shining eyes. 'Sir, you did say you should be told when the doldrums began. And they have begun! About six bells all the stars went out, one after the other right over the sky, and there was the most prodigious thunder and lightning, better than any Guy Fawkes' night; and the sea comes from every direction at once. There are three boobies on deck, perfectly amazed, just abaft the blue cutter. Do come and see, sir. It might all fade with the sunlight.'

It did not fade with the sunlight, which did little more than make a slightly greater extent of white-capped sea visible. The sun rose, to be sure, but it scarcely diminished the brilliance of the almost continuous lightning-flashes — the sheets, even, of lightning — that raced across the low dark base of cloud-cover, while the thunder scarcely left them a moment's silence.

'Do you see the sea, sir?' called Hanson in his ear. 'Ain't it turbid?'

'Lurid too, in a way. Pray lead me to the boobies.'

'Let me give you a hand, sir,' said Davies, dangerous in temper, not very clever nor much use except in an engagement, but much attached to Jack, Hanson, and even, in a somewhat condescending way, to Stephen.

Man-ropes had been rigged, fore and aft, and he was led, staggering, to the blue cutter. No boobies. A bosun's mate, strengthening the clamps that held the boat to the deck, said, 'Boobies, sir? Mr. Harding tossed them over the side.'

'Did they fly?'

'They flew perfectly well. They were just swinging the lead, the creatures.'

'Do you know why he tossed them over the side?'

'Why, they were *brown* boobies, sir. And you can't have unlucky fowl of that kind aboard the barky.'

'Ah? I did not know.'

The bosun's mate sniffed, and in the sniff could be read, among other things, that the Doctor, though a worthy soul, could not really distinguish between larboard and starboard, right and wrong.

From that truly apocalyptic beginning, the doldrums necessarily diminished to a rather commonplace dull, calm, low-skied greyness — commonplace in everything apart from the truly exorbitant heat. The thin cloud, though low, seemed if anything to increase the power of the sun, which showed right through the day, a vast ball, tolerable to narrowed eyes yet so powerful that, as all hands had foreseen, it brought the tar dripping black on the holy deck, angering the cats beyond description. They had been silent, meek, aghast, hiding in corners, grateful for comfort when the ship was so horribly buffeted; but now they stalked about, sometimes howling, sometimes treading in the liquid tar and withdrawing their paws with cries of disgust, perpetually searching for something like coolness, which was nowhere to be found, even deep in the hold among the great water-casks.

They complained above all of the lack of

air: in reasonably hot weather it was their custom to lie their full length at the lower end of the wind-sails that ventilated the sick-berth; but at present the berth was empty both of patients and of fresh air and they stretched in vain. The ship's true sails hung limp from their yards; the log, when heaved, stayed just where it was, not even carrying out the stray-line, so that cast after cast was reported as 'No knots, no fathoms, sir, if you please,' and both smoke and smell from the galley hung about the ship until the next meal was due.

Yet she was not entirely motionless: the slight, obscure, often conflicting little currents that wafted fronds of seaweed along the ship's side, forward or aft, also turned her, almost perceptibly, so that at four bells she would be heading south and at six bells due north. The dog-watches, ordinarily times of cheerfulness, dancing and music, in calm, reasonably temperate waters, were now given over to weary gasping, low-voiced nattering quarrel, and unseemly nakedness.

Yet the immutable sequence of bells, relief of the watch, meals and grog, divisions, and mustering of the watch, kept them in touch with a certain reality.

'Mr. Harding,' said Jack, as he watched

the frigate's toplight soar up, growing dimmer, almost vanishing in the murk as it passed the topgallant yard, 'early in the morning, when the sea may be presumed to be at its coolest, let us rouse up some pretty sound spare topsails, boom them well out amidships with a really handsome span above the surface fore and aft on either side, and so fill them with water for the people to splash about in and be cool for a while.'

These orders were being carried out the next day, after a twilit breakfast; and while Harding, the bosun and the sail-maker were making doubly sure that the swimming-bath was impregnable, even to those jelly-fish that could insinuate themselves through a hole and inflict a shockingly painful sting, Stephen said, 'My dear, should you not like your usual swim? See how the people' — pointing to the naked, frolicking starboard watch — 'do enjoy it. I shall leap in too, if you will, and swim a couple of lengths.'

'Not in this sea, I thank you. It ain't quite to my taste. I was standing at the stern windows when his brethren dealt with our old blue companion. But do *you* go, by all means.'

'Sail ho!' called the foretop look-out.

'Sail one point on the starboard bow.'

As he spoke three ghostly pyramids of sail drifted very slowly across what path *Surprise* possessed. Jack clapped the helm hard over, raced forward and hailed, 'The ship ahoy! The ship ahoy! What ship is that?'

Five seconds of drifting cloud intervened: then came the answer, loud and clear. '*Delaware*. USS *Delaware*. What ship is that?'

'His Britannic Majesty's hydrographical vessel *Surprise*: and pray bear up with all you have. My people are bathing over the side.'

A breath of air not only parted the gloom a little but brought the American voices with their distinctive yet not unpleasing accent as clearly across as though they had been spoken ten yards away. 'He says she's *Surprise*.' 'Bear up, Plimpton: bear up, there.' 'He says his people are bathing over the side.'

The truth of this statement, which was uttered with a certain reserve, became apparent thirty seconds later, when the breath of air, encouraged by the rising sun, tore the veil so wide apart that the mother-naked starboard watch were exposed to the mirth of the Delawares, lining the side of their handsome frigate.

There was a real danger that the two windless ships should run (or drift) each other aboard, tangling bowsprits or otherwise wrecking the perfect order so apparent in both craft; but they had right seamen aboard and within moments booms were rigged out, tipped with swabs, to make any encounter harmless.

The captains' conversation went on: 'It is improbable that you should remember me, sir, but we dined together with Admiral Cabot, when you were visiting Boston. My name is Lodge.'

'I remember you perfectly, Captain Lodge. You were there with your mother, my neighbour, and we talked about her parents' house in Dorset, not far from mine. I hope she is very well?'

'Very well indeed, sir, I thank you. We celebrated her eighty-fifth birthday just before sailing.'

'Eighty-five: that is a great age,' said Jack, and instantly regretting it, he said that he and his officers should be very happy if Captain Lodge and his wardroom would dine aboard *Surprise* tomorrow, wind and weather permitting.

Captain Lodge agreed, but only on condition that the Surprises should come aboard *Delaware* the following day: and then, lowering his voice, he asked whether he might send his master over this evening: they had a slight navigational problem.

The *Delaware*'s master, Mr. Wilkins, came across, sullen, dogged and willing to take offence: his function was to explain the problem, and he was most reluctant to do so, although he was carrying the ship's two chronometers and their last few weeks' workings. 'Well, sir,' he said, when Mr. Woodbine had settled him into his sad, damp day-cabin, with a deep glass of bosun's grog apiece, 'to cut a long story short — not to beat about the bush — we are all human.'

'So we are indeed,' said Mr. Woodbine, 'and many a strange cocked-hat have I produced in my time. Once, when we were running for the Scillies with the wind — full topsails — at east-south-east, it was so strong that I wished I was a Roman so as to be able to pray to Saint Woodbine not to run full tilt on to that wicked reef, like Sir Cloudesley Shovel.'

'Mark you,' said the American, 'I should get it right with a couple of lunars. But there ain't no moon: and my captain is most uncommon particular.'

'Position somewhat astray, maybe?'

'Position? Frankly, taking the average of the two chronometers, there ain't no position, not as who should say *position*. Of course with a couple of lunars I should get it right . . . but for fine work . . . for working through shoal-water . . .'

Woodbine knew only too well what his colleague meant, and he suggested that they should compare chronometers. This they did: *Surprise*'s two Earnshaws agreed within fifty seconds: *Delaware*'s pair showed a much greater and increasing difference, so it was not surprising that the cocked-hat, the triangle of uncertainty, should vary so. The question was, which, without a lunar, a good star observation or even better one of those lovely Jovian moons, should be trusted. Of course this meant most when the ship was approaching a coast: but even in mid-ocean you could run at ten or twelve knots right on to a wicked shoal. Saint Paul's Rocks, Stephen's particular delight, were no great way off.

'I tell you what, Mr. Wilkins,' said Woodbine, suffering cruelly in his uniform coat, best Bristol double-width broadcloth, 'I have a most uncommon mate: he don't need no tables of logarithms — has them all in his head — and he dearly loves a problem. What is more, he has a youngster as is brighter still. But we should be crowded in here; so let us call them up, show them the workings from your last fix — Rio?'

'Rio.'

'And let them work the whole thing through, while we take off our coats and sit in the shade on the fo'c'sle: there is nothing better for a young and active mind.'

'Well, if you insist, Mr. Woodbine, I am bound to yield.'

'So you came round by the Horn, sir?' asked Woodbine, easing himself down on a well-shaded heap of mats about knee high.

'By the Horn, indeed: there's nothing like Old Stiff. For ease, if you understand me? No farting about in doubt — are we there? Aren't we there yet? With Old Stiff you either are there or you ain't: no two ways about it. No more poring over charts till your eyes drop out — how many rotten little islands was that to larboard? No. You are there, or you are *not* there.'

'Much ice about, Mr.?'

'No. Thin sheets now and then, and an odd lump from the glacier behind; but we never shipped a bowgrace.'

They discussed the question of bow-graces, of fenders, and of some very curious objects used by the Greenland whalers: and when they had exhausted the subject twice, the American, (a person from Poughkeepsie), said, 'That smart young fellow, your mate's aid de con, as you might say, is he a prize-fighter?'

'Good heavens no. He is a gentleman.'

'Oh? Well, I meant no harm, I'm sure. But he looks like as if he had played give and take pretty often. Cauliflower ear, and so on.'

'Why, as for a little genteel sparring, our young gentlemen don't despise it. This young cove here, he don't weigh ten stone, but you should have seen him lambaste a big reefer out of *Polyphemus* when we were in the Gulf. Oh dearie me, such swipes in the eye, such bottom: they calls him the Lion of the Atlas in the berth. Aye, and on the lower deck too.'

They rambled along pleasantly, telling of rare old mills they had seen in their time, at fairgrounds, at Blackfriars, at Hockney-in-the-Hole, where there was a chimney-sweep would challenge all comers not above a stone heavier to fight for half a guinea — fair fighting: no gouging, no falling on a man or wrenching his privates.

Neither listened much to the other, but at least there was no contestation, no breaking in with greater marvels: indeed, for an interview with one man who had lost his position and another who was certain of his to within ten miles it might be called unparalleled.

'Now, shipmates,' cried Woodbine, breaking off his account of the great mill between Sayers and Darkie Joe in Coldbath Fields, 'what are you a-doing of?'

'Which we are carrying the watches, sir: and the small Boston job is quite right — dead on — agrees with our Earnshaw to within five seconds.'

'Then what are you a-moaning for?' asked Woodbine, his mind (which did not move very fast) still in the Coldbath Fields of long ago.

'You can't rely on just *one* chronometer,' cried Wilkins. 'What, trust a ship and all her lading, to say nothing of the hands, to *one* chronometer?'

They all fell silent, aware of the breach of good sea-going manners, but unsure of how to improve the position. 'Here is the Doctor,' whispered the armourer's mate, a highly-skilled metal-worker who often helped Stephen with his current instru-

ments and sometimes made him new ones
— few men could set a very fine-toothed
bone-saw with the same smooth precision.

'Well, shipmates,' said Stephen, 'I see
you are busy about the time-keepers, those
most ingenious of machines.'

'Yes, sir,' said the armourer's mate, 'and
ingenious they are, by — very ingenious
indeed. But they can on occasion turn
fractious; and then, oh my eye!'

'But surely, Webberfore, an artist like
you can open the fractious time-keeper,
and very gently bring it back to its duty?'

There was a general confused sound of
disapprobation and denial. 'You must
understand, sir,' said Webberfore, 'that if
you go for to open a time-keeper's case, by
the Articles of War, you are flogged to
death, your pay and allowances are forfeit,
your widow has no pension, and you are
buried with ino words said over you.'

'You mustn't open a chronometer, no,
not if it is ever so,' said the master: and the
company agreed. 'Flesh on Friday ain't in
it.'

The talk ran on in this righteous way for
some time, but Stephen felt that it was
deviously approaching an outlet. 'Of
course,' said Webberfore, 'the *outer* case
may always be opened, for the officer —

usually the master himself,' — bowing to Woodbine '— to wind the machine: and it is always possible for a part such as the ratchet-click to lose its tip, which, having tumbled about with the motion of the ship, interfering with the chronometer's accuracy, works its way down to the winding-hole, from which a skilled hand may pluck it with superfine Swiss pincers. Pluck it out without ever *opening* the watch.'

'Very true,' said the master, looking earnestly at Stephen.

'The ratchet is the piece that rises when you wind the watch, is it not?' They all agreed. 'Like a windlass,' said one. 'Or a capstan: but then you call it a pawl,' said another.

'But surely,' said Stephen, 'if the ratchet fails, the wheel runs backwards without control. It has happened to me. I was winding my watch, and as I took out the key, there was a dismal whirr, and the watch was dead.'

'Certainly, sir,' said Webberfore, 'because the whole of the ratchet's tip had gone and there was nothing to stop the wheel or the spindle as the case may be from turning. But if only a corner of the tip had gone, which sometimes happens with over-tempered metal, the rest would hold the spring wound tight — under tension — so the watch would go — while the odd corner would ramble about making sure it would not keep true time.'

'Well, I am content, Webberfore,' said Stephen, 'and I congratulate you heartily.'

'And so do I,' cried Wilkins. 'By God, navigating with a single chronometer is . . .' He shook his head, unable to express the horror, the extreme anxiety; and then, the men having retired, he asked Woodbine whether they ever smoked or chewed tobacco. Woodbine answered that they did both, when they could, but the ship was on very short cornmons, and they longed for Rio and a fresh supply.

Wilkins nodded with great satisfaction, stowed his chronometers in a padded bag and, taking his leave, he said, 'I believe I am to have the pleasure of dining aboard you tomorrow, sir?'

Tomorrow was another day, at least by the calendar, but the two could hardly be told apart: the heat, the faintly drifting cloud, the ship pitching heavily with no way on her, the flaccid sails, were all the same: to be sure, an outraged frigate-bird had replaced the boobies, and a slightly smaller blue shark now swam under the counter, but the tar still dripped, the hands still cursed and sweated.

'I am sorry not to see *Ringle* yet,' said Stephen, gazing into the general murk.

'I am sorry too,' said Jack. 'But I do not think you need feel really anxious. William is a tolerable navigator and his master is even better — sailed with Cook. Then again a schooner as light as *Ringle* is more affected by these shifting currents than we are. In any case William knows very well that we victual and water at Rio. Stephen, forgive me for saying so, but there is tar on your breeches, and our guests will be aboard in ten minutes.'

Dining to and fro, under awnings that sheltered the deck from the misty yet strangely ardent sun, and from the now more liquid tar, they enjoyed themselves more than it might have been thought possible in such conditions. The Americans certainly had the better of it, they having victualled at Rio and still possessing stores of tropical fruit and vegetables: the Americans had also seen the *Asp* being refitted there, which gave rise to a number of long, highly technical descriptions during which Stephen's attention wandered, though Jack and his officers assured him that they were of the very first interest.

'How particularly agreeable that was,' said Stephen as the Surprise's barge pulled back through the varying mist, the coxswain steering by the sound of a small maroon, booming every thirty seconds. 'It was indeed,' said Jack, and the other officers in the boat mentioned a variety of delights, mostly in the tropical line but some, such as chess-pie, among the foundation stones of the American cuisine: while Candish and the master agreed that they had never drunk such quantities of wine before.

After a reminiscent pause, Jack said, 'Captain Lodge told me that as soon as it was dark and a little cooler, he meant to send his boats out ahead and tow east-north-east for a watch or two, now that they knew their position for sure. He believed there was a fairly steady current — had experienced it before.'

When they were aboard and in the cabin, Stephen went on, 'And I was so pleased with what Dr. Evans told me about young Herapath's medical studies — highly gifted — and the success of his book.'

'Young Herapath? Yes, decent creature indeed: but no mechanical power known to science could ever make a seaman out of him — Lord above,' he cried over an enormous peal of thunder, the cabin lit through and through by lightning just overhead, and the literal crash of rain on the deck, 'those poor souls are in for a ducking.'

The prodigious downpour was so monstrously thick that one could hardly breathe in the open; and after ten minutes naked figures could be seen flitting through the deluge, opening the inlets that would replenish the butts far below with a water as clean and pure as the heavens could provide. All this, however, angered and terrified the cats more than anything that had gone before: the more austere of the two, the long-legged animal with an apricot-coloured belly, flung herself into Stephen's unwilling lap, and could not be comforted.

It was inconceivable that the deluge should last till dawn — the sky could not hold so much — but it did, leaving them stunned, deafened, amazed at the light of day to eastward and the familiar sails of *Ringle* making three or even four knots towards them, the tiny breeze right aft. Incomprehensibly the deck had become littered, even covered in places, with strange forms of deep-sea life, presumably sucked up by some remote series of water-spouts and liberated here.

But Jack Aubrey was having absolutely none of them: *Surprise's* only care, and *Ringle's* too, was to get out of this odious part of the sea without a moment's pause — no breakfast, even, until they were well under way with clear decks, rigging free of seaweed, flying squids and various monsters — Stephen had to content himself with pocketing the less gelatinous creatures and hurrying them below before his stony-faced captain had him forcibly removed.

Still, breakfast there was, in time — at least for those not labouring at the pumps, shooting out thick jets of water on either side — when humanity returned to Captain Aubrey's face and Stephen asked him timidly 'did he think they were out of the doldrums yet?'

'I hope so, I'm sure,' said Jack. 'When the belt — the convergence — is very narrow and concentrated as I think this one was, it sometimes ends in a furious tantrum like this, as who should say . . .' Meeting the cats' steady, attentive gaze, he changed his mind and finished ' "Fare you well, ye Spanish ladies". Killick, Killick there.'

'Sir?'

'Pass the word for Poll Skeeping. Forgive me, Stephen, I trespass upon your ground.'

'Sir?' said Poll Skeeping, tying on a new apron.

'Be so good as to remove those cats. They know perfectly well that they are not allowed in the cabin.'

They did, indeed, and suffered themselves to be carried away, one in each hand, limp, meek, with lowered eyes.

'How glad I was to see *Ringle*,' said Stephen after a while.

'So was I, by God: she is only a little thing; and at times the weather was close on as heavy as weather comes.'

'Would it be improper, unlucky, to ask where we are? I mean, just a very vague approximation.'

'After taking the sun's height at noon, which I think we shall achieve, I hope to be able to tell you in rather finer limits than that: but even now I shall hazard the guess that by tomorrow morning we shall be in the steady south-east trades, not much above a week's sailing from Rio, according to how strong they prove.'

'Good, good: very good. You ease my mind: but tell me, Jack — for I see that in spite of a sleepless night you are eager to be up and about, inspecting booms, gun-wales, lifts . . . Pray tell me when you are inclined to sit down quietly and talk about the less physical aspects of our affair.'

Jack looked at him thoughtfully, revolving the less physical aspects: then smiling he said, 'Although I have a very good first lieutenant, there are many things aloft that I should not rest easy without seeing. And below too, of course. Let us say after dinner, over a private pot of coffee.'

Jack Aubrey pushed back his chair, loosened his waistcoat, and said, 'I had no idea I was so hungry: I am afraid I must have eaten like an ogre.'

Killick could be seen to smile: Jack's appetite always pleased him — his one deviation into amiability.

'Oh come,' said Maturin. 'Six mutton chops is not at all excessive in a man of your weight: an abstemious ogre would call it moderation. Those dear Americans said that the animal came from some favoured state: indeed it was both succulent and tender.'

They toyed with an elderly Essex cheese, much helped by burgundy; and Jack, recalled to a sense of his duty, asked whether Stephen's inspection had been as satisfactory as his own.

'It was pretty well, I thank you: not quite as good, since three recent fractures will have to be re-set. But upon the whole I cannot complain. They were tumbled about, to be sure; yet most — not that there are many in the sick-berth at present — withstood the tumbling and the uneasy motion of the ship very well. I have often noticed that a prolonged and violent blow tends to dispel the megrims; and it may well be that the visible approach of death, the immediate horror of the last, may restore a virtuous equilibrium.'

'Killick,' called Jack. 'Light along the coffee, there.'

It took a little longer than usual and Killick — the door held by his mate Grimble — entered crabwise, the great pot and its cups flanked by a decanter. 'With *Delaware*'s compliments, sir: Dutch schnapps.'

'They have won again,' said Jack, shaking his head. 'How I hope that we gave them *something*, at least.'

'I did have half a carboy of tincture of hogweed conveyed into their boat,' said Stephen in a doubtful voice. 'It was the best hogweed,' he added, with even less certainty.

'Well, may it prosper them,' said Jack. 'Though they are little better than republicans and democrats, may it prosper them.'

'Amen,' said Stephen, and they fell to drinking alternate sips.

'You are in the moon, brother,' said Jack after a while. 'What are you thinking about?'

'My transition to a C major passage in the adagio,' said Stephen, and he whistled it.

'I know the piece.'

'It seemed to me, out of nothing, during the blast, that it was out of place, a little flashy.'

'I should never, never say flashy: but out of place — well, perhaps.'

'Thank you, Jack. I shall leave it out. Now may I pour you a cup of coffee and leap on to Rio?'

'By all means.'

'You have told me a certain amount about Sir David Lindsay, but not as I remember a considered opinion in a consecutive narrative. Do you feel inclined to do so now? He may possibly be of the first importance in our enterprise.'

'That is scarcely my line of country, you know, Stephen. Even a pretty simple dispatch in which I know all the details comes out looking like an unravelled stocking, even when you and Adams have had a hand in it.'

'Certainly: an impersonal account for official publication must be shockingly difficult to write, and the Dear knows that very few admirals or their secretaries manage it handsomely. But as between friends in a ship that seems to be sailing along in an exemplary fashion — these are the southeast trades, I gather? — could you not tell me roughly what to expect?'

'Well,' said Jack, 'no one can say he is not a good seaman. He has fought two or three creditable sloop or frigate actions and he handles a ship well; yet he does not look at all like a sailor. If you were to see him in civilian clothes you might put him down for a soldier; and I think that is because, being rather on the small side, he holds himself up quite straight. He is a gentlemanlike fellow. I know nothing about his family, but they have had a baronetcy for a couple of generations and I believe they live in the north country or just in Scotland. He speaks — perhaps rather too much and too long . . . but Stephen, do not think I am taking the man to pieces: I am just speaking openly, as I would not speak at anyone else.'

'I fully understand you, my dear.'

'Well, since I have said so much, I will tell you that he is extremely touchy — cannot bear interruption, and the least aspersion on his understanding or his knowledge of the world, let alone his family, is very ill-received indeed. Oh, and I should have said before this that he was bred in one of the great English public schools, until an uncle took him aboard as a rather elderly mid. During his time there he did much more reading, came by more Latin and Greek than most people in the service, which is no doubt one of the reasons for his talking so. But to go back to his touchiness: if you go on prating to that extent, somebody is sure to interrupt or contradict, and that, as I said, he cannot bear.'

'Yet he must have borne both at school?'

'And in the midshipmen's berth as well. But once he had the King's commission and the implied licence that goes with it, he had a pretty free hand. He was in fact extremely quarrelsome, and I do not think anyone *went out* in the special sense of pistols for two and coffee for one, so often as Lindsay. I do not think it increased his reputation for courage: probably the reverse, it being forced and exaggerated. Yet courage was there, without a doubt: you do not board an enemy of equal strength and carry her unless you are tolerably brave.'

'Certainly.'

'But it was that touchiness, impatience of control, or possibly courage, which proved fatal to him. During fleet exercises, when his 28-gun frigate was being coppered, he was given a ship-sloop, and he let her fall very badly from her station, spoiling the line in a shocking manner. The admiral sent for him and, from what I have heard, uttered a long and particularly scathing reproach. Lindsay bore it; but in the morning he sent the admiral a challenge. How he induced anyone to carry it I do not know, because calling your superior officer out — above all a flag-officer — is just plain impossible in the service. Calling him out for having given you a punishment or an order or a reproach that you do not like, is just plain impossible, as any friend would have told him. He had few friends, I think. At all event, he was taken up, laid by the heels, court-martialled and dismissed the service.

'For some time he ranged up and down, making speeches about injustice and spending a mint of money on lawyers — he had inherited — and then he vanished, coming into these parts, as I understand it, with the reputation of one who loved freedom and who had suffered for it. There are a good many English merchants in Chile and the Argentine: some of them liked having a genuine baronet about, and some of them and of their South American friends were all in favour of freedom, so long as it was freedom from Spain — freedom to shoot your admiral in Hyde Park was another matter, but it was swept along with the general cry of liberty.'

'By the way, does the gentleman speak Spanish?'

'Oh, remarkably well, I am told.'

Chapter Seven

On a singularly beautiful morning well south of those vile calms and enervating breathless heat the *Surprise* hauled to the wind well off the looming American coast, and Jack, walking up and down with a piece of toast in his hand, said, 'Stephen, do you choose to go into the top? With this gentle, steady roll the masts scarcely move at all.'

'Is it the Sugar Loaf you wish to see?'

'I should be happy to see the Loaf — indeed, I can already make him out on the rise — but for this occasion I could wish him away, since what really concerns me at present is the activity in the port, the coming and going, the yards: and the Sugar Loaf hides almost everything. But I shall have to send *Ringle* in any case, to arrange for victuals, water and wood: perhaps you had rather go in her?'

'Not at all. I am perfectly willing to climb to whatever pinnacle you choose.'

'Mr. Hanson,' called Jack. 'Mr. Wells. The Doctor is going aloft. You will act as hand and foot fasts, as and when required.'

'Aye-aye, sir, aye-aye,' they replied; and he swung himself into the absurdly familiar ladder-way, mounting with the smooth ease of a powerful, very well trained body to the maintop, where he greeted the look-out and drew breath for a while to ease his friend's somewhat more laborious progress.

Stephen arrived, pale and if not anxious then truly worn, followed by his attendants, and they all sat for a while, gazing at the mainland and the schooner with the Captain's glass.

It was quite true: the masts were in no considerable state of motion. Yet even so, at the next stage, the not very awful crosstrees, Jack said that that would answer very well. He gazed for a while, pointing out various remote inland heights; and then, reaching out for a backstay, his own expeditious form of descent, he desired the young men to see the Doctor safely bestowed when he wished to return to the deck, and so vanished.

Arriving with little more than a muffled thump, he caused *Ringle*'s signal to be thrown out, requiring her to come within hail; and then, spurred by the scent of breakfast, he hurried into the cabin. Presently Stephen joined him, paler still, but with the assurance of one who now walked upon comparatively firm ground: Killick plied him with coffee, bacon, sausage, toast; and quite soon his equanimity and even cheerfulness resumed their usual placid height.

'I do hope,' said Jack, 'that Dr. Jacob would be so good as to accompany William into Rio, and speaking Portuguese find out all he discreetly can about the *Asp*: William will know all the questions to ask, but it would come much better through someone not obviously English — someone, say, who was acquainted with her in Valletta, before she left the service, and who naturally takes an interest in her.'

'Am I right in supposing that ideally William should be a passing figure, preoccupied with other maritime affairs, and that Jacob should be an idle passenger, walking about the docks to see something of Brazil, largely ignorant of the sea, but interested in his earthbound fashion?'

'You are wholly in the right of it, brother: that is exactly what I should have asked. A trifle of coffee?'

At this point Killick announced Mr. Woodbine's desire to see the Captain directly or almost so; the near approach of *Ringle*; and the news that those African cats had got at the mangoes — 'And what they ain't ate, they've spoilt,' he added with an obscure surly triumph.

Mr. Woodbine's mission was concerned solely with a certain deviation from truth on the part of the pintles, observed and exactly measured in this pellucid calm — a deviation forecast by Mr. Seppings when he installed the new stern-post, the correction being provided by three simple operations, clearly figured by young Mr. Seppings in a drawing to be found in the case holding the necessary implements. The next interview was nothing like so satisfactory: William Reade did not feel that his explanations of a series of basic questions about the revived *Asp* had penetrated the layers of Dr. Jacob's ignorance of both English and Portuguese nautical language. He knew very well what Captain Aubrey wanted to learn, but he felt that apart from making the usual arrangements for water and stores, he was going on a fool's errand. 'You might as well try to shave with a butter-knife,' he muttered, taking his seat next to a sombre Jacob in *Ringle*'s gig.

On the other hand, Jacob, though indeed as impenetrably stupid in some respects as the most prejudiced seaman could wish, was also a remarkable draughtsman. This was of course most apparent in his beautifully exact and explicit anatomical drawings; but he was perfectly capable of changing scale, attitude and nature of description; and his drawings, produced in the cabin from rough sketches and combined with Reade's vivid technical description, gave Jack Aubrey a very clear impression of the renewed, the almost entirely rebuilt *Asp*.

'I doubt I should have recognised her, sir, with this fine long line running aft' — he traced in on Jacob's profile — 'and I must do the Doctor the justice of saying that he could not have struck it off better had he been bred to the trade. My only question is whether, with these extra feet, she will be as windwardly as she was — her one good point. Faster, for sure: but as windwardly? I wonder.'

'I dare say you are right.' Jack did not choose to be more specific, but he spoke gravely; and as William Reade carried on with his description of the *Asp*'s improved armament, including a most elegant pair of long brass chasers right forward, his face, ordinarily so cheerful, grew graver still.

'My dear,' wrote Stephen, 'many a year have I spent sailing the sea in ships, but rarely have I felt such a corporate sense of concern: it is certainly not a *defined* uneasiness, for the *Surprise* is sound, as all hands know, she is well supplied, and she carries an ample crew of seamen perfectly well used to working together. Yet there is a want of cheer, of those conventional jokes, semi-insults and jocular repartees that make up so much of the very small change in shipboard life; and what puzzles me extremely is that it is quasi-universal. It may spare the midshipmen's berth and the little small gathering of ship's boys, but it is fairly general elsewhere. I noticed it first when we were lying in the wholly sunless estuary of the River Plate, having sent the tender over that vast and as far as I could see birdless waste to Buenos Aires, carrying among other burdens a message to you in which I pointed out the extraordinary contrast between your African water, teeming with both familiar and wildly exotic duck, geese, anhingas, waders from the most minute of stints to *Ardea goliath,* and this prodigious desert, inhabited perhaps to the extreme limit of my glass by one moulting black-crested grebe. How ardently I hope that my note may reach you in Dorsetshire, bearing as it does more affection than is ordinarily enclosed in a common sailcloth cover.

'It is true that I date this — gloom, untoward atmosphere — from our dreary sojourn in the River Plate, and for a while I foolishly tried to account for its mood by the absence of creatures: but of course that was sad nonsense. As soon as the schooner rejoins, and as soon as we resume our course we shall necessarily begin to see the southern birds; already, before we dropped anchor here, a few skuas from the Falklands had been observed and in a very short time the various penguins will be commonplace.

'No. I must find a more rational basis for this prevalent mood. Part of it may arise from the odd in-between nature of the season, neither one thing nor another: much more from the general knowledge that we are to sail into the Pacific by way of the Horn rather than attempt Magellan's Strait, which Jack Aubrey dislikes extremely, taken from east to west, the farther reaches calling for some manoeuvres that are exceptionally perilous in a strong westerly blow.

'I think it may fairly be said that no one man in a ship has as much influence as her captain: and I believe that the strength of that influence is very, very much increased when the captain has commanded the ship, her officers and her company for many years, which is of course the case with Captain Aubrey. His expression, his daily mood, his tone of voice are naturally, automatically and universally observed — not out of curiosity or intense personal interest but as any man — sailor, farmer, fisherman — subject to the weather frequently looks at the sky. Now except as a friend I am not particularly subject to the great man's state of mind, his état d'âme, yet I find myself curiously affected . . .'

Here the letter came to a halt, starting again many days later with a different pen, dipped into a different ink, and written on a somewhat discoloured sheet of paper: 'My dear, it is not without a real regret that I see the absolute loss of so many pages, swept off by an intemperate gust, pummelled and pounded by intrusive sea-water intimately mixed with ice swilling with the utmost violence about the sodden cabin while poor *Surprise* lay on her beam-ends on one of the innumerable uncharted reefs in this forbidding part of the world and while I and the blessed Poll Skeeping bandaged, splinted and dosed the hands injured by a gun forced from its emplacement by the furious thrust of ice. At present we are on an even keel once more, gliding under courses and close-reefed top-sails along the inward — the leeward — side of one of the countless islands that fringe this desolate end of the world.

'These pages, now reduced to pulp, were little more than a kind of diary, a daily musing that I liked to share with you — reports of the increasing numbers of penguins (even some emperors), albatrosses, petrels great and small, seals of course and sea-lions, and that beautiful sinister creature the killer whale, sometimes in numerous bands. But they did contain an apology for addressing you in this familiar style, which I justified by the fact that as I was not an absolutely and formally rejected suitor, such a degree of ease could be considered permissible (though perhaps blameworthy: even indelicate). And they contained a passage that described our coming to the Cape of the Eleven Thousand Virgins, beyond which lay the broad and tranquil mouth of Magellan's Strait, perhaps a dozen miles across: the wind was fair, on our larboard quarter; yet there was no call to change sail or course. The seamen lined the landward side and they watched the strait go by, most with a face as grave as their captain's. No remarks of any kind: the silence broken only by the regular stroke of the bell.

'Since then, and since our passage of the Strait Le Maire, which leads only from one part of the main ocean to a worse part a little south, we have had foul weather, far, far more ice than is usual at this time of the year, and the very strong wind has a far greater southerly component than most ships encounter; and of course this makes the ice much more dangerous, much more plentiful. It is mostly floe-ice, great flat sheets of no great depth, rarely more than our skilled whalers (and we have several aboard) and the bowgrace with which we are adorned can deal with; but occasionally great ice-mountains are to be seen — sometimes, when the sky is clear, of an extraordinary green, blue or turquoise beauty. Our whalers say that as the season advances, above all with so much south in the wind, we shall see many more. From a purely aesthetic point of view, they are a most noble spectacle; for these great and continuous winds, with so very long a fetch, build up monstrous waves, perhaps a hundred feet tall, and when they break against an even taller mass of ice with enormous, deliberate force, it is a very magnificent spectacle.

'Yet their presence, and the presence of the vast waves, the largely adverse winds, oblige us to make what westward advance we can achieve under the lee — the sometimes astonishingly complete lee — of the many, many islands. Sometimes, after days of perpetual and wearing fight against the weather, we will put into a sheltered bay, rest, fish (mostly for a kind of succulent cod) and dredge up enormous mussels from no great depth.

'We are lying in just such a bay at present, and Jack Aubrey and I have supped on these same delights. As I think you know, when he was a boy he was acquainted with the Byron family. There may have been some family connexion — I am not sure — but in any case he knew the Admiral, nicknamed Foul-Weather Jack in the service, admired him greatly and often repeated his anecdotes. You may recall that when he was a midshipman the Admiral sailed in the unfortunate *Wager*, one of the squadron with which Anson made his famous circumnavigation: the *Wager* was wrecked in the Chonos archipelago, and Byron and some of his shipmates lived among the Indians of those parts — lived very, very hard indeed. And he would tell how the women, some of whom were quite kind to him, would do practically all the work. It was they who handled the canoes, for example — fragile craft perpetually over-setting — and few of the men could swim, whereas the women were taught from childhood. And they did the fishing, laying out nets and then setting their dogs to drive the fish into them, little intelligent smooth dogs, sometimes painted, that could dive and swim under water. They cooked too, and made what few clothes any of them ever had: but most went bare, or with just a piece of seal-skin slung about them and kept to windward. The men walked about the strand gathering fuel, sometimes hunting, but not with much success. They did make fires, however, even when everything was sopping wet, as it usually was; and they signalled with the smoke, passing messages to a considerable distance. But, my dear, I wander, and it is time for my rounds. Hands have been piped to weigh the anchor; the deck echoes with the steady tramp of feet, the click-click-click of the pawls as the cable comes home; and I remember now that we were to profit by the making tide to move to a headland from which we could see the main ocean, the open sea.'

Eight bells: the usual morning rituals,

one of which was Stephen's rounds. The sick-berth was sparsely inhabited at present, but one cot, containing a Swedish whaler called Bjorn, who had broken three ribs in a recent blow, already had a visitor — Hanson, to whose division the seaman belonged.

'You are doing very well,' said Stephen in that rather loud, distinct voice that even quite intelligent medical men use to their foreign patients, 'and if Mr. Hanson will call a shipmate to make sure you do not fall, you may go up on deck for a while, now that the ship is so still.'

The morning ceremonies also included breakfast, and while they were eating it, Stephen said, 'It is very pleasant to see how the young men take care of the hands who belong to their division. Ever since the boisterous weather that filled the sick-berth, there has not been a day when two or three of them have not come to ask how their shipmates do.'

'It would be a damned odd, unhappy ship where they did not,' said Jack. 'There is no right feeling where the officers do not feel a real concern for their men: if you were to serve in other ships, I think you would find it much the same throughout the service.'

Stephen did not wholly agree, but he said nothing; and before he had poured his next cup of coffee Whewell, the officer of the watch, came in and said, 'I beg pardon for interrupting you, sir, but we have just opened the strait and I am afraid it is blowing very hard outside, and the making tide is coming through like a millstream, carrying damned — carrying awkward great lumps of ice.'

'I am sorry to hear it, Mr. Whewell,' said Jack, 'but unless our reckoning is very far out it will be slack-water before long. Pray drop a kedge, but keep the breeze right aft, so that we can look through the strait when we choose. I shall be on deck directly.'

'My dear,' wrote Stephen, 'I followed them on deck: we were still in the lee of the tall black cliff to larboard, with just steerage-way on us; but overhead the wind raced across the gap with a deep and steady roar, while through the passage to the open sea the 'awkward great lumps of ice' to which Mr. Whewell referred were irregular masses the size of a moderate haystack, presumably the fragments of some huge ice-mountain that had driven with full shattering forces on the outer cliff. We (though not *Ringle*) might have survived a glancing blow from one of them, but there seemed no hope whatsoever for the canoe that was trying to cross the tide at its farther extremities — I mean on our right-hand or starboard side, where the current ran violently up the shore.

'For some moments I did not understand what was happening, but then Hanson and his seamen quickly explained, and passed me a telescope. In the canoe was a young woman with a piece of sealskin over one shoulder and a paddle in both hands: in the floor of the canoe, covered with nets, half a dozen small crouching dogs, right aft an older woman, completely naked, holding a basket of fish and an equally naked baby. They all glistened with the rain and flying spray: it was just not freezing. The girl, with an extraordinary mastery of her craft, tried again and again to slip between the great blocks of ice, often touching but never being upset. We watched with the most extreme attention and anxiety. At last, the blocks coming in an almost uninterrupted train, she spun the craft round, and now running with the current as it curved across the channel to our side, she ran within hail. Captain Aubrey called out, offering a rope. She dared not take it: I think the check would have destroyed the frail canoe, Bjorn shouted and she replied. Someone threw a blanket, clear into the older woman's grasp: she was seen to smile and they were swept on along the shore, checking their way on a small shingly strand with something of a hovel behind it, smoke from a fire, and some naked men who sauntered down for the fish, the dogs and the blanket.

'Very soon after this, with one of those dream-like changes, the tide fell still. Jack hailed *Ringle*, lying there under our lee, and desired her to look out through the pass, the channel, and report on the state of the sea and the ice. Then calling Hanson and Bjorn, he told them to join us in the cabin: there he gave them some coffee, and speaking mainly through Hanson, who was not only Bjorn's immediate officer but who was thoroughly used to his way of speaking, he asked for a general account of the situation. For example, did Bjorn understand the language of these parts?

'Yes, sir, he did: more or less. Had been wrecked in the *Ingeborg*, out of Malmö, some way to the west, in Wigwam Reach and beyond — ship burnt to the waterline and only five men reached the shore — the people were quite kind — took most of their belongings, but gave them food — they were mad for knives — had no knives, no metal — they gave him a girl for his second-best knife — so after a year or two — he lost count of time — he came to understand them quite well — they were fairly decent people — but they did not know cleanliness. Their language was called Tlashkala: no, it was not spoken right along the Reach: far from it. Another nation lived say fifty miles westward, and they could not understand it at all. When the two nations met they usually fought and the stronger side took everything they could carry. And beyond that nation, the Wona, there was yet another, and so all along Wigwam Reach. Some of them ate men's flesh: some did not. But they all signalled to their friends with smoke. A pause, and Bjorn murmured to Hanson, "Would the Captain know about Wigwam Reach?"

'Hanson blushed, overcame his confusion, and said "Sir: Bjorn wonders whether you know about Wigwam Reach?"

"Please ask him to tell me all he can."

"Well, sir," said Bjorn, "I don't want to shove my oar in, but Malmö and Gothenburg whalers, homeward bound and in no hurry from the far south fisheries, quite often use it, above all when there is so much south in the winds off the Horn, like it is now. The Wigwam Reach is a sheltered passage — not this one just west of us at present, but the next after it. A continual lee, and slow of course; but it goes on and on a hundred and fifty miles or more, past Cabo Pilar into the Pacific. It is the far end of the Magellan Strait. To be sure, the Indians are mostly wicked, which worries the whaling ship: but a man-of-war has nothing to fear."

"Well, thank you, Mr. Hanson," said Jack, standing up. "Thank you, Bjorn; and I hope your poor ribs will be better very soon." '

'My dear,' wrote Stephen again, in a jagged, uneven hand although he and his stool and his desk were so clamped together that nothing but his wrist had independent freedom: the ship and the sea upon which she was at least for the moment suspended knew no such limit, 'we are in the boundless ocean once again, and blessed by what they very oddly call a favourable wind we are sent in our tumultuous headlong way something north of west. We have of course as I probably told you in one of these countless rambling disconnected and profoundly ignorant pages long since rounded the dreaded Cape Horn, and now Captain Aubrey has decided that duty requires him to *waste not a minute* in the placid navigation of slow, sheltered waters, but to press on come tempest, come dreadful ice, come wounded spars and threadbare, wounded ropes: and *now,* come the approach of famine. Our supplies of everything but water are running very, very low.

'The shortage is already perceptible in the sick-bay, where old wounds open for a nothing, where there is evident debility and perhaps the first signs of scurvy. Three men and a boy have died of plain uncomplicated pneumonia, and poor old Mr. Woodbine is sinking fast under a complication of inveterate self-treated maladies: but what can medicine do in such cases other than ease the end without deliberately provoking it?

'Himself, and by that I mean Jack Aubrey for he does indeed personify the ship, has become grave, stern, unapproachable. He asks no man's opinion, and I have the impression that he knows exactly what he is doing — that he sails with the same determination and clarity of mind as the great albatrosses that sometimes accompany us, blackbrowed, wandering, and royal.

'Although I am by now quite an ancient mariner, long accustomed to the ways of the service and the sea, it does surprise me to observe the steady force of usage, custom, necessity and discipline. The people, weakened by loss and now by short rations, are worked very hard indeed: putting a ship about in such seas and with such winds, in very, very cold weather, is extremely wearing: and they have been kept to it for what seems an unaccountably long time. Yet I have heard no complaints, no short answers, no cursing of an awkward shipmate. The gaiety is gone, of course it is: but an astonishing fortitude remains, even among the ship's remaining boys and the midshipmen. Once or twice I have heard the Captain check an officer: but it is very rare.

'He and I eat together, as we have always done; yet this, clearly, is not a time for intimacy. And it is a great while since we candidly exchanged our minds. I only remember him nodding his head over the last of the coffee, and telling me that towards the end of the graveyard watch he had suddenly remembered the *Delaware*'s present of some bottles of Jamaica rum, as yet unbroached in his private store-room. "The men will go through Hell and high-water to save the barky," he observed. "But if you touch their grog, I should not like to answer for even the best of them."

'So the grog is safe for a while at least; and unless I quite misunderstood the conversation in the gunroom, the extreme anxiety of our dwindling stores — our very few casks of barely edible horny beef — is likely to be relieved, since we are steering, or attempting to steer, towards a small group of islands laid down on three separate charts reasonably near what passes for the coast in these latitudes. For this, though you may find it as hard as I do to believe, is the beginning of the Antarctic spring: the whole cycle of life begins again, and we hope thereby to preserve our own. What light there was is fading, but not, this evening, under the usual cloud of small-flaked snow but of a sombre driving rain: and so, my dear, I bid you good night: God bless.'

Some days later, on Thursday, a very weary Dr. Maturin eased himself into the same writing-place, looked automatically at his close-scrubbed hands again, and dipped his pen. 'My dear,' he wrote, 'it is perhaps no more than a piece of hedge-law, but I have heard men say that butchers cannot be allowed on a jury, they being so daily accustomed to blood that all tenderness is washed out of them: and for my own part, during my medical studies, I was intimately familiar with the dissection of the dead. It is true that at first I had to overcome a certain reluctance, indeed an extreme reluctance, but I thought I had conquered it entirely. Not at all. The carnage of yesterday and the day before distressed and sickened me beyond what I had thought possible. The weather was exceptionally kind and we, *Surprise* and *Ringle*, headed into a sheltered bay, there dropping anchor in perhaps twenty fathom of water, pulling in to the shore over a moderate swell, through ice that presented no great difficulty. Yet already there was death at hand: just by the blue cutter in which I sat a leopard-seal made a lunge at one of the smaller penguins which shot into the air like a little rocket or a cork from the bottle, landing on a small ice-floe. The shore itself was a most striking spectacle, divided into rookeries (as they say) for the various kinds of penguin — various levels for the different species —

and then strands, rocky or smooth, appropriated to the seals according to their kind, and one particular cove to the vast sea-elephants, whose enormous males as I am sure you know wear a fleshy great proboscis and rearing up utter a hellish roar. Above them all, on the sparse herbage of the upper island, wheeled terns, three or perhaps four kinds of albatross, petrels and skuas; and with a glass one could make out sitting birds by the hundred.

'As I think I have said before, several of our hands have sailed in whalers or sealers and they were perfectly accustomed to the slaughter: the others, after the initial bawling and excitement, settled down deliberately to knocking the medium-sized seals on the head, while those with some knowledge of butchering cut them into reasonable joints for salting. What merriment or wanton brutality there was soon died away and I was able to prevent some unnecessary suffering with a scalpel. It was an extraordinarily bloody, extraordinarily unpleasant exercise, carried out for the most part in a phlegmatic, workaday fashion. It distressed most of the boys extremely: excited a few others. By good fortune or perhaps I should say good management we had salt in plenty: so there is our hold, and *Ringle*'s hold, filled with barrels of seal and sea-lion flesh, as rich and nourishing a meat as you could wish.

'I did however notice that although the very real fear of running out of provisions in the far south sea had certainly vanished, yet a certain cloud hung over the ship. It disappeared after grog and an enormous supper of fresh seal steaks: and stupidly I did not attend to the proportion of those who were affected and those (mostly countrymen and accustomed to killing as a matter of course from childhood) who were not; yet I did notice, since we were in the same boat, that Hanson and his particular friend Daniel did what little they could to hide their distress in our many bloody voyages to and fro, with the skuas screaming just over our heads.'

Chapter Eight

Jack Aubrey turned away, having said the oh so familiar last words over his old shipmate Henry Woodbine, and he had not walked the length of the deck before the look-out hailed a signal from *Ringle*, far away in the clear north-north-west.

'Jump up with a glass, Mr. Hanson,' he said, and stood there waiting while the young man raced up to the fore-topgallant crosstrees.

'Sir,' his clear young voice came floating down, '*Ringle* says: *believe Cape Pilar north a half west perhaps thirty-five miles.*'

With a greater deliberation but with an even more beating heart Jack rose to an even greater height, settled himself comfortably on his familiar perch and directed his telescope to the horizon well beyond the distant schooner. The cold clarity of the air made for excellent visibility: yet there was the inescapable curvature of the earth's surface, and a moment's calculation assured him that what could just be made out from the distant *Ringle*'s masthead would not be seen from *Surprise* for the best part of an hour, even if she maintained her present beautiful ten knots.

Nevertheless he lingered, the cold biting through his dreadnought griego and his wonderfully unbecoming woollen bonnet; and in time he half persuaded himself that he could make out a nick in the horizon within five degrees of the required position — a horizon otherwise as taut as a hard-stretched line.

Slowly, easily down, and he walked aft through the questioning gaze of the watch on deck — a sadly diminished watch by now — to the cabin, where he found Dr. Maturin stirring a tankard of mulled claret over a spirit-stove. 'Take a sip of this, brother,' said Stephen. 'It will help dispel the cold: I have added a pinch of ginger to the nutmeg and the cloves.'

'It goes down very well,' said Jack, 'and if anything could replace coffee, right Mocha freshly roasted and freshly ground, it would be this. Many thanks. Have you heard the news?'

'Not I. Poll, Maggie and a horse-leech from the starboard watch have been administering enemas to the many, many cases of gross surfeit that have now replaced the frostbites, torsions and debility of the recent past, the very recent past. Strong fresh seal-meat has not its equal for upsetting the seaman's metabolism: he is much better kept on biscuit, Essex cheese, and a very little well-seethed salt pork — kept on short commons. What is the news, tell?'

'William signals land thirty-odd miles to the northward that may be Cape Pilar, which is laid down in just about that position.'

'I am so sorry. I thought we had done with capes. Take a little more wine, for your stomach's sake.'

'Well, if you insist . . . but let me tell you, Stephen, that although Cape Pilar or Cape Deseado as some say, forms part of Desolation Island — yet another Desolation Island, for all love — it is a wonderfully comfortable sight to a seaman bound for the Chilean coast, because just beyond that blessed cape lies the Pacific Ocean.'

'Do you mean we may survive?'

'Oh, I should not go as far as that; but presently I shall desire *Ringle* to reduce sail and ask William to dine with us after we have both made a very, very careful noon-observation. Then we shall compare positions and rejoice or lament as the case may be. Killick. Killick, there.'

'Sir?'

'Pass the word for the acting-master.'

'Pass the word for the master it is, sir,' replied Killick with (for him) an extraordinary degree of good humour.

'And Killick, tell my cook to lay on as decent a dinner as the barky can provide: *Ringle* will be coming aboard.' When Killick had gone, Jack said, 'Stephen, I do not suppose the sick-bay's comforts could be laid under contribution for the feast?'

'I might be able to spare a little, a very little, portable soup,' said Stephen, 'and I will myself look through my stores for two or three decent bottles of wine. And so this, you tell me, is virtually the Pacific?'

'Unless dear William has totally lost his wits with longing, the waters of the two oceans mingle off the seaward point of that Cape Pilar; and the Pacific, you will recall, bathes the coasts of Chile and Peru, stretching up to the Isthmus of Panama, on and on to Nootka Sound and the frigid Canadian shore. Come in, Mr. Daniel: let me tell you that one of your first duties as master's mate of this ship is to make a most meticulously exact noon-observation, For as I dare say you have heard, *Ringle*, far ahead, has signalled a probable sighting of Cape Pilar, with something very near the right bearing. And please tell Mr. Harding, with my compliments, that I should like him to make all reasonable sail to close the schooner.'

Within moments there was the sound of intense activity on deck: the bosun's oddly cracked bellow urging people 'to tally and belay', the thump of racing feet and the creak of blocks; and all the countless notes that made up the ship's voice rose in pitch and intensity, while the run of the sea from her cutwater aft grew more urgent by far.

The sea, if it teaches nothing else, does at least compel a submission to the inevitable which resembles patience. And all those concerned contained themselves with a decent appearance of that virtue through the clear hours of approach. To be sure, for both cabin and gunroorn there was the delightful discovery (at least for those who understood navigation) that their positions coincided in the most gratifying manner; and then of course there was the feast, during which it was found that a really full-bodied burgundy went admirably with seal steaks. But the real, truly relished delight came well after this, when, well topped up with American rum, they stood in the foretop, Jack Aubrey calling up the midshipmen one by one and bidding them take the most particular note of that tall naked mountain at the tip of the island just ahead, the mountain with two pillars of rock on the seaward side, the higher quite black. They were never to forget that landfall, because it marked the western end of Magellan's Strait: and then from these tolerable luck and a west or north-west breeze a ship could be carried through to the Atlantic in a week.

They had perfectly delightful weather after Cape Pilar, with clear skies, topgallant western breezes with none of that cruel bite of ice, a truly blessed sea with great smooth rollers riding gently in towards a shore so distant that it was only the faintest loom, a sea with here and there a whale, and fine fresh fish taken over the side in God's plenty. And above all this sea was *pacific* — no sudden dreadful squalls, never a night when all hands were called, plucked from their half-warmed hammocks to confront hail and ice-caked decks, tops and ratlines: health began to return, and with it laughter, capers, mirth; and at last the African cats came from their refuge in the galley, where they had what very little warmth was available, south of the Horn.

This enchanting weather lasted from one Wednesday until the next, and on the intervening Sunday they rigged church, all hands in pretty good clothes (though few chests had escaped a soaking), trimmed by the barber and his mate, pigtails combed and replaited, and the singers, who made up most of the ship's crew, in good, hearty voice. Jack read them one of Taylor's sermons on intemperance, to which they listened gravely; while the *Ringle*s, just under their lee, had to put up with the Articles of War yet again, Mr. Reade having little confidence in his powers that way.

From well before dawn the following Wednesday it was clear to everyone aboard that they were going to have it rough; but few who had not seen the appalling drop of the barometer could have imagined quite how rough they would have it, or how soon. The wind came dead foul, of course, blowing from the north-north-west with ever-increasing force and against the flow both of tide and of current. At two bells all hands were called to bring the ship to and to veer out a drogue: it was tarpaulins again and ice in the wind; and a freakish cross-current whipped the crest of a tall wave clean across her side, flooding the galley and putting out the fires.

The cold, the hard, hard, very hard toil of keeping her just so, under bare poles forward and no more than a scrap right aft — pumps going without a pause — was about as severe as anything they had gone through, bar the even more deadly threat of the massive far southern ice.

When at last it did blow itself out they were almost too tired for relief, though Jack did observe, with grave approval, that the schooner had come through quite well: her headrails were gone, for the most part; her bowsprit was little more than a stump; and she had had to ship a new bright yellow boom; but she looked more buoyant than the *Surprise*. They were lying there in a still violently agitated, dirty sea, and clearly they were nearer the land than he had reckoned. In this cloudy evening light he could not see it, but all along to starboard there were shattered trees, masses of vegetation, as though kelp-beds had been ploughed up or steep-to land carried away. Far out to westward he thought he could make out a distant light.

'Mr. Whewell,' he said to the officer of the watch, having pondered a while. 'Let us signal to *Ringle make what offing is fea-*

sible.' He saw the coloured lanterns hoisted and acknowledged: told Harding that the watch below might now indeed go below once grog and a reasonable piece of smoked penguin and biscuit had been served out.

He noticed the first lieutenant's glance at the word 'biscuit', but without taking it up he went below. The sick-berth was more or less what was to be expected — indeed dreaded — after so sudden and so severe a blow. *Less* rather than *more,* seeing that there were now fewer to have limbs strained, dislocated, even broken; and now all were seamen, thoroughly used to the most furious extremes of weather and to having one hand for themselves as well as one for the ship. He did what was proper and customary by each, and he observed that Stephen had been as generous as usual with his laudanum where there was severe pain: he had known surgeons who out of something like a vicarious asceticism would allow nothing but liniment for even the worst of torn muscles. 'And for yourself?' he asked privately. 'How have you come through this blow?'

'Tolerably well, my dear, I thank you,' said Stephen, 'but I could do with a biscuit and a swallow of brandy.'

'The brandy we can do, at a pinch. But as for the biscuit . . . when you have a minute, come on deck: there are some prodigious curious trees a little way inshore. But the light is almost gone.'

'I have three fractures to splint, and then I shall be with you.'

The light had indeed faded, but Stephen could still receive the strong impression of an utterly disordered ocean — uneasy, with acres of yellowish scum, irregular and sometimes conflicting waves, and wreckage from the coast all over what coherent surfaces it had — just under the rail where he stood one of those immense Chilean pines with harshly recurved sharp-pointed leaves, was being fended off for fear its trailing roots — its *roots*, the whole hillside on which it grew having obviously been carried away — should foul the rudder.

'It is indeed an astonishing sight,' said Stephen. 'But if you will forgive me, I believe I shall *turn in*. I die on my feet. Do you not find the air growing curiously thick?'

'In another ten minutes I believe we shall not see our own bowsprit. In these waters you often get fog after foul: and by God it was foul.'

Stephen Maturin often thought — had

304

always thought — himself justified in making quite sure of a long night's sleep when he was very tired, by swallowing enough laudanum or anything else that came to hand to deaden a horse. It was therefore extremely difficult to wake him early in the morning.

'Oh go to the Devil, you hideous ape,' he said in a tone of exasperated hatred, and he heaved over in his cot, pulling the pillow over his head.

But it would not do. Slowly, by dint of steady, unvarying repetition, the message came through. A Hull whaler was alongside, her master aboard, pleading for help with a wounded man. A man whose arm, caught in the line running furiously out as a harpooned sperm whale dived, had been horribly mangled three days ago.

'I am no more fit to operate on a mangled arm than I am to bind up a cut finger,' he said, sitting up and looking at his hands. 'What is that smell?'

'It is coffee. The whaler brought us a couple of pounds. Should you like a pot?'

'Well, I might,' said Stephen, looking quite human, even intelligent. And when two or three remarkably strong cups had dispelled some of the poppy, hellebore and Jamaica rum, his deeply rooted sense of duty, of medical duty, began to return; he said, 'What is the name of my loblolly-boy?'

In a conciliating voice Jack said, 'Poll Skeeping.'

'Is the sea calm?'

'Mill ponds ain't in it.'

'You astonish me.'

'Did you not hear the dead flat thunderous rain all night?'

'I did not.'

'What am I to do?' asked Jack, afraid that he should drop off again.

'Why, beg her to go across and take a general view of the patient. She is an intelligent woman — they exist, whatever you may say — she had the good word of my old friend Dr. Teevan: she has had a world of experience, and she will tell my poor battered stupefied mind what to expect.'

She told him, as she put on his clean shirt and tidied his hair, that Saint Luke and all his fellow-apostles could not save the arm now, nor the whole college of surgeons of Dublin; but she thought that his honour, if she might say so, could possibly save the poor creature's life by taking it off at the shoulder, still quite a clean joint: and she had told the whalers what to do, what to prepare; and she had put up the usual implements.

The time to cross two decks and to descend into the well-lit cabin where the patient lay fighting his pain, his grief and his dread, was enough to restore the medical Stephen to life; and after a cursory examination that wholly confirmed what Poll had said, he carried out a rapid, unusually satisfactory amputation with excellent flaps of *healthy* skin, which he had scarcely dared hope for, and he murmured into the patient's ear, 'There: it is over. You will do remarkably well, if you lie quite still and drink no spirits at all for a week.'

'Is it over, sir?' asked the patient. 'I did not know. God bless you.'

On deck he said to the master of the ship, 'You will stay here, beside the ship, if you please. I am reasonably sanguine about your man — your brother, I believe? — and I should like to dress his shoulder tomorrow and show the most intelligent of your shipmates how to carry on until he is quite well.'

'I have always liked whalers,' said Jack, still waving though they were half a mile apart on a blessed calm forenoon with a fine breeze for reaching. 'They have to be right seamen to survive at all. People call them rough and their ships all a-hoo, and to be sure they kick up Bob's-a-dying on shore: but then they live rough, most uncommon rough. Yet for open-handed, I do not know their equal, though in general sailors are not often called skin-flints. Carling there, Joseph Carling, would have emptied his hold if I had let him: but I would not accept more than a couple of casks of biscuit, once I had heard that there was a small sheltered port or rather anchorage within reach, a little place called Pillón where most of the whalers down here go for their stores. The place is kept by a Hull man married to an Indian woman and he knows just what they need.' A pause, and Jack went on, gazing after the whaler, now hull-down, 'It is pleasant to see how sailors recognise one another all over the world: I am sorry you were too busy aboard *Ringle* and with your patients here to dine with Carling and me. You would have heard about some fellow-members of the Royal. Do you remember Dobson, Austin Dobson?'

'The entomologist?'

'Just so.'

'Of course I do. The *Proceedings* would not be what they are without him. There

308

are no less than three beetles named after Austin Dobson: in fact there may by now even be a fourth.'

'Have you heard about his inheritance?'

'Come, my dear, pray do not let us tease one another with question and answer. I find that I am somewhat fractious today — I have been made to work far too hard: I am nourished on most indifferently preserved penguins and seals. And I desire you to give me a plain straightforward seamanlike account of our colleague.'

'Very well. Let us go below and sit in comfort. There: put up your feet and calm your spirit. Austin Dobson, now, had a remote cousin whom he did not know — had barely met — who lived in gloomy splendour somewhere far in the north, where coal is mined and shipped from Newcastle. Now this cousin died, and Dobson inherited some ludicrous sum: millions — I do not know how many, but millions. And he instantly set about doing what he had always longed to do. He bought the Lisbon packet, a very stout serviceable craft designed to make rapid passages across the Bay of Biscay, and with an adequate crew and five or six friends, all Fellows of the Royal Society, botanists or entomologists and one authority on marine life — all men of wide interests — he set off by way of the Cape to India, Ceylon, the Spice Islands and so across the Pacific. They looked into Juan Fernandez and now they are working up the Chilean and Peruvian coasts as far as the Panama Isthmus, where two mean to cross and take ship the other side, carrying the seeds and more delicate specimens — they have university commitments — while Dobson and his remaining friends carry on to Nootka Sound, returning by way of Kamschatka, where two of them mean to study the Economical Rat of those parts.'

'What a noble ambition,' cried Stephen, clasping his hands. 'What fortitude, too: for however comfortable the packet — and those I have known have all been neat, padded and as it were well-sprung — these men have already traversed some waters that call for a certain resolution, continually renewed between Cancer and Capricorn. And even in a very well-found packet there is sure to be a certain monotony of diet . . . no, no, it is a noble way of enjoying an inheritance. I honour him.'

Jack said, 'I am sorry you were not there: you would certainly have known most of them — you go to the Royal much more often than I do, and to the dinners. My friends there, the people whose papers I read with most attention, are the astronomers and mathematicians. These men here, of course, were primarily naturalists of one kind or another, and when the two craft put into San Patricio together for stores they asked the whalers all sorts of things about whales — the various kinds, depth of blubber, pregnancy in whales, where found, numbers in schools — accompanying young? Ambergris, where located?'

They both laughed: Stephen had once been cast ashore on a coral island, where his only companion, apart from a few crabs, was a piece of ambergris.

'Why do we laugh? There was nothing droll about your situation or our anxiety,' said Jack.

'Perhaps because you found me, so it all ended happily. But to be sure, laughter is sometimes wonderfully obscure: whenever my mind moves to that piece of ambergris I feel the birth of a smile: I do hope we meet these men. Theirs is a very respectable curiosity and I for one long to know the answer to some of their questions.'

Jack was called away at this point — something whirling about among the sails, in all probability — and Stephen sank into a by no means agreeable fit of musing. He might not possess the millions attributed to Dobson — and indeed, very large sums were required for that kind of exercise — but he was what most people would call rich or at least quite rich; and yet he had done no more than consider a journey into the Atacama desert to examine the effects of extreme aridity, and another to study the life of the Caucasian snow-cock: and these mere considerations had led to nothing concrete. He had contributed nothing to the sum of knowledge. Some part of his mind at once offered a flood of denials, excuses, attenuating circumstances, assertions of his distinguished merit, his unbroken record of observing Lent as strictly as any man not even in minor orders; but he remained low-spirited, and he was glad to see Jack reappear with the news that 'the damned fore . . . had carried away, but all was fast and a-tanto now.' The words that followed *fore* sounded very like a piece of obscenity far, far grosser than anything that Jack was ever likely to say and Stephen was still trying to recapture the sound and interpret it when he became aware that he was now being told about Daniel's and Hanson's zeal in plotting their course for the whaler's refuge of Pillón behind its protecting island. They had Joseph Carling's bearings, his outline of the island from south-west and due west, his directions for the entrance to the little bay, and an at least approximate table of the tides.

'With this sweet breeze we should be off the coast a little before high tide at nine,' said Jack. 'We shall lie under the island's lee and send *Ringle* in with the two pursers: she can lie alongside much easier than *Surprise* and there is an awkward turn in the channel where we might just touch and she would not. All the whalers know it and take care if they are deep-laden. I could wish the sky looked a little more promising: but a quick turn-round and we are in hundred-fathom water, heading north with a full hold.'

All the whalers knew the awkward turn in the Pillón passage, but they did not know that the frightful shore-tearing storm had combined with a minor local earthquake (usual in those unhappy regions) to block it with a massive landslide; and the Ringles, advancing cheerfully towards the bend, just waiting to put the helm hard over, ran straight on to the sharp-edged new-fallen rocks.

It was a pale and shaken Reade who

pulled round in the gig to report this to Captain Aubrey. 'Never mind, William,' he said. 'Just lead us in, sounding all the way, and we shall see if all anchors out astern and the capstan can heave her off. The tide is still making.'

They did heave her off, with a shuddering groan, at the very height of flood, all hands and all the men of the little village sweating at the bars: and she lurched backwards into deep water. But their triumph was silenced by the rise of broken woodwork from below, from her stem itself and from the larboard cutwater, some of it copper-plated.

They beached her moderately well on a smooth sea-lions' nursery, and at low water they found that the wounds, though horrible, were not deadly. Both carpenters and the few skilled men in the settlement (who felt it extremely, and who admitted that there had been a slight earthquake) worked with the utmost concentration, and at the next high tide she floated.

Clearly a well-equipped yard was necessary, the complex assembly of her bows, though nowhere wholly pierced, had been cruelly wrenched: she could not bear anything even near half-pressure on her foremast, and although she could make some modest way if she met no really savage head-seas, she would need a dry-dock and highly-skilled hands to bring her back to fighting trim.

'My dear,' wrote Stephen yet again, but now sitting in reasonable comfort at his desk, 'I have no doubt that you remember that exceptionally amiable young man with one hand replaced by a steel hook: his name is William Reade, and I have been attached to him these many years: but he alas was in command of the poor schooner when she ran full tilt into what amounted to a bar of rock and very nearly destroyed herself. Now that sheltered piece of water was perfectly calm; the awful crash of rock loosened and cast down by an earthquake had long since died away; and an estimable whaler who knew the small harbour intimately had laid down the bearings of the passage or channel with meticulous accuracy: the poor young man is in no way to blame. Nobody, least of all Jack Aubrey, who brought him up from childhood and who loves him and esteems him, does blame him. Yet he walks about bent, weighed down with imaginary guilt. I have prescribed (for she carries no surgeon, poor thing) a modest cathartic, and tonight he will sleep, will sleep indeed, with a seasonable amount of help from me and the blessed poppy, together with a few minims of hellebore, God love him.

'But otherwise I must say that although the southern parts of this prodigious continent are forbidding and bear such well-deserved names as Port Famine, Cape Froward and Desolation Island, if one does but survive and persevere, one comes to regions, to whole stretches of coast where the southerly current is both constant and wholly favourable, and where the breezes often favour a gentle northward movement, which is all that we can reasonably desire or pray for until we reach San Patricio with our poor crippled *Ringle* and, I trust, a cure for poor dear William's melancholy, which moves his people so that I have seen them shake their heads and clasp their hands as he goes by.

'At present this most curious sea, this piece of the enormous ocean, is filled, *filled* with utterly innumerable small fishes so very like anchovies that I doubt if I could distinguish between the'species (or genera) unless I had the true Mediterranean creature in my hand for comparison. A little trawl, negligently drooped over the side, provides us with a dish of whitebait (rather large whitebait it is true, but eminently palatable) in a trice. But our pleasure is as nothing compared with that of the seabirds of this region, above all — or at least most obviously — the vast bulky pelicans: they circle about us with rapturous cries, plunge, gorge, rise into the air mute while they are cramming down their prey, dive, rise again, and so it continues. There are rocks and headlands all along this coast, where these birds, too heavy at last for flight or merely sated, spend the later part of the day and the night until dawn, when they begin again, their voices as fresh and piercing as ever: and these rocks are white with their droppings. Indeed, these deposits, this *guano,* is said to have a depth of ten feet and even more.

'At present we coast very gently along — I think we have no more than double-reefed topsails abroad — and the distant, somewhat veiled shore, with here and there a remote white gleam from the still more distant Andes, scarcely seems to move; yet our devoted navigators take careful observations every watch, and every watch the pins on the chart advance perceptibly north towards San Patricio, where we are confident of at least three capital yards. Indeed, so near are we now that Captain

Aubrey is having the barge carefully over-hauled and beautified, to run in with me so that the chosen yard shall be ready to start as soon as *Ringle* comes. He takes me, not as you may well suppose, for my advice in sailing the boat, but merely for my ability to speak Spanish.

'Horatio has just come to tell me that the headland marking the southern end of the estuary on whose shores San Patricio has its present being, is now in sight, and that the Captain will soon have the barge afloat. I must fetch some respectable clothes: but first I must tell you that San Patricio, like many another settlement on this uneasy shore, has already had other sites, destroyed by earthquake or fire or its opposite, a vast engulfing wave that seems connected with the earthquake and that not only destroys the ruins even more thoroughly but that will carry a ship, an eight hundred ton ship up and *through* the town, sometimes setting it down, as by a giant's hand, upright on the debris: though it is possible that I may confuse San Patricio with other towns — so many on this unstable shore have suffered from all these calamities, as well as from pest, plague and piratical rapine too.'

★ ★ ★

Leaving the frigate at anchor on good holding ground well off the coast, *Surprise*'s barge pulled smoothly up the confluence of two rivers towards San Patricio: and as she was coming into the fairly well-inhabited part of the town — the docks and wharves to starboard with a good many craft and a few ships alongside — plain astonishment burst through the ordinarily mute coxswain's reserve and he cried, 'By God, sir, there's the old Lisbon packet, painted blue. Painted blue, by God. I beg pardon, sir.'

'So she is,' said Jack, following his gaze, and the gaze of all the bargemen. 'So she is: but what a difference the colour makes. I am not sure I should have recognised her.'

'God love you, sir: I was a boy aboard her, and being she was a packet, they liked her to be kept Navy-fashion, and there ain't a brass handle, knob or bolt I don't know. Watch your stroke there, bow-oar.'

Jack turned to Stephen, who was watching a flight of pelicans, and said, 'Four craft along, to starboard, there are your friends, I do believe. Our colleagues of the Royal.'

'Oh,' cried Stephen, 'but they have

painted her blue. Could the boat row over, do you think, so that we may hail her?'

Jack gave the necessary orders and they moved gently across the stream. 'Take care of the paint, you moon-struck bastards,' called an angry voice in Chilean Spanish.

'Watch out for the paint — do not touch it for your life: by God, it's Maturin! And Aubrey! How very pleasant to see you here, dear colleagues. Pray thread your way through to the wharf, to our other side, which is quite dry, and come aboard. We have some really excellent lemonade.'

How they talked, how they quaffed the excellent lemonade! The bargemen were dismissed to an eating-house on the open quay a little way along, and the Fellows told of the horrors and delights and discoveries of their respective voyages, several of them talking at once now and then and all as hoarse as toads by the time Jack stood up, begged leave to go and look at the various yards for his wounded tender, and engaged them all to dine aboard *Surprise* tomorrow. 'And if I may, gentlemen, I will pluck Maturin from your bosoms: he speaks the Spanish, you know, which I do not.'

'One hears very high opinions of Lopez,' said Dobson. 'And he was certainly most obliging with our paint and a small leak.'

'It is the second yard on the right as you go up the stream,' said an eminent botanist. 'The first is occupied by the Chilean navy.'

They got along but slowly, partly because there were several small yards on either side, whereas they had heard of only three, and partly because parties of waterfowl passed overhead, sometimes in great number, and Stephen would come to a stand, cursing the absence of his telescope and trying to make out the birds' nature despite the absence.

They were approaching yet another quay and Stephen threatened to come to yet another halt as a very lofty flight of long-legged, long-necked crane-like birds came across the sky, when they heard a voice from the other side of the road. 'Aubrey! How glad I am to see you here. Are you looking for *Asp*?'

'Lindsay! What a pleasant meeting: it must be years and years since I last saw you.'

'Yes, indeed,' said Lindsay, walking over: he was wearing a uniform very like that of the Royal Navy, but with rather more lace. 'I dare say you are looking for *Asp*?'

'At the moment I am looking for Lopez' yard.'

'It is just beyond the theatre — but perhaps you do not know the town?'

'Lord, no. This is the first time I have ever been here, and apart from drinking lemonade with some Fellows of the Royal Society we have done nothing but walk along this quay.'

'Fellows of the Royal Society? Those men in the former Lisbon packet? I dare say you were very much at sea in that learned company?'

Their slight acquaintance did not at all warrant this familiar tone and Jack left a distinct pause before he said, 'May I introduce my political adviser, who is also a Fellow? Dr. Maturin, Sir David Lindsay.'

'Your servant, sir,' said Lindsay, somewhat confused. And to Jack, 'Should you like to look at *Asp*? She is just across the way, in the naval basin.' They crossed, and with increasing confidence Lindsay pointed out the various changes he had made, particularly the lengthening of the deck for more guns a side. Jack had reservations, but he did not utter them, contenting himself with the observation that the *Asp* must have made a remarkable passage.

'Good God, yes: but I was in a hurry; and as you know I have never been afraid of cracking on: so I took the Strait. Some people say it is dangerous and prefer to creep round by the Horn; but I don't mind a little danger, and I took the Strait. At one point just after the Second Narrows, when we were very nearly close-hauled, the wind began to back before we were handsomely round the cape and with tears in his eyes the master begged me to put into the sheltered bay. But "No," said I, "in for a penny, in for a pound", and we rounded the point with barely a fathom to spare.'

'Well done, well done,' said Jack, feeling that it was required of him; and for a while Lindsay stood relishing his feat and murmuring 'In for a penny, in for a pound'. But then one of the circling crane-like birds dropped a turd on his hat: he wiped it fairly clean with a piece of sea-wrack, and then went on in a more matter-of-fact tone, 'I was in a hurry, of course, as you will understand; and I got here in very good time. I have already looked at almost all my bases, almost the whole of my command — Concepción, some of the smaller island places, Talcahuana, and now this. But I must tell you, Aubrey,' he went on, after a significant pause, 'I must tell you that the discipline, sense of order, and indeed elementary cleanliness, to say nothing of seamanship, are not what we could wish: that is one of the many reasons why I am so happy to have a man like you — of your reputation — under my orders.'

'What you say is particularly kind and flattering,' said Jack after a considering pause and a glance at the wholly impassive Maturin, 'but I am afraid there has been a misunderstanding. As a post-captain on the active list, on detached service, I am under the orders of the Admiralty and of nobody else on earth.'

Lindsay reddened, and after two false starts he said, 'I am commander-in-chief of the Junta's naval forces, and as such . . .'

'How do you mean, Junta?'

'The combination of authorities that make up the Republic.'

'The republic of the whole country?'

'The entirety — apart from a few dissident northern bases near the Peruvian frontier that will soon be liberated. And as such,' he went on, resuming his official voice, 'it is within my power to press your men and impound your vessel.'

'Gentlemen,' said Dr. Maturin in a voice that expressed neither authority nor impatience but that did stress the need to speak in a lower, more adult tone and to abandon rhetoric, 'it is surely time to sit in the shade; and although tea can scarcely be hoped for, yet coffee may well be had, or maté. There is an agreeable awning at no great distance.'

'The gentleman, as I believe I said before, is my political adviser,' observed Jack. Lindsay bowed again, and said that coffee, iced coffee, was indeed to be had under the awning.

It was with evident relief that they descended from this near crisis and sat in the shade, called for their coffee and talked for a while like ordinary human beings, discussing common acquaintances, the few ships still in commission and the fate of officers, particularly junior officers, flung on shore and living there on half-pay. Then Stephen, having found that Lindsay was somewhat less foolish than he had appeared at an earlier stage, laid out the position (or a chosen part of the position) as it was seen in London. Government was in favour of Chilean independence: it did not much care for some of the members of the southern junta or group of juntas and had not committed itself to anything resembling recognition; it was on better terms with those in the north, and there had been a certain indirect intercourse, a certain understanding. But if any vexation, let alone any violence, were offered to a ship even remotely connected with the Royal Navy, the effects on Chilean independence would be disastrous, disastrous: whereas a more or less tacit co-operation in suppressing Spanish privateering or the like, to say nothing of Peruvian invasion, would have entirely the opposite effect. Sir David was no doubt perfectly aware of *Surprise*'s force, her fighting reputation, her superbly well-trained crew: her prime and ostensible function was hydrographical — above all surveying — but in the course of her activities she might well have many and many a chance of helping the infant republic to full and acknowledged independence. If Sir David would make all these facts clear to the many influential men with whom he was in contact, he would do both countries a very great service indeed.

They parted with expressions of good will and assurances on Lindsay's part of the most wholly discreet cooperation in case of need; and when they were separated by a decent stretch of ground Jack said, 'How can that young man have been so bubbled, so wildly deluded, as to think that I had come out to join him? I am deeply puzzled. For as you have observed, he is not altogether a fool: yet he really believed what he was saying. And to believe that even in peace-time a post-captain quite high on the list and not reduced to actual beggary should consent to act in such a wholly unauthorised caper — and to serve under him . . . it passes imagination.'

'Certainly I can advance not a shadow of official approval or qualified assent, no instant solution, no convincing hypothesis at all. But a line runs — or rather limps, for I do not think I have it right: *"Jockey of Norfolk be not so bold, For Dickon thy master is bought and sold."*'

A few yards farther and he said, 'I have had a certain experience of juntas and I must say that quite often those combinations for a common aim bring out the worst in men, they generally having private ends in far greater mass than the common aim. And Jack, it is my belief that you too have been bought and sold, some considerable member of the northern junta that first approached you having defected to the south and having transferred your services, as he might those of a common mercenary, to his new friends. But I speak very much at random and must submit my notions to Jacob's vastly superior local knowledge and connexions. I hope to see him in Santiago: but meanwhile we have done no harm.'

Chapter Nine

'My dear Sir Joseph,' wrote Stephen, 'how I wish I had the words to express my admiration at the celerity of your message and at your very particular kindness in sending down to Dorset for as much as the ladies concerned could write while the chaise was turned round. The celerity of course owed a great deal to Mr. Bridges' ingenuity together with his profound knowledge of Andean passes, and to the most uncommon physical powers of his Indian runners, but even more to the network of republican Masonic lodges that found us here rather than at our southern port. Yet the kindness was yours alone and I thank you very heartily, enclosing the briefest of all brief replies. Now as for the actual posture of affairs here in Santiago and the rest of Chile, the varying composition of the juntas (roughly one for each considerable stretch of territory) and their convictions, to say nothing of their desire for power, makes any prediction so tentative in my present state of knowledge that it is scarcely worth writing down; yet I will say that O'Higgins, the Supreme Director, appears to be losing popularity, together with San Martín, whereas the Carrera brothers and Martinez de Rozas are certainly increasing theirs. When I have been here a little longer and have spent more time with the invaluable Dr. Jacob, I shall send you a more considered, better-informed account of the shifting, almost impenetrable political scene: but for the moment I shall close, if I may, with my sincerest thanks for the increased grant, and a few words on our naval affairs. The first of these words is a little discouraging, since it must state that His Catholic Majesty's heavy frigate, renamed *O'Higgins*, of no less than fifty guns, is now found to have become wholly unserviceable, through age and decay: and the republican ports are very short of all naval stores. On the other hand, Captain Aubrey and Sir David Lindsay have reached a working agreement: and *Surprise* is now lying off a small port in Chiloé, which is still held by the royalists, who have a considerable base there as well as two or three of moderate size. But the port in question is a commercial harbour in which a notorious Spanish privateer has taken refuge — a vessel that *Surprise* means to board and take by night at slack water, so that if the wind should fail, the ebb will bring her out. Aubrey is attended by three republican sloops, which, says he, know nothing of their trade but are pitifully willing to learn: each has an experienced RN master's mate or senior midshipman to help them. And Heaven knows the Republic has a very great and urgent need of sailors who possess at least the rudiments of their calling, when the naval force of Peru is considered, with their thirty-two gun, quite new frigate, others somewhat older but serviceable, several ship-sloops and brigs, manned by a body of competent professional officers and seamen, and commanded, in effect, by a viceroy perfectly loyal to his king and bitterly resentful of the royalist defeat at Chacabuco. The Peruvian army may be discredited, but this most certainly does not apply to the Peruvian navy: and while the Spaniards still hold the southern base of Valdivia and those on the important northern island of Chiloé, the new republic's trade, its sea-borne trade, is in constant danger, and swarms of privateers, under royalist licence or no licence at all, take whatever ships they can overtake and overwhelm.

'Now until I have the honour of writing more fully, after consultation with Dr. Jacob, I shall just append a provisional list of the juntas of which I have personal knowledge, encode the whole, and end, with the utmost gratitude, dear Sir Joseph,

> Your humble, obedient, and
> most affectionate servant,
> S. Maturin'

Before encoding the whole, however, S. Maturin looked at the two scraps of paper that had come with Blaine's message: one addressed to him, the other to Jack. Unfolding his own he read, with infinite tenderness, 'from two very close friends at Woolcombe, with their dearest love. Brigid and Christine', but hearing someone at the door, he thrust it secretly into his bosom.

The sound at the door was of course Jacob: unlike many orthodox Masons he had no strong prejudice against these somewhat irregular republican lodges in Chile; but he did deplore their loquacity.

'At least,' he said, sitting down heavily

and taking snuff, 'I did learn that the younger O'Higgins, the one you were so friendly with in Peru, will be here tomorrow.'

'Ambrosio? Yes, I did like him, and could wish to see him again. A deadly shot, and a not inconsiderable botanist. Would it be sensible to invite him, do you think?'

Jacob considered, took more snuff, and said, 'It would be noticed, of course: particularly if we went to Antoine's. But I do not think it would do any harm. Rather the reverse.'

'Then I shall invite him. Never was a more permeable frontier. We have a reasonable number of agents there, I believe?'

'Tolerable, tolerable . . . we could certainly do with more.'

'See if you can find a couple of reasonably intelligent, reasonably truthful men with some nautical experience to keep an eye on the state of naval preparation in Callao. There are rumours of unusual activity. Amos: forgive a personal question, I beg, but do you put crumbled coca-leaves into your snuff?'

'No. I have more respect for the septum of my nose. I keep to mere tobacco. It is not so good, admittedly; but it revives me after the dreary meetings. And as you see,'

— tapping it — 'my septum is intact.'

'Long may it remain so. For my part I prefer to chew, or swallow. In moderation, in moderation, of course. Should you like to cast an eye over my synthesis of your information on the juntas and their political colour?'

'Certainly.'

'And I shall encode my piece for Whitehall, and then, with the blessing, we can dine. The day after tomorrow, having seen young O'Higgins, I mean to go down to Valparaiso: Captain Aubrey should be back by then. Will you come?'

'I had rather stay, if you do not mind. Two or three agents will be coming here from Lima.'

As Stephen rode down on a fine smooth-paced dapple-grey mare he turned a towering shoulder of rock and there was the ocean before him, an enormous, magnificent sea stretching to the horizon, and beyond the horizon, if his memory served, to China, Krim Tartary and the countries beyond: but here, close at hand — relatively close at hand — was the dear *Surprise*, unmistakable with her towering thirty-six-gun frigate's mainmast, and accompanied, which was by no means unusual, by a prize, a moderate ship-rigged privateer, now with drooping ears and in her turn accompanied by three republican sloops. These little vessels, though new to the game, knew enough about the ways of the prize-court to remove everything of value aboard, whether it was screwed down or not; and even from this distance they could be seen swarming over the side with their booty, like a body of ants.

At this early stage, when the foreigners — and nothing could have been more foreign in Chile than Jack Aubrey, fair-haired, red-faced, massive, his officers and most of the hands — were looked upon as valued, welcome allies, it was a pleasure to walk about Valparaiso, with smiles, bows and cheerful cries — Merry Christmas! Good night! — on every hand, and when he had confided the mare to a stable that she obviously knew and liked, Stephen walked into the Capricorno with a mild satisfaction if not complacency, instantly succeeded by open astonishment as he recognised Dobson and his shipmates sitting at a punch-bowl, all delighted by his surprise. They made him sit down with a variety of delights. 'I had no idea you would be so far north already,' he said.

'Oh, the *Isaac Newton* can be induced to go at an astonishing speed; and having a professional master and his mate, who knew her very well on the Lisbon run, we can even sail by night, you know.'

'There is that amiable young man of the schooner, Mr. Reade,' said another Fellow, interrupting his account of a dicotyledonous plant unknown to science. 'Let us be mute, and see his amazement.'

The amazement reached their highest expectations, and they sat William Reade at the top of the table. 'Tell me, sir,' said Stephen's neighbour in a low voice, nodding towards William's hook, 'does the young gentleman ever feel the effects of electricity, of static electricity?'

'I do not believe so, sir,' said Stephen. 'But then there is a considerable amount of insulation between the steel and his flesh, you know.' A pause, and he went on, 'I am wonderfully ignorant of the whole subject: is there yet a general theory of electricity — electricity, what it is?'

'Not that I know of. Its effects can be seen and measured, but apart from that and some pretty wild unsubstantiated statements I do not think we yet know the ABC. Though Lankester may — he has done a great deal of work recently with copper wire in coils. Mr. Lankester . . .'

'Well, Aubrey,' cried Mr. Dobson, 'welcome ashore. All we need now is Noah, Neptune, and a couple of tritons, ha, ha, ha,' and he called for another bowl of punch.

Punch or no, they listened very attentively to Jack's brief play-by-play account of boarding the privateer from the landward side while *Surprise*'s few mortars, briskly served, pooped up various lights into the seaward sky, varied with flashes and shattering bangs.

This really finished the day. After a somewhat rambling and hazy supper, three or four Fellows were led up to bed, and the rest sat under the starlit sky, sobering themselves with the iced juice of various fruits.

'What was the damage aboard?' asked Stephen as they walked back to the mare's agreeable inn.

'Extraordinarily little,' said Jack. 'Nothing that dear Poll could not deal with. Those fellows, those Chiloé privateers, knew nothing about action: they sailed their ship quite well, but as for fighting her . . . On the other hand, our young fellows really pleased me — our Chileans, I mean. They handled their craft quite well on the way over, and they boarded her like good 'uns, cutlass in hand.'

'Shall you ride back tomorrow? I have two men to see, and then I am away.'

'I do not think so. Since I speak no Spanish, I am not much use in Santiago, now that I have done the civil thing, with your help, by all the proper authorities. No. Down here I can really accomplish something, according to our agreement with the Supreme Director: they have good yards, decent craft up to a hundred tons or so, and at this time of year the breezes are reasonably steady and kind; and above all the eager young men learn very quick. Harding and Whewell speak a little Spanish, so do a few of the petty officers and hands, but the great thing is that most of them grasp the idea from good will and example. A rolling hitch is not all that simple, the firrt time: but I only had to show Pedro once, and he did it again and again, laughing with pleasure and asking my pardon for laughing.'

'I am heartily glad to hear what you say, my dear. We may have great need of young men that can tie a hitch . . . but as for laughter, open, audible laughter, I quite agree with your Pedro. There is something curiously offensive about it: above all when it is not truly amused, deeply amused. A parcel of excited young women screeching aloud and agitating their persons and limbs is enough to make one retire to a monastery. Our Fellows did not present a very elevating spectacle.'

'I did notice some of the Spaniards looking rather grave, and I did regret the last bowl of punch. Yet on the other hand, ours is an eminently respectable society: the *Proceedings* are known all over the learned world, and the men of the *Isaac Newton*, however bibulous on occasion, carry recommendations to the government, foreign office and universities of whatever country they visit. I do assure you, Stephen, that our connexion with them, with the Society as a whole in its most sober and learned mood, is a singular advantage to us.'

'My dear, I am entirely in agreement with you, no other Fellow more: yet even so, I could wish they would not laugh; or at the least, if they are truly amused, that they would laugh like men rather than eunuchs.'

'Oh, dear Jack,' he said, pausing at the door, 'I had almost forgot a note for you in Sir Joseph's packet.' He passed it over, a more substantial letter than his own, and written very small.

It was some time before Stephen came back to their inn, for he had found the small Catalan colony in Valparaiso dancing their native sardana in the square outside St Vincent's and he walked in smiling, the familiar music still running in his head. But the smile was wiped clean away by the sight of Jack so reduced with sorrow, deeply unhappy, red-eyed and bent. Stephen had often deplored the tendency of the English to display their feelings — their emotional weakness — but now looking sharply at his friend he saw something quite out of the common run: and indeed Jack stood up, blew his nose, and said, 'Forgive me, Stephen: I do beg pardon for this disgraceful exhibition: but Sophie's letter quite bowled me over.' He held up the almost transparent pages. 'She is so brave and good — never a harsh word, nor a hint of complaint, even though the girls have been really ill and Heneage Dundas is not quite pleased with George's conduct in *Lion*. She brought the whole place so alive, Stephen — I could see it all, courtyard, stables, library, farm-land and common. And she said such kind things about Christine and your Brigid: . . . Lord, it quite unmanned me. Strutting about on the other side of the world, leaving everything to them . . . I had no idea how attached I was.'

Stephen took his pulse, pulled down his eyelid, and said, 'It is very, very hard: but in the first place you are to consider that the dear west wind will waft us through the Strait, and then, which is not improbable, if you accompany the squadron, it will almost take us to the Cape. And there with the liberation of Chile behind you, you may bring Sophie down and any others you choose, to a delightful healthy country, new sights and admirable wine — Sophie dearly loves her glass, God bless her. And as a physician I do assure you, Jack, that we must sup extremely well, on thick beef-steaks, with a large amount of burgundy (I know where Chambertin is to be had), and then a soothing draught to take to bed.'

The next morning, having fondly visited both men-of-war — how very much at home he felt in either — having greeted all his old shipmates, and they reminding one another of cruel hard times — how the Doctor had declined a gravid seal's burden

— and having conferred with Poll and Maggie about their cheerful, well-bandaged patients, he rode away.

With the dusty town behind him he struck into the main Santiago road, almost deserted that day. Up and up on the fine-pacing mare, and quite soon he reached that stretch of fissured, apparently soilless shoulder of rock so remarkably studded with the small, extraordinarily spiny cactus locally called the lion's cub. It took them an hour and more to round this vast mass and reach the farther stretches where the winding road rose and fell through almost barren ground — barren, except for some botanical wonders; and, for so bare a countryside, remarkably well populated by birds of prey, ranging from a minute shrike to the inevitable condor. The rise took up at least nine tenths of the way, a steady, inevitable rise with every now and then a descent so steep that he dismounted and took the bridle. And all the way along this prodigious highway through the mountains, whether he rode or whether he walked, there before him, at various distances, sometimes diaphanous, occasionally sharply focused and clear, he saw not indeed Christine but various aspects of her: and the miles went by unnoticed, until the mare stopped at the usual resting-place and turned her mild gaze upon him, with a hint of reproof.

On the next stretch they passed through an invisible barrier into a thinner, cooler air, and there were his — not illusions: *perceptions* might be the better word — of Christine again, clearer and sharper now, particularly as she moved across a dark wall of rock. A tall, straight, lithe figure, walking easily and well: he remembered with the utmost clarity how, when she was reading or playing music or training her glass on a bird, or merely reflecting, she would be entirely apart, remote, self-contained; and then how she would be wholly with him when he moved or spoke. Two strikingly different beings; and the delight in her company, as he delighted even in the memory of it, seemed to him essential happiness, fulfilment. Of course he was a man, quite markedly so, and he would have liked to know her physically: but that was secondary, a very remote stirring compared with gazing at this phantasm — this now remarkably clear and sharply-defined phantasm against the rock-face.

He had gathered that she was respected

but not particularly liked in the colony, where her most uncommon beauty seemed to pass if not unnoticed then at least sometimes unadmired. In a crowded gathering he had heard a conventionally pretty woman say 'I can't think what they see in her', referring to the group of young and middle-aged men who rarely moved far from where she was standing.

In Stephen's long-considered opinion the most striking thing about her was the change from a perfectly well-bred woman, little given to personalities or colonial chit-chat, reserved but not at all woundingly so — the remarkable transition to warmth and sympathetic exchange with someone she liked. When this took place her whole physical attitude altered with it: at no time did she ever hold herself stiffly, but now there was a suppleness in her whole stance; and Stephen, who had watched her more closely than he had watched the rarest of birds, could tell by a minute change in her complexion whether she was going to like her companion or not. 'Besotted I may be,' he said aloud, 'but that spontaneous confidentiality . . .'

He did not finish even the thought, because at a corner immediately ahead appeared the leader of a mule-train, an aged animal with a hat on her head, accompanied by a man who in an enormous roaring voice that echoed in the chasm, desired Stephen and his mare to step aside into the appointed nook.

Isobel, the mare, knew exactly what to do, which was just as well, since Stephen was so deep in his own discourse, so intent on his wonderfully convincing (though distant) illusion, he had not noticed for the last quarter of a mile that they had been walking on the edge of a sheer, a truly appalling, precipice, the road having been cut across the face of a cliff.

'Go with God,' called the man at the head of the train as he passed, and those at the end blessed Stephen too — comforting in so very lonely and inhuman a spot. But when they were round the comer and plodding steadily upwards in the fading light through the now much narrower valley, his illusion (always a perfectly silent illusion), was no longer there. No searching, no effort of the imagination could call it up: what is more, the nature of the landscape had changed. One more sharp turn and directly before them there was the dip in the skyline that showed the high pass, and well below it, on a smooth, almost domestic slope, the lanterns of their inn.

A frosty morning, and they crossed the pass, coming to a much more populated road, somewhat tedious and commonplace: another inn, with even poorer food. Up and down: up and down: no illusions, alas; but towards the end of a weary day, Santiago. Isobel, rubbed down and filled with a fine warm mash, could go to sleep in her accustomed stable, her head drooping: and Stephen returned to his hotel, where he found Jacob in an unusual state of agitation. 'So you have come back,' he cried.

'I could not agree more,' said Stephen. 'Pray help me off with these boots.'

The boots off, with a final gasping heave, Jacob said, 'Unless these two new agents lie in their teeth — and I could swear they are independent, each ignorant of the other's enquiries — there is anxious news from both Lima and Callao. The viceroy has decided on invasion, to be preceded, with the full consent and approval of the naval staff, by an attack on Valparaiso.'

Stephen nodded, and Jacob went on, 'But this, above all the naval part, requires more stores than they possess, and the people concerned — the various boards — are running up and down buying rope, canvas, gunpowder and so on. Fortunately for us, many of those involved, the manufacturers of rope, canvas and gunpowder, have either, as you may well imagine, raised their prices or concealed their wares until the prices shall have reached to what they suppose their limit.'

'Can such things be?' asked Stephen. 'But in any case, before sending off post-haste to warn poor Captain Aubrey, I must be fed. I smelt the homely scent of an olla podrida as I came up the stairs. I have eaten my fill of fried guinea-pigs between here and Valparaiso and back again and I tell you most solemnly that I absolutely must be fed.'

'Well, if your god is your belly, I suppose you must worship it,' said Jacob; but he did touch the bell.

Within moments the fragrant olla, which stood perpetually simmering, perpetually renewed, on the rim of the kitchen hearth, reached the eager table.

Repletion came at last, and Stephen pushed back his chair: from an inner pocket he drew the pouch in which he kept his coca leaves, the lime and the necessary outer wrapping. He had no particular urge to chew coca at this moment, but he knew how a meal as substantial as that which he had just eaten dulled the mind. He desired that his wits should be as sharp as possible, and while he carefully dosed his proportions he said to his friend, 'Amos, when you used coca in considerable quantities, did you observe a difference in reaction according to altitude? I know that porters in the Peruvian Andes, when they have to carry a heavy burden over a very high pass, will increase the dose to a surprising degree. They seemed to take no harm and I supposed that physical energy, physical endurance and freedom from hunger was all they sought and all they derived. But have any other effects come to your attention?'

'Not in the north: no — apart from compulsive habituation, of course. But as you know there are many sorts of coca: down here they use the Tia Juana. And here, in the case of asthmatic patients or those afflicted with migraine there have been reports of hallucinations, their strength and frequency varying with the height — not with exertion, but with altitude.'

Stephen separated the ingredients of his little packet into their different compartments, and said, 'Thank you, dear colleague; but I do not like the notion of a vegetable providing my beatific vision: if it chooses to sharpen my intelligence, to

348

allow me to multiply seven by twelve, well and good: but the sacred emotions, no. Amos, we must go down to Valparaiso directly, though I quite dread seeing that road again.'

'If only you could overcome your prejudice against the mules, as I have said many times before, I could show you a quicker, easier road. True, there are a few very steep passages that only a goat or a mule could venture upon without dread, but you can always leap down after they have shown you the way.'

'Then let us call for excellent mules, with an equivalent number of muzzles, and a warranted muleteer.'

It so happened that Stephen was on a particularly kind and amenable mule whose good will he increased with a piece of bread at each halt; but even she grew excited and inclined to caper as they came down into Valparaiso. The place was filled with soldiers; and the cries and acclamations very soon made it evident that Bernardo O'Higgins, the Supreme Director, was in the town with his powerful escort of picked troops, many of whom had been at the decisive battle.

They led their mules and the muleteer to

their hotel by back ways, and there they met a profoundly discontented Killick, who snatched their baggage from the muleteer with a suspicious look and who told them that the damned place was crammed with bloody soldier-officers and he had only kept the Doctor's room by force, while the poor Captain had had to give up his drawing-room to an effing colonel, on the grounds that the effing colonel spoke English. Which *Surprise* was in the port, admired by all hands, and Captain Aubrey had taken General O'Higgins across the bay in *Ringle*, and if they survived they were all going to have dinner aboard *Surprise* tomorrow, gents.

The word *tomorrow* sent such a gust of impatience racing through Stephen's mind that he missed some of Killick's later information, but later the more phlegmatic, less-concerned Jacob passed it on: Lindsay was at sea, protecting republican trade from privateers; and about four hundred of the troops were going on to Concepción, which should make Valparaiso less whoreson crowded and noisy.

The people of the hotel were making up a bed in Stephen's little room and Killick was angrily trying to put clothes away in inadequate cupboards when the door opened: Stephen looked in, thought that anything would be better than this and retired. Almost at once he met an officer who stopped, bowed, and said, 'Dr. Maturin y Domanova, I presume? Allow me to present myself: Valdes. I used sometimes to come to Ullastret, to hunt the boar, and I believe we may call kin.'

'Why, you must be the Cousin Eduardo, of whose English my godfather was so proud, so rightly proud! I am delighted to see you.'

'And I to see you, Cousin Stephen.' They embraced, and Stephen suggested that they should go down into the patio and drink to their better acquaintance under the vine.

In the daylight Stephen saw that his new cousin was a colonel, and one who had obviously seen a good deal of service: a soldier, but a thoroughly civilised soldier, who was now speaking of Jack Aubrey in terms of the highest, almost enthusiastic praise. '. . . such a fine fellow: don Bernardo took to him at once, and at this moment they are tearing about the bay in a schooner . . .'

'Well done, cousin: it was long, long before I learnt to call it — to call her — a schooner.'

'Ha, ha,' said the colonel with evident satisfaction. 'But tell me, I beg, how does one say *Director supremo* in English?'

'There you have me,' said Stephen. 'Director-general smells of commerce, and Protector of that villain Cromwell. Perhaps Head of State?'

They exchanged alternatives, but neither was satisfied by the time Jack and the Supreme Director himself came in, a fine-looking man, obviously of Irish extraction, followed by several officers. He and Stephen were old friends, and the conversation carried on, still in English. After the first civilities — immense delight in *Ringle*'s sailing qualities on O'Higgins' part, compliments on the Chilean soldiers' past deeds and present civility on Stephen's — the conversation continued and Stephen said, 'Sir, I have just come down from Santiago, on a *mule,* on a mule, sir, on the quick but perilous road or rather path, through La Selva, because I had some information that I thought should be conveyed to *you* with the utmost rapidity.'

O'Higgins studied his face, looked round the patio, and said, 'Let us walk on the battlements. Please come with us, Captain Aubrey. And you too, Colonel: but first be so good as to place sentries to ensure the privacy of our conversation.'

From the high battlements they could see *Surprise* and the schooner looking quite beautiful, excellently lit by a declining sun: *Surprise* being tittivated to a truly remarkable extent, for the Supreme Director was to dine aboard her tomorrow.

They paced along four abreast, and Stephen told the essence of his news: the Peruvian viceroy's decision to invade, crossing the frontier with horse and foot once the Peruvian navy had destroyed the Chilean men-of-war in Valparaiso — the embarrassment of Lima and Callao where stores were concerned — the strong probability that they would seek them in Valdivia.

'Thank you very much indeed, Doctor,' said O'Higgins. 'This thoroughly confirms the less reliable, less precise intelligence that has reached me.'

'Sir,' said Jack Aubrey, 'may I suggest an immediate reconnaissance? The wind serves admirably and in all likelihood it will bring us back. I have rarely seen a more promising breeze.'

'Dr. Maturin,' said O'Higgins, 'did your informants speak of the Peruvian navy's state of preparedness?'

'Not directly, sir,' said Stephen, 'but by

implication, and by the already soaring prices, it is clear that their only heavy frigate, the *Esmeralda*, of I think fifty guns, is by no means ready to take the sea. As for the smaller craft, I gather that they are even more dilapidated.'

The Supreme Director considered, and said, 'If I know anything of those people in Lima they will be circulating minutes and memoranda from ministry to ministry for at least ten more days. We have the time. Dear Captain Aubrey, if I may I will come aboard you to dine, as you so kindly suggested: and while we are eating, let the ship move gently, almost imperceptibly, round the southern headland and then sail with all diligence for Valdivia, to come off the port rather before sunset, so that we may look into it with the light behind us. I shall bring what we have in the way of charts, drawings and plans.'

'Very good, sir,' said Jack, unable to conceal his satisfaction.

It was a curious dinner, much commented upon. As far as the ship's crew were concerned, it started naturally enough, before dinner, with the ship and all her people being brought to an even more unnatural state of cleanliness and, where possible, of polish. It was natural too that the great man's approach should be marked by a roaring of guns that did not leave a single bird on the water: and that the side should be dressed as he was piped aboard: but even at that early point there was something odd in his being brought out by the Captain's barge, together with a colonel, who made a proper soldier's job of coming aboard; and it was odder still when, well on into the cabin's dinner the order came to get the barge aboard and start untittivating the ship, stowing the beautifully ornamented man-ropes and getting everything back into sea-going order.

'I tell you what, Maggie,' said Poll Skeeping to her particular friend, 'I think there's something fishy going on.'

'The minute I saw Joe Edwards and his mates unpicking those man-ropes, with the gentlemen still at table, nowhere near their port even, I smelt a rat.'

To keep so very complex an entity as a man-of-war functional, all hands and most of the gear must be able to face a great number of widely differing events, circumstances, emergencies very quickly indeed; and in a man-of-war so highly worked up as the *Surprise*, with a crew of right amen, this could usually be done smoothly. But virtually all sea-borne emergencies have a certain pattern, a sequence, however disagreeable; and once that pattern is very grievously upset, confidence dwindles. The unpicking of those man-ropes did much more harm than the raising of the barge to its usual place on deck — in itself most unusual, reprehensible, but not downright insane, or even worse, unlucky.

As Jack's dinner carried on with its agreeable progress, the decanters making their steady round, most of the frigate's people spoke of their uneasiness, usually confiding in their tie-mates, the friends to whom they would entrust their pigtails for combing and replaiting, but sometimes to others, quite far removed even by watch, with whom they had a particular sympathy. These friendships were by no means uncommon, but few were as improbable or as wholly unequal as that which had sprung up between Horatio Hanson and Awkward Davies — awkward, not because of his uncouth motions but because of his truly awful rage if crossed. They were working together on a new log-line and a new sounding-line, placing the marks with the extreme accuracy required for exact navigation.

'Sir,' asked Davies, in a low and anxious tone, 'did you ever see a man-rope stowed, unpicked and stowed, when guests were still aboard?' They were certainly still aboard, their voices, eagerly discussing the politics of juntas, could be heard quite clearly where the new log-line lay.

'Oh, as for that,' said Horatio, 'Poll mentioned it when I went below for a flannel rag, and I told her to be easy — it was the Captain's orders.'

'Ah, the *Captain's* orders . . .' said Davies, and he sighed with relief.

Shortly after this the Captain's orders came on deck again in the form of a rather small, still immaculately neat midshipman called Wells, who smiled nervously at Hanson and said, 'The Captain sends me with orders for Mr. Somers. We are to weigh.'

'You will find him in the head,' said Hanson.

Very shortly the word came aft, and re-assurances with it. They were to prepare for weighing: they were to drift with the ebb and then spread the close-reefed fore-course until they were round the headland. The ship was filled with intense activity: but a calm and relatively placid activity. They knew where they were now — *Sur-*

357

prise was to steal away on the ebb, according to the Captain's long-considered plan — steal away with the lowering sun in the casual watcher's eye — and then, once round the headland, make sail and bear away on this fine easterly offshore breeze in whatever direction he desired, carrying the country's ruler and his mate. With great zeal but with even greater discretion they weighed the best bower and the kedge, taking great care that there should be no clashing as the anchor was catted and fished, yet finding time to watch *Ringle's* boat come across for Mr. Reade, who hooked himself rapidly down the frigate's side without the least ceremony, urged his men to a frenzy of activity and instantly set about getting the schooner into a similar state of discreet motion.

Night: and this being the dark of the moon, an actual instant brilliance of stars. But neither O'Higgins nor Cousin Eduardo was the least degree concerned with astronomy or navigation; and both, as hardened guerrilleros, knew the value of sleep. They smoked a cigar apiece on the quarterdeck, tossed the still glowing stubs into the spectacular wake and went straight to bed, leaving Jack Aubrey to show Daniel, Hanson and Shepherd (a midshipman whose intelligence was beginning to develop) the moons of Jupiter, not indeed as objects of beauty or curiosity, but as valuable elements in fine navigation.

The next morning, at a particularly cheerful breakfast, O'Higgins begged Jack to keep well out to sea when they were at the height of Concepción. 'My dear sir,' said Jack, 'that is not likely to be much before five in the afternoon.'

'Indeed? Yet I thought you had been driving along at a furious pace. But then I know very little of the sea.'

'Well, we did manage a little more than ten knots: we could have made more sail, but I understood that you wished us to come off Valdivia in the last hour or so of the sun.'

'So I did, of course: and no doubt you have portioned it out.'

'So I have. Nothing whatsoever is sure at sea, nothing at all. But the barometer is steady; the breeze has every appearance of remaining true; and if we do not see Valdivia before the sun has set, I will give ten guineas to any church or charity you choose to name.'

'Come, that is encouraging,' said O'Higgins with an eager smile, 'and I will do the same if you succeed.'

This very soon, and by the usual channel, became known throughout the ship: although there was scarcely a man aboard who had not left Gibraltar heavy with gold — several years' pay at the least — most had used their not inconsiderable ingenuity to get rid of it. True, some had made really important allocations home: but in any case the ship's company's old sense of values had revived, and when they heard that ten guineas, *ten guineas,* were at stake, they kept the barky at it with the same zeal that they showed when there was a chase in sight. The officers and reefers were also very busy, but there was scarcely one but Harding who was such a good seaman as the older hands, and no one who knew the barky better. All orders were anticipated, and when at about five o'clock in the afternoon Stephen and Jacob made their perfunctory rounds — two of the usual hernias that would yield only to rest, and a couple of obstinate poxes — and drank their habitual cup of tea with Poll and Maggie, they heard Captain Aubrey's very powerful voice telling the Supreme Director down there on the quarterdeck that the blur of smoke one point on the starboard quarter was Concepción.

'I am heartily glad of it,' replied

O'Higgins, directing his voice upwards with all the force he could manage. 'And I hope all my people have settled in comfortably.'

Jack Aubrey had always meant to take in topgallants and even topsails well before standing in for Valdivia, at about the time Cape Corcovado bore due east; but the favourable wind, the current, and above all the people's zeal showed him the Cape on the larboard bow long before it had any right to be there, long before the sun was low as he could wish. He shortened sail, and when everything was neat, quiet and properly coiled down he said to the Supreme Director, 'Sir, it occurs to me that you and Colonel Valdes might like to practise climbing into the top in preparation for our closer view of Valdivia a little later, when the sun is nearer the horizon?'

'I should be very happy,' said O'Higgins: and Colonel Valdes could hardly say less: but they concealed their happiness quite remarkably as they climbed up and up, with a wooden stoicism, until they reached the modest height of the maintop.

'We can go much farther up, you know,' said Captain Aubrey.

'Thank you, I can see perfectly well from here,' said O'Higgins, rather shortly: and

Colonel Valdes asked whether telescopes might be sent up. In the case of those unaccustomed to going aloft, there was the danger of an involuntary, purely muscular, trembling of the hands if one were required to go up and down repeatedly. He was perfectly ready to stay in the top until the true reconnaissance should begin: it could not be long now — he could already make out several familiar stretches of the shoreline, and the sun was no great way from the horizon.

Rather than distress them by remaining in the top, Jack vanished over the seaward side and returned to his cabin, where once again he studied what O'Higgins had brought in the way of charts, views and town-plans of Valdivia. The charts were of consequence only to the seamen, but those of the views that could be rolled up he tucked into his bosom and a fairly large panorama could be carried on deck by hand. There, he saw Daniel and Hanson taking the bearings of many a peak. Hanson, by this time, was one of the nimblest topmen in the ship and Jack said to him, 'Mr. Hanson, be so good as to sling this over your back and deliver it to the gentlemen in the top: if you take the windward shrouds I will take the leeward.'

At present O'Higgins and Valdes were a good deal easier in their minds, and since this was country they both knew quite well they pointed out many of the small villages and churches along the shore.

'It will not be long now,' said the Director looking eagerly southwards. Nor was it. One small cape: another, and there was the half-ring of fortifications guarding the port of Valdivia: the whole of it and the more distant town brilliantly lit by the lowering sun.

Jack called down a low order and a backed forecourse reduced the ship's way quite remarkably. The two Chileans searched port and town with their telescopes: a port empty but for some smacks and a trading brig; moderate activity on the far side of the fortification.

The Director-general and Colonel Valdes had seen a great deal of fighting, conventional and otherwise, and when Valdes named two hundred and fifty men as the force he thought adequate for taking the place, Jack believed him — though it seemed trifling for such an expanse of solid masonry and embrasures for so many guns on the massive dark walls.

'Sir,' said O'Higgins, turning towards him, 'may I ask your opinion? I dare say you have had more experience of attacking fortified ports than we.'

'Well, sir,' said Jack, 'the seaward approach is obviously quite different from the way soldiers might envisage the affair on land. I have been looking at that important fortress, the outermost part of the defensive chain, with some people walking about in front of it. It occurs to me that if its defenders are not uncommonly seasoned and courageous the place ought to be taken by a two-sided attack; and if that fort were taken, the two arcs of the semicircle would find it extremely difficult to cooperate, to mount a counter-attack. Look at the slope of the shore.'

They discussed this for some little while, the Chileans, who knew the quality of the troops in Valdivia, clearly coming round to Jack's view of the matter.

'Very well,' said O'Higgins, in his decisive way, 'I shall beg Captain Aubrey to carry us back to Concepción as quickly as possible — could the ship hold two hundred and fifty men?' he asked, turning to Jack.

'Not in any comfort, sir: but if this beautiful wind lasts, and I think it will, they will not have to suffer long. And there is always the *Ringle* to take a score or so. Furthermore, I may add that I can contribute at least a hundred thoroughly experienced able-seamen, accustomed to the naval side of the attack I have in mind.'

'That would indeed be a very welcome contribution, most gratefully accepted.'

'Very handsome, upon my word,' said Valdes.

'Now,' went on O'Higgins, 'if we can but get down on deck in safety, and if the ship can slip quietly away towards Concepción, I should be most obliged if you would give us your general notion of a combined plan of attack by sea and land.'

'Very good, sir: I think that for the actual descent, Colonel Valdes should take precedence.' And raising his voice to its usual pitch. 'Pass the word for my coxswain and Davies.' Then some seconds later. 'Lay aloft, lay aloft, there, and guide the gentleman's feet. Now, Colonel, this is the lubber's hole, and if you will lower yourself through it, powerful hands will guide your feet to the horizontal cords that act as steps.'

Valdes made no audible reply but he bowed and very cautiously let himself half-way down. 'Handsomely, now, handsomely,' called Jack and the look of extreme anxiety faded from the Colonel's face as competent hands seized his ankles and set his feet on the ratlines.

'Now, Excellency, it is your turn,' said Jack, 'and may I suggest that when you have rested and looked at the charts again, we should sup and then discuss the possibilities?'

'Very happy,' replied O'Higgins, with a face even graver, more concerned than the Colonel's.

However, they were both cheerful, seriously cheerful, when the supper table was cleared and they sat with charts and views spread out before them, and coffee at their sides with brandy for those that liked it.

'Now, sir,' said Jack, 'since you have asked me to begin, I shall start by saying that the gunner and I have overhauled his stores and that materially the scheme that I shall propose is feasible. In essence it is this: having embarked your men at Concepción — they will be men picked for courage, agility and freedom from seasickness — we, the schooner and the frigate, will return a little before dawn, landing all the soldiers and the seamen accustomed to mining, blowing up and destroying gun emplacements, at this point, Cala Alta. The boats will return to the ship, which will then make sail and proceed to a station off the fort, which she will most deliberately bombard from ranges suited to the accuracy of the defenders. But at no time will she fire on the great gate leading to the mole. During this bombardment the soldiers and seamen will advance along the path on the inland side, and I think the intensity and the noise of the bombardment will prevent the defenders — the comparatively unseasoned and inexperienced defenders, as Colonel Valdes tells me — from noticing their approach. But whether or no, the seamen's task is to fire rockets and stinkpots into all embrasures, filling the whole place with vile, unbreathable fumes and stench, and to mine all emplacements with guns in them. All this time the soldiers will keep up a steady fire, shrieking and bawling like fiends . . .'

'What is fiends?' whispered Valdes in Stephen's ear.

'Demonios.'

Then followed a whispered Spanish conversation in which Valdes described a pillar in a cathedral of his childhood which showed devils tormenting the damned in Hell, uttering shrieks as they did so.

When this was over, Stephen's closer attention returned to Jack Aubrey's discourse: '. . . and my reason for leaving the northern wall and its gate-house untouched is that I am convinced that the defenders, unless they are hardened grenadiers, will very quickly sicken of the bombardment and the sulphurous fumes and stench, and seek to escape by rushing out of the gate and running along the mole to the next strong-point or the one beyond if not to the town itself, or at least to the store-houses, and as they flee we can pepper them with the grape and then pursue . . .'

He paused: the Chileans looked at one another, and O'Higgins, sure of the reply, said, 'Colonel, may we hear your opinion?'

'Excellence,' said Valdes, 'it seems to me an eminently feasible operation.'

'I entirely agree. Dear Captain Aubrey, may I beg you to desire your people to sail the ship back to Concepción as rapidly as may be convenient?'

'By all means, sir. But as I believe you noticed, we altered the frigate's appearance — remarkable to any seaman — and to return to Concepción with any speed we must restore her mainmast. The one in the middle,' he added.

'Certainly: the central mast — can it indeed be changed at sea?'

'With a strong crew and a moderate sea, yes: but it takes time, and you might think it prudent to send your orders in to Concepción by the schooner. She will get there much sooner: and when we arrive, if all goes well, your men should be waiting on the quay.'

'They shall be written at once, in emphatic words suited to the meanest intelligence: and as I recall the men are to be picked for courage, agility and freedom from seasickness.'

'Exactly so, sir: and as soon as they are written, I shall entrust them to Mr. Reade, who commands the schooner, with orders to proceed to Concepción without the loss of a minute, there to embark the troops named in the margin, and to return with the utmost despatch. And as soon as he is under way, it may interest you to see a brutish, stumpmasted, unmemorable frigate transformed into something truly glorious by the towering mainmast of a thirty-six-gun ship! And then when all is a-tanto and belayed we shall set out with a press of sail for Concepción.'

Out and back again, still on this glorious and even strengthening west wind, a splendid piece of sailing — so splendid that it reconciled the sombre infantrymen crammed into the two vessels, so that at times they burst into song. They had a likeable, fairly intelligent set of officers to whom the largest plan of Valdivia had been shown, spread out in the gunroom, while the fairly simple plan of attack was explained again and again. Two of the officers knew Valdivia well and they pointed out the store-houses at the end of the mole, with the treasury behind them.

A little before dawn, with Mars rising astern, the galleys in both crafts were heated to something not far from incandescence and the cooks and their mates served out a royal breakfast to all hands, not a crock nor a pot nor a square wooden plate being left unfilled.

By now the mountains were filling a quarter of the sky; a few scattered lights could be seen ashore. *Surprise*'s and *Ringle*'s officers were very busy in getting their boats over the side, formed into two trains, ready to be manned. Jack, right forward with his night-glass, saw the Cala Alta clear, and the central fortification looming up behind it. He had already reduced sail: the ships' people were extraordinarily silent, almost the only sound coming from the breeze (much less inshore) whispering through the rigging and from the water running gently down the side.

With the Cala Alta close on the larboard bow Jack called 'Let go' and a kedge was lowered into the sea, bringing the ship up just abreast of the rock. The boats put off one by one: five dark lanterns in each: the seamen ran them beyond the tide mark: the silent lines formed up, glimmering light between each band: Harding, in charge of the detachment of heavily laden seamen, said, 'Give way,' and they stepped out, followed by the soldiers.

'Kedge,' called Jack. 'Hands to the braces.'

The frigate's yards came round, her sheeted sails took the wind, and she moved forward, faster, faster, and the main fortress came abreast of the larboard beam: lightless, blind, except for a single window. He glanced aft: no sign of the marching column yet. 'Mr. Beeton,' he called to the gunner. 'What do you make it?'

'A trifle above five hundred yards, sir.'

'Try a sighter, mid-high.'

'Aye-aye, sir: mid-high it is.' And the gunner's voice was cut off by the bellow of his gun and the shriek of the recoiling carriage. The wind swept the smoke forward and all eyes strained to see the impact.

Nothing could the most eager make out in the darkness, but almost at once the windows came to life, row after row of lamp-lit squares.

'Fire as they bear,' said Jack, still in little more than an undertone: and louder, 'A rolling fire, there.'

This was not a time for broadsides, nor yet for the regular fore to aft of target practice: 'I do not wish to strain the ship's timbers,' he said in a much louder voice to the Chileans behind him. And louder still. ' 'Vast firing — Mr. Wells,' — to his attendant midshipman — 'tell the officers commanding the guns that I am going to move up a hundred yards or so.' By this time the fort was replying with a crackle of musketry and the odd bullet passed overhead.

'Mr. Daniel,' he called, 'move her up, if you please, until we can see the gate-house and the mole.' Then to the guncrews, 'Fire at will.'

Now there were as many as three great flashes, hungry darts of flame, at once, lighting the wall; and it was clear that the fire was having its effect — two windows beaten into one, fallen masonry, a small blaze inside a room, the whole outer wall pock-marked. The lit windows began to move aft, the guns still firing briskly: but they had not gone beyond *Surprise*'s mizzen mast before a violent explosion shook the back of the fortress, followed by musket-fire and then three more explosions, even deeper.

The gate-house came in sight, well in sight, and now the *Surprise*, swinging slightly to larboard, could send a cross-fire into the shattered centre. This she did, while on the far side the mining and the musketry increased until the noise reverberating from the mountains behind the town was perfectly shocking.

'One would say a heavy artillery battle,' said Colonel Valdes.

'Mr. Wells,' called Jack, 'run and tell them not to touch that God-damned gate-house.'

Now the musketry from the fort diminished: and the mining increased.

'It is unbelievable that they should have carried all that powder,' observed Stephen.

'Any minute now,' said Jack. 'Mr. Daniel, lay me for the mole, just abaft those two smacks, the instant that door opens, and stand by to make her fast. Mr. Somers — Mr. Somers there: let the armourer and his mates serve out cutlasses, pistols, boarding axes . . .'

A great roar all along the deck drowned

his last words. The gate-house doors burst open and a dense crowd of men rushed out, trampling one another and racing along the mole.

'Reload with grape,' called Jack, and they had half a dozen rounds before the ship ground against the dolphin of the mole.

'Starboard watch make fast fore and aft. Larboard, charge.'

By this time the soldiers behind the fort had seen the flying garrison on the mole and they joined the pursuers. The seamen flung down their heavy crowbars and sledge-hammers and caught up with wonderful speed. 'Surely,' gasped Stephen, as he ran, 'it is very strange that the zeal of the pursuers should be greater than that of the prey?'

Strange or not, it was true: the fugitives had no sooner reached the next fort than those who were not killed had to run again, often being caught and knocked down. And so it went, fort after fort, until the miserable remnant ran clean away up into the town, leaving the entire port and all its naval equipment to the victors' discretion.

In this case the victors showed no discretion whatsoever. Some of the Chilean soldiers knew the port well, having worked there, and they showed their allies a perfectly extraordinary treasure of rope, sail-cloth, blocks, firearms great and small, timber, powder, ammunition, medicine-chests, and, what pleased them even more, the treasury. It had armoured doors, of course: but the seamen, running — running — back for some of their heavier tools, made short work of armoured doors, or the pillars that supported them.

Inside there were four large chests of silver and a moderate chest of gold: curiously enough they were only closed with a hasp, and on seeing their contents a soldier who had been in the *Surprise* said they had all risked their lives to gain this wealth and that in his opinion it should be shared out equally at once: now, now, equally and at once. His opinion was supported by several men there, but O'Higgins said, 'A fig for your opinion,' and shot him dead.

With so much death in the forts, all along the mole and in the lesser fortifications this made no great impression; but it did restore order, and Captain Aubrey suggested to the Supreme Director that the right and natural place for all these things was Valparaiso, to be conveyed in the *Surprise* as far as the chests were concerned, while the huge accumulation of marine stores lying outside the magazines, lofts and victualling buildings should travel in the two large smacks lying just beyond the frigate outside the mole.

Once the treasure-chests had been moved across the yard on rollers (cut from new topmasts) to the *Surprise* and taken aboard by those ingenious cranes improvised by seamen, zeal began to flag. People (particularly soldiers) looked at the massive cables with distaste and showed a disposition to creep away. Stephen, however, asked Jack to have the head of a barrel containing Chilean aguardiente taken off for Dr. Jacob, and he called upon all hands, in both necessary languages, to form in lines and to advance in turn. This they did; and each man passing Jacob was given a cup from the barrel; then moving on to Stephen he received a very considerable dose of prime coca, with its usual accompaniments.

Within a remarkably short space of time (so long as time in the ordinary sense still existed in their circumstances and their very recent, very violent past) the atmosphere changed entirely: strength returned, and good humour with it. The daunting heaps lessened, dwindled, vanished entirely into the smacks, amicably chartered with the help of the golden chest;

and the cobbles lay bare under the indifferent moon.

'Cousin,' said Colonel Valdes, embracing him, and they standing alone in the five-acre yard, 'that was a glorious victory: a most glorious victory.'

Interchapter

'My dear Christine, if you will allow so free an expression,' wrote Stephen Maturin, 'we won a famous victory in Valdivia not long since, when Captain Aubrey and his seamen, with General O'Higgins and his soldiers, having destroyed the main fortress, drove the royalists out of Valdivia, secured their immense stock of naval stores and their treasure, returning in triumph to Valparaiso, to rejoicing, cheering crowds, to fireworks and music, three separate bull-fights, and of course to dancing. None of our people was killed; their few wounds are healing well; and all hands are delightfully elated, at least in part because of their coming wealth when the prize-money from the captured treasure is shared out. I too was elated with them — happiness is charmingly contagious — and I celebrated the occasion by indulging myself in an emerald. As you may know, my valued friend and colleague Amos Jacob is descended from a family of merchants dealing in precious stones: he understands and loves them, and like many of his calling he has acquaintances or connexions in Golconda and other places where gems are found, including Muso in the Andes, no very great way from here, so justly renowned for its emeralds. I therefore desired him to procure me a specimen: and here it is.' He turned the oblong stone in his hand: a splendid wealth of green, but finest of all from its perfect face. 'I shall wrap it in jewellers' cotton wool, enclose it in a packet for Sir Joseph that must leave this evening and beg you to accept it as a small token of my esteem — a trifling return for *Ardea goliath*.'

Here he paused, shook his head, and walked up and down the room, glancing at his watch. Up and down: it was most unlike Jack Aubrey to be late, and although the Indian runner did not mean to set out much before dawn, he was uneasy.

He sat down again, returning to his letter. 'But now, my dear, I grieve to say that our joy has diminished to something not very far from grief. The triumph at Valdivia, after the first explosion of popular joy, gave way to a singular but ever-increasing jealousy and resentment. It was the victory of what is seen as the English and of O'Higgins, the one the hereditary enemy of Spaniards (and republicans or royalists the mass of Chileans are essentially Spanish) either as buccaneers or raiders like Drake and national enemies in times of war, and the other disliked, even hated, by many of the leading men in the various juntas for curbing their pretensions, for his love of law and order, and for his opposition to a dominant Church. To some degree this growing resentment unites the juntas, but just to what extent I do not know because Jacob is away, gathering information: yet it is a fact that the treasure we captured has not been shared out, the seamen have not been paid, and that for some days past I for one have met with open rudeness in the streets of Valparaiso. O'Higgins, his personal friends and guard have retired to Santiago or perhaps beyond: and we have no news. What is more, and perhaps worse, is that Sir David Lindsay, resenting an incivility, has been challenged by one of his own officers: they are now on the ground.'

'I am losing my wits entirely,' he murmured to himself, drawing a careful line round those parts of his letter that were suitable only for Sir Joseph, and in encoded form: the line was not finished before he heard a step, a knock, and he called out, 'Come in.'

It was Hanson. 'Oh sir,' he cried, much upset. 'He was hit. The Captain sent me: the surgeon said there was no hope.'

There was indeed no hope. 'Aorta,' said the Chilean medical man, motioning towards the great dark pool under Lindsay's body.

'No hope?' asked Jack, and when Stephen shook his head, 'Mr. Hanson, double up to the ship again and tell Mr. Harding that I should like four stout hands and a stretcher to carry Sir David's body down: and a sheet to cover him.' To Stephen. 'We shall bury him Navy-fashion, the way he is used to.'

This caused a movement of uneasiness among Lindsay's remaining Chilean friends — his opponent and the seconds apart from Jack had disappeared — and one of them said to Stephen, 'The Prefect of the port will have to view the body, and approve the burial.'

'It is the *custom*,' said Stephen with grave emphasis. 'The ancient naval *custom*.' The word had such force for the Spaniards that their murmuring ceased: they stayed until the stretcher came up from the port and then when Lindsay was laid on it and covered, the military men and sailors saluted as he was carried away, while the few civilians took off their hats: though one, standing next to Stephen, murmured that this would no doubt offend the prefect extremely.

Jack told Harding to slip his moorings and to take the ship to twenty fathom water outside the mole. There, when he had taken everything that should go to Lindsay's family, he called for the sailmaker and two round shot and when Lindsay was shrouded Navy-fashion, Jack buried him before the assembled crew with the full ceremony and honours due to his former rank, saying the ritual words as he went over the side.

Then the *Surprise*, doing away with the formal signs of mourning, returned to the harbour, returned to her former place. 'In almost any breeze this allows me to get out to sea,' he said privately to Stephen, 'I have already seen enough to make me uneasy, and I have no doubt you have seen much more.'

'Yes,' said Stephen, 'and I am only waiting for Jacob to come back with fuller information about the southern juntas to know whether I should officially advise you to withdraw from the political enterprise entirely and devote yourself to pure hydrography or not. The Chonos Archipelago is virtually unknown.' And who knows what unknown wonders its flora and fauna may reveal, he added inwardly.

They were in the cabin, drinking tea, and after a long silence Jack said, 'Stephen, what I am going to say will probably sound sentimental to you, but several of those young fellows I have been training show every sign of becoming first-rate seamen, and for this reason among a host of others, I have been turning a plan over and over in my head. As you know, it was only the treasure of Valdivia that like a fool I handed over to the authorities: the naval stores we turned to our own uses, as far as our needs went, and the barky is now almost entirely new-rigged, stuffed with powder and shot, worn cables replaced, sailcloth to clothe a ship of the line, prime victuals overflowing. So my plan is to attack Callao and to cut out *Esmeralda*. I put it to Lindsay but he said it was impossible: the fortresses would sink us before ever we came to grips. And coming to grips with a massively built 50-gun frigate was no task for 28-gun *Surprise*, even supported by the *Asp*. He was fundamentally opposed to the plan — called it foolhardy, which surprised me, knowing how many times he had been out. But I shall say no more about him, poor soul.'

'God rest him.'

'No more . . . So that, Stephen, is what I mean to do. Do you like my plan?'

'My dear, I am tolerably good at carrying out a suprapubic cystotomy. You are an expert in maritime warfare. Your opinion in the first case would not be worth a straw: nor would mine in the second. If you are content, I am content.'

Nevertheless Captain Aubrey went on arguing his case. 'It was true that Peru was a neutral state, a Spanish colony: but Peru had repeatedly invaded the independent republic of Chile, and if the Spanish viceroy succeeded next time, the infant Chilean navy (so promising and zealous) would be wiped out. There was everything to be said for . . .'

'Beg pardon, sir,' said a midshipman, 'but with Mr. Somers' duty the Lisbon packet is rounding the cape with someone very like Dr. Jacob waving a red handkerchief in the bows.'

'Thank you, Mr. Glover: pray tell him that I should like a signal thrown out inviting her to come alongside.'

Jack went on prosing away about the advantages of surprise, almost certainly superior gunnery and attention to duty until at last they heard the gentle glancing impact of the packet against the fender, the usual shrieks and cries of those throwing and catching ropes, and Jacob appeared. 'By God, sir,' he cried, addressing Jack, 'now the fat is in the fire! The burying of poor Sir David — God rest his soul — before an official enquiry was perfectly illegal and has given the prefect just the excuse he wanted: the ship will be impounded at nightfall — it is known as far down as Villanueva, where the local junta has handed out arms.'

'Has the order to seize the ship been given?'

'I believe so.'

Jack rang the bell, said, 'Pass the word for Mr. Harding,' and to the lieutenant he said, 'Mr. Harding, there will be no shore-leave whatsoever this evening; and if any boats approach, they are to be denied admission. And I am going aboard the packet.'

'But sir,' cried Jacob, 'I have been too hasty — first I should have said that Colonel Valdes is marching his troops back from Concepción and messengers have already been sent to the Supreme Director.'

'Even so,' said Jack, 'I shall carry on with

my plan.' He left them there, went on deck and dropped down into the packet. 'Gentlemen,' he said to the company of Fellows, 'may I beg for five minutes of your time?'

They all murmured agreement, and Austin Dobson invited him below. 'Am I right in supposing that you are now heading for Panama?'

'We are indeed,' said Dobson. 'Sclater and Bewick' — nodding towards the two ornithologists — 'are eager to cross the isthmus quite soon, there being the possibility of no fewer than three ships leaving for England in the third week of the month, and they would like a few days with the terns on the Pacific side.'

'In that case, dear colleagues,' said Jack, 'you can, if you choose, do me and Maturin an essential service. You are all acquainted, I believe, with the very delicate state of this country and the likelihood of O'Higgins being overthrown and the consequent anarchy and an, inevitable Peruvian invasion?' They nodded; and an entomologist murmured, 'Those vile juntas.'

'At the moment it is nip and tuck: or touch and go. But I mean to sail for Callao tonight with the intention of cutting out the Peruvians' fifty-gun frigate *Esmeralda*, of carrying her back to Valparaiso and of manning her with picked men from the Chilean navy trained by poor Lindsay and myself. That should put the balance of power more strongly on the republican side, even before the return of O'Higgins and the troops from Concepción.'

'Certainly,' said an astronomer, 'but, my dear sir and colleague, we are men of science, not of war.'

'Just so,' said Captain Aubrey, 'but as scientists you are accurate observers: you will very soon make out whether the battle is won or lost; and the first of my two requests is that you will send the result, either way, to the Admiralty with the utmost dispatch. And as scientists you will understand the importance of my second: our brother, Stephen Maturin, has left all his collections at our inn in Valparaiso. I, and this ship, have incurred the enmity of the local authorities: I dare not let him go ashore. You under the aegis of the Royal Society may do so without fear: you may sup agreeably at the Antigua Sevilla, gather his belongings, and so join *Surprise* and her tender, the schooner *Ringle*, just a mile off the harbour at midnight.'

Chapter Ten

It was a strikingly beautiful morning in November: but a November morning some twelve degrees south of the equator has few associations with Guy Fawkes or bonfires. The dear topgallant breeze had chased away any hint of mist the night might have left and this was a light-filled day with a deep blue sky from horizon to horizon — a transparent air that allowed small details to be seen a great way off, and although when the sun reached his zenith — the exact height to be measured by every soul aboard who could command a sextant, quadrant or backstaff — his warmth might be troublesome, but euphroes were already at hand for the awnings that would moderate his zeal, and while the bosun and his mates were laying out the intricacies of their lines, fore and aft, Jack Aubrey stood leaning on the elegant taffrail of the *Surprise*, gazing somewhat eastward of her wash at the boat pulling towards her from the vessel registered as *Isaac Newton* but universally called the Lisbon packet, that having been her vocation before her owner (as unlucky in cards as he was in love) sold her to a penurious entomologist who, having inherited a prodigious fortune, indulged himself and his colleagues of the Royal Society in an equally prodigious voyage. One of the friends sailing with him, the foremost European authority on voles, was also in holy orders: and this being Sunday he was coming aboard the frigate to officiate and perhaps to read a sermon.

'He will not be disappointed,' observed her captain, having glanced forward and aloft at the snowy canvas, in charming contrast with her yards, gleaming with Mr. Harding's blacking — though to be sure the sails were somewhat given to flapping now that *Surprise* had started her sheets to allow the boat to catch up. But the person to whom the remark was addressed gave no more than a brutish grunt, clapped his telescope to, and said, 'He is only an aberrant frigate-bird. Those curious marks were certainly the excrement of some companion.'

Jack was on the edge of a witty reply, but before he could both formulate and utter it the boat was alongside: the guest had to be received with due ceremony and led below to drink a glass of sherry and to put on the rolled-up surplice that was handed up after him. Yet since the Reverend Mr. Hare had by now been afloat for so many thousand miles it was reasonable to suppose that he might like to have some of the new-rigged *Surprise*'s perfections pointed out: but Jack might as well have addressed his words to a vole, for Hare was as insensible to the blacking as he was to the unusual cut of the flying jib. In fact he quite dreaded reading his sermon, and once below he gulped down his sherry and looked wistfully at the decanter.

However, when he came on deck again into the presence of the scrubbed, new-shaven, neatly-clad ship's company with their officers sweating in formal broadcloth under the torrid sun, the familiar cry of 'Jews and Roman Catholics fall out' comforted him and he walked with an assured, seaman-like step to the small-arms chest that served as a lectern. The Jews and Roman Catholics did not in fact fall out any more than the various kinds of Muslim, the Orthodox Christians, or the plain wicked heathens. The congregation looked grave, and even blank; but they grew more cheerful when Mr. Hare (an aspiring author) began his hesitant reading of a neighbour's sermon based upon a text from Job: 'Oh that my words were now written, oh that they were printed in a book'. Then came some familiar hymns, in which Poll Skeeping and Maggie Tyler, who knew the words, distinguished themselves, and a psalm, which Awkward Davies sang in a strikingly true basso profundo.

Mr. Hare dined in the cabin with the Captain, of course, the first lieutenant and the surgeon, dined remarkably well, Valparaiso's victuals and livestock still being plentiful, and the chief supplier having thrown in a score of prime guinea-pigs by way of, compliment, while the exceptionally good Chilean wine positively encouraged excess. Not that Parson Hare needed any encouragement in his heartfelt relief at having delivered his sermon without a single blunder: indeed, it could not truthfully be said that the wine was his undoing — the blame for that, if one is to censure unsteady gait and a certain garrulity, must be ascribed to the United States' rum, some bottles of which had survived the wicked cold and the even more wicked seas off the Horn. Jack Aubrey was not much given to censure, apart from instances of poor seamanship, being too conscious of his own faults in that direction (more than once he had been obliged to be wheeled aboard in a barrow), but when it was time for leave-taking he said that he and Stephen would see their guest home, not only to greet their fellow-members of the Royal Society but also to view the packet, and to ask her master about her behaviour under various combinations of sail in given winds.

It was too reasonable to be refused, and when the *Surprise* was heaved to so that the *Isaac Newton* could come closer, all three went on deck. The frigate's hands had been particularly gratified by the presence, the temporary presence, of an undoubtedly certificated parson, an admirable preacher, and as he took his seat in the bosun's chair, a kindly device that would raise him from the deck, swing him out over the side and so lower him into the boat without any exertion or ability on his own part, a disorganised cheer arose, gaining in unity and volume as the barge pulled over to the packet, where Hare's shipmates, aware of his weakness, had already rigged another chair to bring him aboard.

'What an obliging fellow your master is,' said Jack, coming back into Dobson's cabin after his inspection of *Isaac Newton*.

'He answered all my questions like a right seaman — he has in fact sailed with several friends of mine, renowned as taut captains — and he told me many interesting things about Magellan's Strait, too. What is more he said that you had spoken a barquentine which had touched at Callao, where there were two other fair-sized merchantmen, one from Boston, the other belonging to Liverpool, as well as the *Esmeralda*, moored over on the man-of-war's side. Now that brings me to the favour I have to ask of you.'

'I should be very glad to hear it,' said Dobson, looking at him earnestly.

'It is my intention to stand into Callao, wind and weather permitting, fairly late in the evening of tomorrow or the next, and then endeavour to cut her out. We shall enter not disguised but with a peaceable, mercantile appearance, carry her by boarding in the dark and if possible carry her out. I shall take all the hands *Ringle* can spare, but leave her enough to bring the outcome to you, lying off the port: she will also bring out a written account, a dispatch, and you would oblige me extremely by confiding it to your friends bound for England, begging them to deliver it to the Admiralty.'

'I shall certainly do that, and I am sure I can answer for my friends. Crossing the isthmus to the Atlantic coast in only a moderate day's ride, and I know they can expect no less than three ships ready to sail to the Pool of London.'

'God give them a good wind, and us a happy dispatch.'

'Amen, amen, amen.'

'For if it is even moderately happy, I should very much like my superiors to have it before they have completed the new South African squadron.'

Most ships have a Killick or two aboard, but naval history records none with a more intense, persistent curiosity and want of scruple in employing his talents — so long as he was the only soul in the ship's company to know what the authorities, above all his captain, meant to do, the means were of no consequence; and they ranged, of course, from listening behind doors to the reading, lips in motion, of obviously extremely private letters. But this time he was disappointed; and if he had so low and false an opinion of his lower-deck shipmates, a seasoned band of fighting seamen, as to suppose them ignorant of the destination of the iron balls they had spent hours upon, chipping the iron off them and restoring their perfectly spherical appearance and thus their power to fly straight, then he deserved to be.

On Wednesday evening, the *Surprise*, looking as much like a merchantman as she decently could without culpable falsity, sailed into Callao with little abroad but her topsails and a jib, leaving *Isaac Newton* hull-down in the west and *Ringle* about a mile off the coast, there to wait for a signal, though most of her able hands had already been drafted to help serve the frigate's guns.

With no appearance of haste, therefore, they glided in just before the top of the tide, her very young master steering her into battle according to naval custom.

'Lay me for her larboard broadside, Mr. Hanson,' said Jack. 'And then bring her up when we are beam to beam.'

Already the *Surprise*'s larboard watch were preparing the boats for launching: they were equipped with cutlasses, pistols and sometimes, as in Davies' case, with a terrible boarding-axe. Gently the frigate began her left-hand turn. The captains of the starboard guns kept them on their target with iron levers until Jack, taking the distance and the angle to be just so, gave the order 'From forward aft, fire as they bear'. And to Hanson, 'Back the fore and main topsails.'

After the first three unanswered, murderous broadsides they hammered one another with shocking speed and ferocity, the *Esmeralda* replying very nearly shot for shot at first. But then, before the way was off her, Jack gave the order to fill the sails and put the helm hard over, bringing the fresh gun-crews into the most violent action. The Peruvians' rate of fire diminished, as well it might with four of her twelve-pounders dismounted.

For nearly two minutes she was silent, for a shocking accident in the magazine meant that the guns could not be reloaded. Almost at the beginning of this ghastly pause Jack cried 'Boarders away', and leapt down into his barge. The larboard boats came round and up the Peruvian's side as Jack's band made their way on to her deck, Awkward Davies uttering his horrifying roar.

The Peruvians were now attacked before and behind, and although they rallied again and again they were not used to this kind of battle, whereas the Surprises were: and use makes master. Gradually the most part of the Esmeraldas were forced to escape below. But now the light was fading fast and now the inexplicably silent artillery in the fortress guarding the naval port opened fire, each heavy gun shooting out a great tongue of flame.

Jack's uniform had necessarily caught the Peruvian officers' attention and for some time — as far as time can be reckoned in such encounters — he had been extremely busy. Yet even so his eye, the practised eye of a predator, had caught the hoists of coloured lights rising to the mastheads of the two merchantmen in the harbour — position lights, obviously agreed upon beforehand.

He backed out of the fray and roared for his coxswain. 'Take any of the bargemen and any boat and pull like fury back to the ship. Tell Mr. Whewell from me to hoist coloured lights instantly and move the ship about. Cut along.' He raced back into the dense mob fighting two and three deep, fighting all round the main hatchway and a pistol bullet struck him in the left shoulder at very close range, knocking him flat, while a dark-faced man with a fixed devilish grin passed a sword clean through his thigh.

The next moment Dark Face was utterly destroyed by a blow from Awkward Davies, an appalling blow: young Hanson, unhurt so far, stood over Jack until he could pluck out the sword and the two dragged him back to the Peruvian's shattered side. There, although for the moment he was unable to move he saw with satisfaction that the gunners up there were now confused, firing at everything. He also saw with great relief but no very great surprise that the only Peruvians who had not gone below were now surrendering. He called to a group of Ringles he knew well and told them to stand by to unmoor. They stared at him with the wild, half-mad look of men who were or who just had been fighting to the death; and he hailed one of them. 'Mr. Lewis, get these men to stand by to unmoor. And if you can lend me a cravat or a large handkerchief to tie up my leg I should be obliged.'

But now some of the forward gunners there, gathering his intention, redoubled their fire. Fortunately it was not very accurate, and some were still concentrating on the Boston and Liverpool ships. Even so, if the *Esmeralda* were to be cut out at all, it would have to be done quickly. Helped by a seaman called Simon he got to his feet and staggered to the starboard bow and the mooring: the frigate was very strangely made fast to the mole by a cable, a remarkably stout cable. He bawled 'All hands to loose topsails', fell forward and saw young Hanson, with an absurdly curved but obviously very sharp scimitar cutting away at the enormous rope while Davies levered it taut with a gunner's handspike. Hack, hack, a deep breath and a third blow with all his strength. The cable parted, and the ship, feeling the growing force of the ebb, swung free and moved a little way from the mole.

Joy and even a certain strength flooded into Jack's being. 'Hands loose topsails,' he cried. 'All hands there.' Then hoarsely, 'Thank you, Horatio: you are a very good fellow. Now take her out, will you?'

Take her out he did, the ship being hit once or twice but not seriously: out beyond the sheltering mole and into the darkness; and Jack felt a charming ease rise through the pain of his wounds, a pain that did not die away until he lost consciousness as they handed him down into his own sick-bay.

He was aroused not by the piping of All Hands just before eight bells in the middle watch, nor by the bosun's mates bawling 'Starboard watch ahoy! Rise and shine: rouse out there! Starboard watch oh!', nor by the dread sound of eight bells, nor yet by the noises of cleaning the decks with water, sand, and holystones, then swabbing them dry. What woke him from an unimagined depth of sleep was Stephen's whispered explanation of the mangled state of his shoulder: 'The bullet struck the buckle of his sword-belt, do you see, flattening both metal and leather entirely, but leaving the bone intact.'

'I see the crown deeply imprinted in his flesh. Yes, indeed. Surely he is beyond all reason fortunate, when you consider that his thigh was also transpierced without a single important artery being severed,' replied Jacob.

'Gentlemen, a very good morning to you,' said Jack out of the immense happiness that was welling in his full consciousness. 'Is *Esmeralda* under our lee? Have we made a decent offing?'

Somewhat taken aback, they said that she was; and that the shore could not be seen.

'Give you joy,' said Jack. He vented his own, a bubbling exaltation, in a croak of laughter, and said, 'Pray give me something to drink: I am horribly dry.' Stephen held a jug to his lips and he drank like a thirsty horse.

They looked at him with a certain disapproval, and both felt his pulse. 'It is scarcely reasonable,' said Jacob, aside. 'But then he always was a full-blooded man.' And much louder, 'Give you joy of your victory, sir: give you joy.'

'God bless you, my dear,' said Stephen, gently shaking his hand. 'It was a noble feat. But tell me, Jack, do you feel much pain?'

'Not lying on my back: not to stop me sleeping — Lord, how I slept! Now I am aware of my shoulder, and the bandage on my leg is a trifle tight. But God help us, after such a thrust it ain't surprising. Tell me, could I be fed? Just a little thin gruel, if you like, but something to set me in train: I have a most important letter to write.'

'Fed?' they cried automatically; but then Stephen, who had known Jack's iron constitution for many years, said, 'Thin gruel will not set you a-going. An egg, beaten up with milk, should make a splendid dispatch.'

'Lord, how well that went down,' said Jack some minutes later. 'Killick, pass the word for Mr. Harding.'

'Which he is aboard the *prize*, sir,' said Killick, exulting. 'But we will hail her.'

'Of course you will. Stephen, pray heave me up. I cannot dictate an official letter lying flat on my back. You have already washed my face, I find. Thank you. Killick, there: pass the word for Mr. Adams.' And when his clerk came in, 'Mr. Adams, a good morning to you. I am about to write an official letter, so let us have excellent paper, excellent pens, and right black ink — Mr. Harding, there you are.'

'I will take my leave,' said Jacob. 'Once again, sir, many, many congratulations.'

'Thank you very much — Stephen, pray do not stir. Mr. Harding, a very good morning to you. How does *Esmeralda* swim?'

'Like a swan, sir: very easy indeed.'

'Not much damage?'

'Well, her larboard upper works are tolerably battered, her mizzen shot half through just under the top and I have had to strike three guns down into the hold: and I am afraid the fore part of her magazine is a wreck. But she is dry — no damage beneath the water-line — and with single-reefed courses and topsails she goes along very well.'

'I am very happy to hear it. Now I have to write the official letter, so please let me have the butcher's bill for both sides and the usual details. You are happy to sail her to Valparaiso, I take it?'

'Oh Lord, yes: and all the way home, with some moderate patching, if you choose. But I am afraid their losses, with that dam — that horrible explosion in the magazine, were very heavy. Yet the officers are a decent lot: most of them wounded, and very grateful to Dr. Jacob for his care. And the hands are much the same now: their bosun and the carpenter's mate — the carpenter himself was killed — have done what can be done to her mizzen until she can go alongside a sheer-hulk. Our losses were fairly light; but there were some good seamen who will be sadly missed. I thought you would need it, sir, so I have scribbled an exact list on our side, and just approximate numbers on theirs: though I did put their captain's name.'

'Thank you very much, Mr. Harding. I shall get my letter off as soon as I can, to Panama with the packet and so straight to London. Is there anyone you would particularly wish to be mentioned?'

'Well, sir, there was Linklatter, carpenter's crew, who made us fast to her bows at the cost of his arm; and of course there was Mr. Hanson who stood over you when you were pistolled by the main hatchway and who gave some shrewd blows: but I daresay you remember that.'

'Indeed I do, though I was half-stunned for a moment. And I shall certainly remember Linklatter. Thank you, Mr. Harding. By the way, where is *Ringle* lying?'

'About half a mile on our larboard quarter, sir.'

'And the packet?'

'Perhaps another half mile beyond her.'

'I could not ask better.' And when Harding was gone, 'Stephen, I should not like to lose a moment having this letter fair-copied, so I shall say it slowly, deliberately; and if you hear anything that is low or bad grammar or just plain wrong, pray hold up your hand and we will mend it before Adams has time to write it down.'

'Brother,' said Stephen after a moment's hesitation, 'you have reflected upon the peculiar difficulties of this letter, sure?'

'Oh, this is not the first I have wrote, you know: dear me, with guardian angels hovering about me like a pack of rooks I have been blessed with occasion to write a dozen at least, some of them printed in the *Register*. They are difficult, of course, and there are certain forms you have to learn: I generally begin with a usual and quite proper opening: *Sir* (or *My Lord,* as the case may be), *it is with the greatest satisfaction that I have the honour to acquaint you, for the information of the Lords Commissioners of the Admiralty, that* . . . and so on, always taking care to get your position, your latitude and longitude, just so.'

A pause, and Stephen said, 'My dear, you are forgetting that this is not an ordinary matter for the Board. You, in command of *Surprise, formerly* a vessel belonging to the Royal Navy, brought her here on a hydrographical expedition with the added, but I think not expressed, condition that you should help the independent and republican Chileans to form a navy. It is true that some one of the many juntas appointed Lindsay, but since his death I think it can be assumed that you command what naval force there is to be commanded: and it is surely to the rulers of this country that your letter should be addressed — to don Bernardo O'Higgins, the Director Supremo, or his successor. After all, as I understand it, you mean to take the *Esmeralda* back to Valparaiso: and the possession of that very considerable man-of-war, together with what the Chileans already possess, absolutely guarantees the independence of their country. Everything depended on naval superiority: and now it is ours.' With infinite concern he had been seeing Jack age before his eyes: it was not that he grew pale — he could not have been much paler — but all the living joy had drained out of his face; and now it was that of the Jack Aubrey of seventy or even more. 'Never grieve, brother,' Stephen went on. 'The essence of the matter is unchanged: only the appearance has seemed to alter. All this has been entirely in line with the Ministry's intentions: but they cannot yet be publicly expressed, far less avowed in print. Believe me, Jack, the Admiralty will be as pleased with this victory as if it had been won over an acknowledged enemy; and I do not doubt that they will take as much notice of your recommendations, while I am very sure that the Supreme Director, on hearing the more than happy outcome will absolutely assert that you did not exceed local orders given in a great emergency — Peru was actively preparing to invade the country. Dear Jack, I *know* about these things. Let me write a private letter to Sir Joseph, send it over by our brethren in the packet, and then a Spanish piece, announcing the Chilean victory that confirms the country's independence to San Martín and O'Higgins, thanking them and their colleagues for their directions and their unfailing support. This, when you have signed it, will go racing on before us to Valparaiso.'

Jack smiled — a smile that was neither forced nor constrained but that betrayed an immense weariness — and said, 'I do beg your pardon, Stephen. My wits were astray and I was forgetting my real status: I should be most grateful if you would write both. And in Sir Joseph's letter, if you think proper, pray mention Horatio's conduct: after all he did unmoor *Esmeralda* and sail her out under very heavy fire.'

'I shall do that. And my Valparaiso letter will go by *Ringle*, with all her amazing speed, for if I do not mistake, we and our prize must carry on at this sober pace. But Jack, my dear, you have lost a terrible lot of blood; your mind is sadly agitated — far more agitated than the situation warrants — and it is my considered opinion that you must eat as large a quantity of chicken soup as you can hold, and then take the comfortable draught that I shall mix you while the bird is preparing.'

All this time the *Surprise* had been filled with the innumerable sounds of a ship being brought back to a state of high perfection, having been battered out of it, the continuous thump of caulkers' mallets all along the frigate's engaged side being the most obvious of the great variety: surprisingly great, since a good half of the ship's company were aboard the crippled prize, which had been hit very hard not only in the naval battle but also by the fortress's thirty-six-pounders. And it took Stephen some little time to find Killick, who was furtively smoking on the seat of ease: but when, with some vexation of spirit, Stephen at last had the nourishing broth in preparation, he and Jacob set themselves to composing and encoding the singularly difficult letter to Sir Joseph.

At something very near the most critical point a knock on the door almost wrecked their tense concentration. 'Beg pardon, sir,' said Killick, timidly now, although he was backed by Maggie Tyler. 'Which Poll says the broth is ready.'

'Very well,' said Stephen, darting a furious look at him. 'Maggie, as soon as it is cool enough, spoon it into the Captain until he can take no more. No forcing him, however: do you hear me, there?'

'Yes, sir,' whispered Maggie, aghast.

'And he is to take this draught' — holding up a purple phial. 'Three teaspoons; and count sixty after the first and second.'

'Sixty it is, sir. As much as he can hold, then the draught: three teaspoons, and count sixty between the doses.' She had never seen either doctor look so very severe, and she bobbed a double courtesy as she backed out, treading on Killick's feet.

Another hour of intense concentration; and since they used a particular ink that could neither be effaced nor altered nor blotted, another hour of increasing squalor, then, when both were satisfied and neither had quarrelled (which, where an encoding is concerned, says a very great deal) Stephen thankfully sealed the frail sheets and carried them first to the cabin for Jack's wavering signature ('Only half of him there at all, the poor dear soul,' said Stephen to himself) and then on deck. 'Mr. Whewell,' he said to the officer of the watch, 'I should like to go aboard *Isaac Newton*, if possible — the Lisbon packet — and it does not seem worth troubling *Ringle*, particularly as the Captain wishes her to make for Valparaiso as fast as ever she can sail.'

'Why, sir, we will lower down the blue cutter in a trice — she is easily the best sailer we have. Mr. Hanson, the blue cutter, if you please. Doctor, may I ask how the Captain does? The people are right uneasy.'

'I do not think they need to be. He was indeed dreadfully knocked about yesterday, particularly on the head and shoulder, and he lost a power of blood; but he has eaten well, and I think he is now asleep. Or very soon will be.'

'Thank God,' said Whewell: and several hands within hearing distance nodded with grave satisfaction.

Even before he had begun to think of himself as part of the Navy (and that, because of strange but extensive areas of physical, mental and spiritual incompetence had been a very long period) — even before his acceptance of a life as gregarious as that of the honey-bee, Stephen Maturin had had a respect for the service and a kind of puzzled affection for sailors, particularly when they were aboard their own ships, those extraordinary hollow dwellings, sometimes as beautiful as they were comfortless. But never had he been so impressed as he was now, when a war-battered vessel, not a full day away from her bloody victory, produced and lowered down a trim, spotless cutter at no more than three words from the officer and two notes from the bosun's pipe, stepped her mast and sent a boy running up the side to guide him down into the stern-sheets, the cushioned stern-sheets.

'Where away, sir, if you please?' asked the coxswain.

'The Lisbon packet — but tell me, how is your William?' 'Well, sir, he copped it good and hearty, something cruel; but Dr. Jacob hopes to save the leg. Mind your head, sir: we are going about.'

The *Isaac Newton*'s master altered course to close the cutter and within a few minutes Stephen was aboard, clutching his bosom with maniac force lest the papers that had cost so much and that carried so much should escape during his frog-like progress over the gap between the cutter and the packet: he was safe, but he gasped for a while before handing the wrapper to Dobson, his very old friend and, as an entomologist, a familiar of Sir Joseph Banks. Then, though he very earnestly wished them on their way — particularly Sclater and his friend, who were to traverse the isthmus and take ship at Chagres on the Atlantic coast — he received their very hearty congratulations and gave them a brief account of the action, as far as it could be made out from the surgeons' station in the cockpit.

Back aboard the frigate Stephen went straight below to his invalids: Jack, of course, was still asleep, and would be for a good while yet, if poppy and hellebore retained any virtue, but what was much more to the point was that his face had recovered a little something of its youth and happiness — at least it was no longer mortally stricken — while his shoulder, though an undeniably hideous bruise, showed no signs of infection, nor yet did his leg, which was distinctly less swollen. Stephen remembered how once he had spoken of Captain Aubrey's power 'of healing like a young dog'; but under the influence of a certain piety or perhaps of mere sea-borne superstition he brushed the thought aside and hurried into the sick-bay to confer with Jacob, Poll and Maggie — satisfactory upon the whole — and so on to the cabin, where he threw himself into the composition of his letter to the Chilean authorities with great zeal and conviction.

'A very fine letter indeed, dear colleague,' said Jacob. 'Even if I could suggest any change, which I cannot, since it seems to me that you have summed up the situation admirably well, insisting upon the imminence of the Peruvian invasion, the urgency of the Director Supremo's request and the wholehearted support of your political advisers. But even if I could suggest any changes, I say, I should not, because I know how you long to send *Ringle* away to Valparaiso, and any recopying for the sake, let us say, of a mere subjunctive, would fret your spirit intolerably. Let us seal the letter, direct it to San Martín, and send it off without the loss of a minute.'

'What a good creature you are, Amos,' said Stephen, shaking his hand. 'Pray warm the wax.' And a few minutes later he said, 'Mr. Harding, the Captain is still fast asleep. In his condition, sleep, quietness and rest are of the very first importance and I should be most unwilling to disturb him. Yet the news of the victory should reach Valparaiso as soon as possible, and I am willing to take the fullest responsibility for desiring you to put a letter addressed to the Chilean authorities there aboard *Ringle* and directing Mr. Reade to deliver it as soon as ever he can.'

'The letter is of course agreed between

you and the Captain?'

'Yes, sir.'

'Then I shall make *Ringle*'s number at once.'

It was a joy to see the schooner come swiftly, smoothly under *Surprise*'s lee, the stiff breeze being in the west-north-west, pick up the message, repeat the orders, and pelt away southwards under such a press of canvas that she was hulldown before Stephen left the deck.

By all accounts the reception of the news in Valparaiso had been ecstatic — music and dancing all day and all night, speeches, more speeches, heroic drinking on the part of the Royal Navy and some Indians from the inland parts, widespread allegations of unchastity. But the beautiful west winds that Jack Aubrey had so often praised as being perfect for the Strait of Magellan and that had indeed brought *Ringle* down at such a pace, often touching fifteen knots watch after watch, soon turned foul: dead foul. When they were trying to beat round Cape Angamos the prize lost her mizzen with its top and everything above, which delayed them horribly.

Still, they did arrive to a fair amount of popular enthusiasm, to official speeches by the score, and of course to splendid dinners: and it was while he was preparing for one of these, said to be the last before Carrera's departure, that Jack's ill-temper, his invalid's ill-temper, worried Stephen extremely, as the possible sign of a late-developing complication from one or other of his wounds. He had been extremely active, getting up long before Stephen and Amos thought wise, and throwing himself into the repair of *Esmeralda*, the refurbishing of *O'Higgins* and Lindsay's *Asp*, and the fitting-out of the little squadron of sloops in which he and some of his officers trained the abler young Chileans, a singularly agreeable band. This time he meant to take them on at least part of his surveying of the Chonos Archipelago; but that depended very much on how his plans for the evening went.

Extremely active, and now he was extremely tired, as well as somewhat irritable, not to say cross-grained: he was much thinner, he walked with a stick, and he was more snappish than his oldest shipmates could remember. 'I do wish you would stop pressing the God-damned place,' he said to Stephen, who was dressing the leg again before he put his breeches on. 'It is hellish tender . . .' He checked himself. Stephen took no notice: he was wholly intent upon searching for proof of the deep infection that he dreaded and that he had seen before in just such a wound; but finding neither confirmation nor disproof he bound up the gash again, whipping the bandage round and crosswise with a wonderful dexterity. 'I could not do that,' said Jack when it was finished. 'Thank you very much. I am sorry I called out just now. You are a forgiving creature, Stephen . . . I am afraid I need a good deal of forgiving these days, you know. Of course, I am out of sorts, in spite of our battle, with many good men lost, old shipmates, and the frigate so knocked about. But what really worries me, Stephen, is the discontent. The hands have not been paid: the prize-money has not been shared out: and the men will not be able to afford a sailor's pleasure, and you know what that is as well as I do — indeed almost certainly better, from the sick-berth. They know it is dangerous, but they do love it, and if they cannot have it they grow chuff, rough and — pushed too far, downright mutinous.'

'I know very well what you mean.'

'You do, do you?' asked Jack, looking at him intently but asking no questions. 'Yes:

and the other officers have seen signs of it. If we were well-found and at sea, I should not worry, but we are likely to be ashore, off and on, for a fair while; and Jack ashore is often an ass. Apart from anything else he can desert: furthermore, as well as many well-tried old shipmates we have some right hard men aboard. We are all right for stores for the next few weeks, and I have told Adams to hand out two dollars a head: but when stores and dollars are gone . . .'

'I could wish you did not have this dinner,' said Stephen. 'But you will go easy with the wine, will you not?'

'If you see me offer to take even half a glass too much, pray give me a kick.'

This would not have been difficult, since the invariable practice at these often-repeated ceremonies, was to seat Dr. Maturin between Captain Aubrey and the most important guest, so that Jack's unwavering ignorance of any foreign language (other than a very, very little French) might be less of a hindrance.

'I hear the trumpets,' said Jack; and indeed at all these splendid entertainments, although he was conveyed by coach, he was attended by drums and trumpets, which even now still evoked a fair amount of cheering.

The guests were very politely received in the great hall, and Jack was seated at the right hand of the junta's president, Miguel Carrera, with Stephen, smaller than either and on a somewhat lower chair, interposed for translation. Jack had never grown used to the Spanish hours of eating and his appetite had vanished even before it smelt the soup: but Stephen (who had been brought up to these times for meals) admired his steady calm as the many, many courses dragged their slow length along. He did speak from time to time, by means of Stephen, usually answering questions about the men-of-war, the quality of the young men training to be naval officers — excellent, said Jack, with strong emphasis: excellentissimo. Stephen did sincerely admire his steadiness, his frequent smile; but it was with dismay that he heard Jack's discreet murmur, after a capital dish of strawberries, desiring him to tell the president that Captain Aubrey begged the favour of a word once the feast was ended.

'Of course,' replied Carrera. 'I should be honoured: and please tell the Captain that I have had very good news from Santiago: the Supreme Director tells me that the grant of the estate has been confirmed by a unanimous vote. And please convey my very best congratulations.'

Stephen did so, and he saw Jack smile, bow, and say that he earnestly hoped all due thanks for the present might be transmitted to the Director. Scarcely were these words uttered but the bishop's chaplain, followed by all others present, rose to say grace.

The whole company waited for the bishop and his attendants to leave, bowing as the old gentleman passed, and then Carrera showed Jack and Stephen into a domed octagonal room with Moorish sofas and coffee, and a Christian decanter of brandy.

'I was so glad to be able to bring you the news of your great estate,' said Carrera as they sat down. 'It is a little far away and it has been neglected by the former owner, a royalist of course: but with the river just at hand there are great possibilities of irrigation. And after all six thousand acres is scarcely negligible.'

As he listened to Stephen's expressionless translation, Jack looked at the ground. It was pretty gross: surprisingly gross in a Spaniard. Clearly the man was uneasy, as he might well be, the land in question lying in an arid stretch of country south of the

Bio-Bio river, inhabited, as far as it was inhabited at all, by Araucanian Indians, the most formidable and warlike of their kind, while much of the land was thickly covered with the Chilean pine, the puzzle-monkey tree.

'No, indeed,' said Jack, 'and as I have said, I am sure you will convey all suitable expressions of my gratitude to the Supreme Director. But for the moment I am primarily concerned with my men. As you are aware, they have not been paid. The very considerable mass of treasure seized at Valdivia has not been shared out. And the people of the prize-court here say that no decision on the *Esmeralda*'s value can possibly be reached this year. No: let me finish speaking if you please,' he said, holding up his hand; and Carrera obviously thought his cold fury as impressive as did Stephen. 'Since I reached this country,' Jack went on, 'I have been referred from ministry to secretariat, from high-placed men to influential friends and back again: and my people, in the height of victory, have not sixpence in their pockets for a pot of beer. And I tell you, sir, this will not do. You, a man of great standing in the republic, are going to Santiago: I desire you to tell Mr. O'Higgins and your other colleagues, that this will *not* do. I must have money: and only a great deal of money will satisfy my officers and men. They must have what they have earned and what they have won; and they must have it by the end of the month. Do you understand me, sir?'

'I understand you, sir,' said Carrera, 'and you will allow me to say that I very much regret the preseint state of affairs. I must set out for Santiago early tomorrow morning, and there I shall lay the matter before those who make decisions. But before I go I shall do myself the honour of sending a letter to your ship, to your most distinguished ship.'

'You are very good, sir,' said Jack, standing up with the help of his stick, 'and it only remains for me to thank you most heartily for this truly splendid feast — I particularly valued the Christmas pudding —' he added with a look of fury, 'and for your comprehension. Finally, may I beg you to tell your colleagues that the end of the month is my fortunate or unfortunate day, as they shall decide.' With this he held out his hand and said farewell.

'By God, you did that in style, brother,' said Stephen, when they were in the coach.

'I could not dislike the man, although he

is a politician,' said Jack. 'And I believe he loves the service. He has a nephew aboard *Gladiator*, who speaks perfect English, and thinks of himself as at least half a sailor already; and he is not far wrong.'

It was the early-rising half that was entrusted with the letter, and it was delivered aboard *Surprise* before Jack's vile morning draught, which Killick brought with eager punctuality at four bells and which had to be swallowed before he might open the envelope.

'Go and see whether the Doctor is about,' said Jack, 'and if he is, ask him to look in, when he has a moment.'

'Which he is in the fish-market, turning over some old-fashioned lobsters. No. I tell a lie. That is him, falling down the companion-way and cursing in foreign.'

Stephen, dusted down and tweaked into good order, his wig restored, was led into the cabin.

'Good morning, Stephen. Would you cast an eye at this?'

'Bless you,' said Stephen. 'I might: *Don Miguel kisses your hands, thanks you for honouring his frugal repast, and has the happiness of enclosing two papers, the one being addressed to the chief cashier and requiring him to deliver five thousand pieces of eight to*

422

any inferior officer whom you may choose to send, the other to the official in charge of naval stores charging him to send over every-thing of that kind you may require. He begs your pardon a thousand times for so brief a scribble, but his horse, a desperately impatient animal, is at the door, only just held by two straining grooms.'

'By God, that is very handsome of him,' cried Jack. 'As soon as we have had breakfast, let us call upon the dear cashier with a couple of powerful holders, and then confer with the master, purser, bosun, gunner and anyone who is concerned with stores to find just what we need: I know the cupboard is most uncommon bare.' He went on about its barrenness at considerable length, a length matched by his own exhilaration; but when for a moment he paused, Stephen said, 'Will I tell you something?'

'By all means. It will probably be even more interesting than the number of swabs we need.'

'Listen. I was walking along the dock-side where they are repairing the big Chilean frigate.'

'*O'Higgins.*'

'No, sir, if you will forgive me: they are changing it to *San Martín.*'

'Are they, by God? That is a damned unlucky thing to do to a ship. And it may be unlucky for us, too. Clearly the tide is changing. O'Higgins was our friend. What little I saw of San Martín I did not care for, and I doubt he really loved me. But there is little we can do about it, apart from knocking the place down about their ears with their own powder and shot; and that I hesitate to do, having several friends in the town. No. I think we must carry on with our survey: and if they turn awkward, if they shuffle or back-water, why, damn them all, I shall ask you to write me a handsome letter of resignation, pray for a steady west wind, and sail home. But first, until the month is out, I must fulfil my promise and take the young men, the pick of the young men, surveying the Chonos Archipelago: and before that we must fill the ship with stores.'

At four bells in the forenoon watch the next day, a very pretty day with Jack's beloved westerly breeze rippling the harbour, *Surprise*'s gunner, in answer to a nod from Somers, fired the foremost larboard gun. All those who had been poised to act, waiting for this signal, instantly cast off moorings, raced aloft, and watching *Sur-*

prise with the closest attention, followed her movements with such exemplary success that the whole squadron of four ship-sloops and one frigate moved steadily across the harbour in an exactly straight, exactly spaced line, and, amid the cheers and applause of the multitude, into the open sea, where, again following the example of *Surprise*, they all steered south-west by south, to allow for the heave of the moderately powerful swell and making tide.

According to local custom, the sloops had two captains, a first and a second; and Jack had them on the quarter-deck by turn, each daylight watch — or to be more exact, from four bells in the morning watch until the end of the first dog — to show them how things were done in the Royal Navy. Three or four of them were quite fluent in English, particularly young José Fernandez, Carrera's nephew, a natural-born merman if ever there was one; but even so the monoglots imposed a dreadful burden on Dr. Maturin, who, though he knew a few nautical terms, such as starboard and larboard, in English, had no notion of how to say 'Come up the tackle-fall' in Spanish or any other language.

'How I wish we had Jacob,' said Jack,

one day off Talcahuano.

'It was entirely with your own consent that we left him in Valparaiso for the possible transmission of a particular message,' said Stephen.

'You are entirely right: I beg your pardon, brother: it was just for the relief of bewailing my lot. An ignoble relief, I admit.'

'Captain, dear, a glass of wine with you.'

In his youth Jack Aubrey had served under two taut captains, remarkably taut even for those rigorous days, and when he said exercising he meant it to a degree that left the poor young men pale, wan, and almost dropping as they stood; but after a few days their young frames, having slept like the dead and eaten like hyenas, gained strength: above all as his own young midshipmen and younger officers raced them from one dizzy eminence to another. And although they had already been through some fairly serious naval training, Dr. Maturin had to treat many a blistered hand and rope-burnt thigh. Yet in all this there was none of the harsh driving so usual at sea: and as far as cheerfulness and good nature were compatible with reefing a foretopsail in a very fresh breeze, the days were upon the whole cheerful and good-natured. The only occasions upon which Jack was less than kind were those upon which the young Chileans showed a really grave ignorance of navigation, of determining the ship's course and position by the principles of geometry and nautical astronomy: here he found Daniel and Hanson of the greatest use, and although a lunar observation was harder to understand than a sheet-bend, most of the young men were convinced of the subject's importance, and several learnt to take the sun's altitude at noon. They were invited, usually in pairs, to dine in the cabin or the gunroom; and although language sometimes presented a certain amount of difficulty, voracious appetites made up for it.

'What a pleasant set of young fellows they are, to be sure,' said Jack Aubrey as he and Stephen walked on a strand by the mouth of the river Llico, 'and many of them have a real sense of the wind and the sea. At least half a dozen will make real sailors — Lord, what a change after those miserable, untrustworthy politicians.'

'Sure, you are in the right of it. But tell me, Jack, what are they doing to the poor *Surprise*, all awry there on the face of the ocean?'

'Why, since it is so still and we so prettily embayed till the turn of the tide, Harding thought of showing the rest of the boys, those who did not pull us ashore, what half-breaming is like. Do you see, they have heaved her down as far as they decently can and they are scraping the weed from what bottom they can reach . . .'

His explanation went on, but presently he noticed that Stephen was looking very fixedly at a bird, by now quite remote. 'I do beg pardon, Jack,' he said, 'but I am almost certain that was a snipe. Do you see it yet?'

'Certainly not. And should give it no countenance if I did. A snipe in Chile, for all love. I should as soon expect a beaver in the Royal Exchange.'

'And yet that dear boy José, whose uncle is a great shot, told me that the snipe — *becasina,* Gallinago gallinago — the same bird as ours — was the very first of breeding birds that come down here on migration. Bless you: here I had been, cursing the day and kicking the ground itself because we were making this voyage, as we have made so many a voyage, in that dismal gap when the winter migrants have departed and those of the spring have not yet arrived. I am filled with hope.'

Filled he may have been; but days, even weeks later, he was sitting on the grey pebbles of an island, one of the innumerable cold grey Chonos islands, sullenly training his glass not on any wildly exotic migrant but the commonplace resident blackish (but white-footed) oyster-catcher wading about in search of its living. Farther along there was another, a lacklustre female; and neither betrayed the slightest interest in the other: clearly this was not their breeding season, whatever the snipe might think. Not the season of sudden joys, although it was indeed the thirtieth day of the month and tomorrow must decide Jack's fate one way or another, neither leading to any evident happiness.

Beyond the hen oyster-catcher a brig came into view, rounding one of the countless rocky eminences that Captain Aubrey and his pupils had surveyed that morning with infinite care — they were now surveying another a little way to the south out of Stephen's sight but within that of the brig, which now increased its already headlong speed with yet more canvas. A green brig familiar to Stephen, used as a yacht by a wealthy and amiable Chilean gem-merchant, one of Jacob's friends, who lived in Valparaiso.

He fixed it with his telescope, and there indeed was Jacob looking at him through another and making signs — untimely mirth? Whatever the signs were they were very soon lost as the brig rounded yet another great sea-worn cliff in the direction of *Surprise*, and Stephen's attention was at once seized by a very noble sight — two black-necked swans flying steadily south, quite low over the water, so low that he could hear the rhythmic beating of their wings.

'I cannot just sit here, watching pale-footed oyster-catchers,' said Maturin aloud. 'But what other course is open to me?'

No other course, during the passage — always north to south — of three skuas and that revolting carrion-eater the crested caracara. Hung about Stephen's neck and wrapped in waxed-silk bags, one inside the other — the replacement of a small and very beautiful repeating watch chimed two quarters and would have chimed a third had he not caught sight of the frigate's jolly-boat pulling fast into the contrary wind. He leapt up and waved and hooted, terrifying the oyster-catchers but making quite sure that he was not marooned.

He came up the ship's side with his usual elegance, and he was greeted by Dr.

Jacob, on whose brow a knowing eye could read A CODED SIGNAL HAS COME THROUGH. Stephen was led below to one of the really discreet parts of the ship and in a low voice Jacob said, 'Jaime brought it just after the government messenger had arrived from Santiago,' and although Jacob had not decoded anything like the whole there was an important section that he perhaps mistakenly thought should be transmitted to the person concerned at once. From the jerk of his head and upward look Stephen grasped that he was speaking of Jack: and this became yet more certain when Jacob spoke of his delight when the brig overtook and passed the heavy sloop-of-war that had set out from Valparaiso before he could find the owner of the brig.

'You have the original and your transcript?' asked Stephen.

'The original, but only a little of the transcript: let me show you how far I went before deciding to come out.'

Stephen held the rough draft to the gunport and said, 'Certainly you were quite right, dear Amos. We must tell him at once.'

'No. He is your particular friend. Here is my copy of the D2 key: there are some difficult combinations that I did not trouble with, but the essence is quite plain and we can worry them out later.'

Stephen nodded, shook his hand warmly, thrust the papers into a pocket and walked quickly out. Almost running into the clerk he said, 'Mr. Adams, pray do me a service. I should like a private word with the Captain: I shall be in the cabin.' Adams stared at so very extraordinary a request, but he saw that Stephen was in earnest, said, 'Very good, sir,' and hurried on deck.

Stephen was gazing out of the middle stern window when the Captain came in, looking surprised and a little concerned.

'Jack,' said Stephen, 'a signal has just come in. It has not all been decoded, but the opening is addressed to you by name and ship and if you choose I will read you what has been made out and try to decode the rest as I go — it has been crumpled in the journey and I may miss some words. But here is the essence: *Immediately upon receipt of the present order you will proceed to the River Plate, there joining the South African squadron: you will go aboard HMS Implacable, hoisting your flag, blue at the mizzen and take command of the blue squadron.*'

Jack sat down, bowing his face in his

hands: he was almost unmanned, but after a moment he did say, 'Read that again, will you, Stephen?'

Stephen did so, and Jack said, 'By God, Stephen, I am so glad it was you brought me this news. Sophie will be so happy. By God, I never thought my flag would come.'

'And there are some other things. Very hearty congratulations from the Duke of Clarence for the Callao action, a personal message to Horatio Hanson and a request that you should send him home as soon as possible to sit for his lieutenant's examination. And there are great quantities of political considerations from Sir Joseph that have yet to be decoded . . . May I too congratulate you, Admiral dear?' He embraced Jack, who took it quite naturally, in something of a daze: but then he said, 'It is all very glorious, brother, and I am glad they are pleased with us. But I am tied by the leg, you know. I am engaged, committed, to the Chilean government.'

At this point the Chilean government, in the person of Carrera, was coming up the *Surprise*'s side from the heavy ship-sloop, carrying a letter. He was properly received by Harding, and permission having been sought, he was shown into the cabin, where Jack offered him some sherry and begged pardon while he read the letter.

'I am very sorry for what it contains,' said Carrera. 'Sorry and ashamed: the men in Santiago beg for another three months, and then all debts will be paid.'

'It grieves me to say this to you,' said Jack, 'but you will recall our agreement. I must desire you to take your young men, your excellent and most promising young men, aboard the sloop. For I am required to sail in another direction. But please rest assured of my personal esteem for you, and of my very best possible wishes for the Chilean navy of the future.'

The transfer took a considerable time — a very cheerful, good-humoured transfer — and the ships parted with hearty reciprocal cheering.

After a last salute Jack glanced aloft — still the sweet west wind — and then he looked fore and aft: a fine clear deck, hands all at their stations and all beaming with pleasure; and turning to the master he said, 'Mr. Hanson, pray lay me a course for Cape Pilar and Magellan's Strait.'

We hope you have enjoyed this Large Print book. Other Thorndike Press or Chivers Press Large Print books are available at your library or directly from the publishers.

For more information about current and upcoming titles, please call or write, without obligation, to:

Thorndike Press
P.O. Box 159
Thorndike, Maine 04986 USA
Tel. (800) 257-5157

OR

Chivers Press Limited
Windsor Bridge Road
Bath BA2 3AX
England
Tel. (0225) 335336

All our Large Print titles are designed for easy reading, and all our books are made to last.